Good Night Sweet Prince

Nightmare in Iran

Henry Jay

GOOD NIGHT SWEET PRINCE
NIGHTMARE IN IRAN

This is a work of fiction. All of the characters, names, incidents, organizations, and dialogue in this novel are either the products of the author's imagination or are used fictitiously.

iUniverse books may be ordered through booksellers or by contacting:

iUniverse
1663 Liberty Drive
Bloomington, IN 47403
www.iuniverse.com
1-800-Authors (1-800-288-4677)

ISBN: 978-1-4917-6732-0 (sc)
ISBN: 978-1-4917-6733-7 (e)

Print information available on the last page.

iUniverse rev. date: 07/03/2015

Chapter 1

August 25, 1977

The PANAM flight from New York's Kennedy airport to Heathrow in London would take nearly ten hours. Sitting alone in a window seat two rows down from the enormous wings of the plane, Jordan surveyed the cabin, which was gradually filling up with passengers, many of whom were formally dressed, the women in stylish dresses or pantsuits, and the men in two or three-piece suits. The stewardesses, smartly dressed in blue and white uniforms, walked up and down the aisles helping passengers stow away their luggage in the overhead bins and settle in their seats. The last passenger had been settled in and the stewardesses had retired to their positions for takeoff, when the captain began his spiel over the intercom.

Jordan didn't think she would meet anyone she could talk to, although she hoped she would. Luckily, she had brought along Keats' Collected Works as traveling companion, and settled down to the long flight ahead of her resignedly. Turning to the odes, she began to read as the plane picked up speed for take off. However, a few stanzas into the Ode to A Grecian Urn, Jordan's eyes began to feel heavy, and soon she was fast asleep. "Heard Melodies are sweet, but those unheard are sweeter," she heard someone say in a confused dream, and she woke up for a moment.

In the last few months she had been giddily waiting for this journey into the unknown. I'm certainly looking forward to my unheard melody, she said to herself determinedly. Hope sprang eternal that the unknown she was flying into would be as sweet as the waiting for it had been. The drone of the jet plane's gigantic engines and the silence in the enormous cabin as the passengers settled down to the long night flight across the Atlantic acted as a joint soporific and Jordan slept through most of it. It was around noon when the Boeing 747 landed in Heathrow. She disembarked and went looking for her connecting flight to Tehran.

Jordan wished she had had the time to do some sightseeing in London, but the connecting flight to Tehran was in two hours. She sat in one of the little airport cafes and sipped Earl Grey English Breakfast tea and munched on a scone. Although generally a coffee drinker, she had deliberately decided to have tea for two reasons. First, she wanted to see for herself what the English saw in tea; they could literally not do without their 'cuppa'. Secondly, she had been tutored by her mother that the people in Iran were great tea drinkers, and so she wanted an easy transition to 'when in Rome.'

When the London-Tehran flight was announced over the intercom, Jordan hurried to gate 16 in concourse B and joined the motley line of passengers, a large number of Americans whom she identified by their non-stop chatter, and an equal proportion of Asians, many of whom she imagined were Iranians going home. Two little boys who were just in front of her with a woman whom Jordan supposed was their mother, were very well-behaved, unlike most American kids, she thought, as she watched them standing quietly, and then she saw the enormous candy bars they were munching on. That's one way of keeping them quiet, she thought amusedly.

Jordan walked down the left aisle of the Boeing 747 looking for row 37; her seat was 37H, by the window. The mother of the two boys occupied the aisle seat. Jordan deposited her little carry on bag in the overhead bin, and excusing herself, eased into her seat. The "fasten seatbelt" sign came on, and a series of clicks like crickets in the night, assailed Jordan's ears. Jordan reached into the seat pocket in front of her and extracted the in-flight shopping magazine and began thumbing through it.

The woman in the aisle seat turned to Jordan smiling. "Hello," she said in a British accent, "are you American?"

"Yeah, I'm from New York. My name's Jordan. Where are you from?"

"I'm Iranian. Going back home on vacation. My name is Soraya Tehrani. I've been living in London for the last five years. The two little guys you see across the aisle are my two sons, Daniel and Samson," she added enthusiastically. It was as if she had been waiting to talk to someone. Feeling a little forlorn herself, Jordan warmed up to the conversation.

"They're cute," observed Jordan glancing across the aisle at the six and eight year old boys, sitting seemingly under great duress under their mother's watchful eye.

Slim and pretty, Soraya's peaches and cream complexioned face was framed by her thick black hair tied up in a stylish coiffure, giving her a very confident, even professional look. What struck Jordan, though, was the easy pleasantness with which she spoke and her warm friendliness, and Jordan thought if all Iranian women were like Soraya, she would have no problem getting along with them. Iran, here I come, she exulted.

"Hey, you've got two famous names," observed Jordan, silently thanking her Mom for filling her in on important names from the recent history of Iran.

"Well, my first name is not the only thing I share with the Shah's former wife," confessed Soraya ruefully, "I'm a divorcee, too. My ex-husband was a professor at Tehran University."

"Oh? That's where I'm going. I'm going to teach English there."

As the plane flew into the eastern night, Jordan and Soraya chatted on about the East and the West, men and relationships.

Jordan learned many things about Iranian men and women, their likes and dislikes, attitudes and mores and concluded that people were the same everywhere. There were jerks and nice guys, bitches and nice gals in every place, she thought.

"Hey, you must come to my house some time, before I get back to London. I'll call you."

"I'll look forward to that. Hey, you know what. You're the first Iranian I've met!"

"That's wonderful. Hope I'll not disappoint you! Oh, by the way, my brother will be picking me up at the airport. Can I drop you somewhere, Jordan?"

"Thanks Soraya, but there will be someone from the university to pick me up. I guess I'd better go with them so I can sort things out."

"Yes, that's right," agreed Soraya, "first things first, eh?"

When the plane landed at Mehrabad airport, Jordan felt both relief and a slight feeling of nerves. It was her first time out of the US, and she was relieved that the long journey was over, yet a slight feeling of apprehension lurked at the back of her mind. It's quite natural, she rationalized. After all she was entering uncharted land as far as she was concerned, but she knew she had nothing to worry about. She was landing in the kingdom of Persia- the land of the Shahanshah- the king of kings. Iran was one of the safest places in the Middle East, the closest ally of the US next to Israel. Besides, she was going to make a lot of money, for the salary that had been promised her was nearly ten times what she had been earning as a school-teacher in Albany.

And I already have a friend, she mused happily.

Chapter 2

Jordan began to recall what she had read about the land of Persia. The second largest producer of oil, Iran was the oldest monarchy in the world. The great Persian Empire, had reached its zenith under Darius II five thousand years ago, battling for supremacy with Alexander the Great.

Mohammed Reza Pahlavi, present incumbent of the Peacock Throne, had been at the helm since 1954. In 1921, his father, Reza, an army officer, and the politically erudite Zia-od-din Tabatabai, had organized a coup d'etat bringing to an end the Qajar dynasty established by Agha Mohammed Shah in 1797. A Constituent Assembly replaced the monarchy.

The British, hovering in the background, were eager for greater influence over the oil reserves of the country. They realized that a grateful monarch, installed by them would be more maneuverable than a Constituent Assembly, and encouraged Reza to grab the reins. Supported by the British, Reza the new monarch, albeit nothing more than a pretender, flexed his muscle and the Constituent Assembly voted to establish a monarchy under Reza Shah Pahlavi, and Reza Shah ascended the Peacock throne in April, 1926. The Pahlavi Dynasty had begun.

Jordan's Mom, who now had a vested interest in Iran had started reading up on the country, and shared whatever she picked up with Jordan.

"The Qajars were not interested in the welfare of the people. They often ruled irresponsibly and selfishly," she told Jordan, "All they were interested in was their power and wealth. In fact they entered into many injudicious alliances with various foreign powers at the expense of the people."

The people looked upon Reza to lead the people to freedom and prosperity. Reza, emboldened with good intentions, started on a program of hitherto unimagined modernization of the country. The under-educated masses, totally under the control of the clerics, to whom modern education was anathema, watched in hope. The clerics, too, watched with rancor, for Reza's actions would only erode their influence over the simple rural majority, who had been coaxed, cajoled and sternly regimented by their theology to look to the after life for their rewards rather than fight for a better life on earth.

"Actually, Reza was determined to veer the country away from the influence of the clerics as fast as he could," she said.

Sadly, however, he ignored or did not discern two of the most crucial elements of the Iranian psyche: first, their unshakable devotion to Shia Islam, and second, their unequivocal commitment to nationalism and nationhood. The Iranian culture was firmly rooted in the Shia faith, which they saw as an equalizing force promising justice for all within the framework of kinship and religion, working as complementary rather than opposing elements.

Therefore for centuries their kings had not interfered with the clergy, and similarly, the clergy concerned themselves with the spiritual rather than worldly affairs.

"I was reading this history of the Iranians, and it seems the Iranian psyche is rooted in the history of the Shia religion. After the death of Muhammad, Ali, his closest blood relative and ally, was ignored and the first caliphate was passed on to another, less deserving and certainly less popular individual. Ali had to wait his turn, and by the time that came around, the power struggle between those of Mecca, in Saudi Arabia, who claimed suzerainty over everyone else, and the Shia, supporters of Ali, representative of the weak and the oppressed, brought about a schism in the Islamic establishment," she said.

Jordan herself had read that although Ali's caliphate had lasted a mere five years, it had brought about a new kind of protest movement that stood for even-handed, fair and righteous rule, which the powerful Sunni establishment had little or no respect for. "That is why Ali represents for the Iranians a fine blend of all of the kingly virtues of Cyrus, and what the Prophet had taught and stood for. And like Ali, his son, Hussein, who chose martyrdom at the hands of a more powerful tyrant, remained an icon of the virtues and the expectations of a just and benign king" thought Jordan.

Mohammad Reza's rise to power was as incredible as it was phenomenal. Starting as a young soldier in the Cossack Division of the Russians who had ruled the north of Iran, he turned tables on the Russians, as well as the weak and vacillating king, Sultan Ahmad Shah, and the British by taking over complete authority, liberating the land from the foreigners and their lackeys in Tehran, for whom he didn't even try to disguise his contempt.

"It's ironic," declared Mom," the Bolshevik Revolution, which gave birth to the Union of Soviet Socialist Republics on the northern border of Iran had a considerable effect on Iranian affairs. The British, feared unpleasant consequences of the Bolshevik presence in the north, and demanded the command of the Cossack division. However, officers of the division, with Reza at the helm, had other ideas, for they demanded freedom from foreign control, capitalizing on a hitherto inactive, but dormant sense of Iranian nationalism."

"With a raggedy band of three thousand soldiers, Reza marched on Tehran and demanded that he be appointed commander of the armed forces," she declared dramatically, bringing a smile to Jordan's face. "Nobody opposed him. From that day in 1921, until he was forced to abdicate in 1941, he remained the absolute ruler of Iran." Jordan was impressed.

"I've heard that the clergy have a fair influence over the people," Jordan interjected.

"Absolutely. In fact the clergy in the city of Qum were not happy with Reza's early attempts to turn Iran into a republic. Reza knew that. And he wanted to wean the people away from that influence. It was turning into an irreconcilable conflict. However, the pressure that they brought to bear on Reza made him equally adamant to enforce his will on them, and be rid of clerical influence for good and all.

Reza was not only a strong-willed man with a mission; he was also very much in a hurry. His programs of reform were shadowed by a sense of urgency typical of a soldier on an urgent campaign. He started by changing the traditional name of Persia to the more nationalist Iran. As a first step in reducing the dominance of the clerics on the Iranian masses, he brought into place certain changes to practices, which he considered remnants of Arab influence that were detrimental to the progress of his people.

First, he banned the traditional veil for women, a first step in reducing the social gap between men and women common in Arabic cultures."

"Power to the females," intoned Jordan, "Isn't that wonderful. Here we are fighting for ERA, and Reza was already fighting for the women himself," she added in adulation.

"Not only that, he wanted to liberate the men, too, this from religious indoctrination. He forced the men to wear peaked caps, which would prevent their foreheads touching the ground at prayer for he saw the touching of the forehead to the ground as demeaning to the male image. These changes incensed clerics no end, but there was little they could do against the onslaught of his indomitable will. He brooked no opposition or disagreement. Any protest that came up was mercilessly crushed, often with more force than was necessary. His opponents were either imprisoned or simply murdered; the more fortunate of them fled the country," continued the historian, and Jordan was mesmerized by the image of the powerful though Machivellian monarch the shades of Machiavelli he seemed to have possessed.

"Sadly, the country still remained burdened by economic obligations to the British, and Reza lacked the ability to make any significant economic reforms that would ease the burden on the people," she added, regret in her voice.

Picking up the trend of what had brought about the demise of Reza the Great, as he was still referred to, Jordan lamented, "Had he been able to bring some form of economic relief to the people, his sudden social and religious reforms might have been justified. He failed to see this, and was unhappy with the pace of modernization and secularization, so he resorted to greater repression of the people."

"You're absolutely right, but one of the cardinal sins he committed at this time was to envision for Iran a form of government modeled on the fascist dictatorships of Mussolini, Franco and Hitler. Deceived by the rise of Nazism in the early years, he had allowed the Nazis a free hand in Iran. He might also have felt an affinity to the so-called Aryan element of the Nazis, the Persians themselves being descendants of the ancient Aryan tribes of Indo-Europe. In any case, the Allied powers were no respectors of history or tradition. The British and Russian forces routed the Nazis in Iran and put them to flight. Reza Shah had backed the wrong horse and met his Nemesis; he abdicated in September 1941, and the country was carved up: the North to the Russians, and the South, with the all-important oil reserves to the British, prompting Churchill to gloat over Iran as 'a prize from fairyland beyond our wildest dreams.'"

"And thus ended the soldier's dream," exclaimed Jordan unnecessarily.

The British tried to revive the Quajar dynasty but failed, for the Iranians would have none of that decadent monarchy which the great soldier had got rid of. Goaded by the fear of communism on the one hand, and the equally fearsome clerical rule on the other, the British had little time to think of a better alternative. They chose the best they had. They simply placed Mohamed Reza, son of the disgraced Reza Shah on the Peacock Throne, lending a new lease of life to the Pahlavi dynasty.

"Oh yeah, the Peacock Throne. I saw a picture of that in an old history book," said Jordan, a tone of wonder in her voice, "I shall look forward to seeing that. It's supposed to be open to public viewing along with the Crown jewels."

"Maybe we could see it together when I come to visit," said Jill, half humorously, "Wouldn't that be awesome."

As history had recorded, the Allies made good use of the plentiful supplies of oil and established important supply bases for their military operations in the Middle East and North Africa. The Iranians suffered great economic hardship and food supplies were scarce, for the Allied military forces took precedence over the citizenry. As long as the war went on, the people were kept under control with all dissent being harshly silenced for the sake of the war effort. Gen. Norman Schwarzkopf built up a ruthlessly constructed power base for the new, wet-behind-the-ears-Shah, silencing all dissidents and opponents.

In their struggle against poverty and extreme suffering, some Iranians turned to communism. The local communist party, the Tudeh, was born in 1942, and became the party for the liberals, reformers and social activists. So everyone waited for the war to end with sanguine hopes for a new beginning-and a new nation to take the place of the old.

The Russian Bear, in the north, watched developments carefully extending its support to the communists, who seized power in 1944. Reza feared Tudeh, the local Communist party, and Iran's giant northern neighbor enough to let the communists carry on unhindered for a while. However, a little over a year into his presidency, a man who had no connections at all with the Tudeh party, attempted to assassinate the Shah. The Shah was injured, but not seriously. The event was carefully manipulated to place the blame on the Tudeh party, and fully exploited to enforce a major crackdown on the Communists. Clandestine support from Britain emboldened the Shah enough to enforce a ban on Tudeh, which he accused of being responsible for the attempt on his life. Many Communist leaders were imprisoned, while others fled the country. British influence took a firm hold in the country, especially on the oil industry. The Anglo-Iranian Oil Company (AIOC) was established, with Britain providing all technological support and management of the lucrative oil reserves. Most importantly, Britain, 'the Nation of Shopkeepers,' managed the AIOC accounts. Britain supplied the majority of the technical staff, while the Iranians were lucky if they could find a job at the lowliest level of labor. Of the annual profit of forty million pounds from the oil industry, Iran received a paltry seven million, and Iranian oil workers lived in abject poverty, their wages limited to a measly fifty cents a day.

"Isn't it sad that the second largest producer of oil in the world could not afford to feed and house her people," quipped Jordan, fresh out of college, somewhat oblivious to the way the world worked.

"Sad, but true," agreed her Mom.

The Shah was obviously very grateful to the British for his position of power, so he looked the other way, thought Jordan.

But not so the Majlis-the Iranian parliament. Protesting at every turn, the Majlis enacted a bill annulling the concessions to Britain. Under the new legislation, Iran and Britain were to receive equal shares of oil revenue. Attempts by the Shah to force the Majlis into submission by tactics such as election rigging failed miserably, and the Shah was forced to give in.

At first Britain attempted to force Iran into submission by sabotaging the oil industry. Britain threatened to withdraw all technological support and shipping facilities. Next, international embargos were threatened. Nothing seemed to have any effect, however, for the geopolitics of the region had changed for good and American influence in the country was on the ascendant.

"So we came to Iran's aid," said Renee, jubilantly, "Engaging the support of the US to ward off the threat of communism in the region, the Shah leaned more and more on America, the rising superpower. He visited the US, hoping to obtain the military hardware and logistics that would protect him from the increasing popularity of the communist leaning Tudeh party, but President Truman, the Democrat, had other ideas. He advised the Shah to bring about greater social reform, which would steer the country away from Communism. The Shah was ready to follow that advice; in fact, he would try anything to scramble back on to the Peacock Throne. However, by the time he returned to Iran, the charismatic leader of Tudeh, Mohammed Mossadegh had firmly entrenched himself in power. On March 1, 1951, the Iranian oil industry was nationalized. The British, playing the injured innocents that had lost their investments in Iran, turned to the powerful new kid on the block, the US, to shake Mossadegh off his perch. Truman, politely declined to intervene in what he saw was an internal matter for the Iranians to settle."

The US presidential election of 1952, which brought General Dwight Eisenhower into the White House, saw a complete change in American policy toward Iran. A little known US civil servant, albeit a shrewd schemer, Kermit Roosevelt-grandson of President Teddy Roosevelt, was dispatched to Tehran to put things right. Eisenhower obviously knew what would happen to American oil interests in the Middle East if the commies got a foothold in the oil rich kingdom. With the support of disgruntled elements in the Iranian military, as well as certain clerics, who had a morbid fear of the Communists, Mossadegh was deposed and placed under house arrest.

"Mohammed Reza was at the helm once again, and the honeymoon between the US and the Pahlavi dynasty began," shrilled Mom, happily.

Now, securely ensconced on the Peacock throne, Mohammed Reza had a lot to be grateful for to the United Sates, which gradually made him virtual policeman of the Middle East. First, the US provided Reza Shah with all the technical expertise and personnel for its enormous oil industry. Over forty thousand American technicians, engineers and other professionals, as well as many anything-but-professionals, took flight to Iran to rake in the profits of the black gold.

The US also provided the country with a powerful arsenal of state-of-the -art weaponry which had other countries in the region not just in awe, but in extreme envy of Iran's meteoric rise to power. Iran's oil revenue, a mere twenty million dollars in the 50s, jumped to twenty billion by 1975. The Shah, emboldened by his new found economic power, and political importance in the Middle East went on the most extraordinary shopping spree for military hardware, spending over four billion dollars in 1973 alone. His list of toys included a hundred state-of-the art F-4 Phantoms with laser-guided bombs, and a fleet of KC-135 aerial tankers to refuel them in flight. Complementing this awesome aerial fire-power was a colossal fleet of C-130 helicopters, and the largest single purchase of military hovercraft made by any single country in the world. On the ground stood row upon row of gigantic Sherman tanks capable of reducing whole city blocks into rubble in a matter of minutes. Iran's military capability stood fifth or sixth on the planet, yet the only occasions when the Shah had to even flex his military muscle was to quell a little communist uprising in Oman, and a couple of insurgencies in the region!

In the meantime, most of the corporate heavyweights of the US that mattered moved to the new pasture, scenting mega business, for here the grass was infinitely green. Allied Chemicals, Northrop, AMOCO, Lockheed, BF

Goodrich and Bell Helicopters set up shop in and around Tehran. The food and beverages followed: Coke and Pepsi, McDonalds, KFC and Pizza Hut opened outlets in the capital and bigger cities. The major houses of fashion, jewelry and cosmetics served the demands of the newly liberated young and not so young ladies of Persia who had not the means of shopping in Europe as the wealthier segments of society did. In fact, the access to money brought about by the oil in general, and the emancipation of women to seek jobs in the cities afforded Iranian women greater buying power than they had ever known in recent times, and they were ready to use it so much so that the average Iranian working woman spent over fifty percent of her salary on clothes and fashion accessories. Those who covered themselves in the forbidding black chador were no exception, regaling themselves in Dior and splashing on Chanel as they went about their work both at home and outside. The oft-repeated joke doing the rounds was that the 'chadoris' as they were humorously referred to, always made it a point to crack their chadors seemingly involuntarily flashing what they really wore under the shroud.

There were social consequences, too. The youth, especially in the big cities, loved coke and Pepsi, and wolfed down the hamburgers and hotdogs with gusto. They loved American music, and disco dancing which had opened up a magical world of fun and romance for them. Dressed in blue jeans and T-shirts with C-A L-I-F-O-R-N-I-A (sometimes C-A-R-I-F-O-R-N-I-A) and N-E-W Y-O-R-K emblazoned across their chests, they danced the night away in the numerous discos that opened up a romantic wonderland for them. The charm of the Western pop scene epitomized by GREASE at one end and Donna Summer at the other had them captivated enough to raise the collective blood pressure of the conservative elements in the country, who chafed at the American presence in such large numbers-estimates had them at a mammoth two hundred fifty thousand.

The Americans, on the other hand, never had it so good, enjoying the money and the benign protection and favor of the Shah. Conscious of the fact that they were brought in by the Shah to fill an important gap created by the dismissal of the British, and earning five times the salaries they would earn for the same work in the US, many of them did not possess the sensitivity that living harmoniously in a completely new culture required. In fairness to them, it was the lack of experience and even education in some of them that led to this failure. They did not see the depth and richness of the Persian culture, and looked upon the Persians as heirs to a camel culture, often referring to them as stinkies and bedouins. Young Americans staggered and swaggered around the cities, engaging in drunken brawls and fights, which were rarely, if ever, seen among Iranians, who preferred to solve their disagreements through peaceful discussion. The loud music, even during the holy months of Ramadan, and worse at Ashura when the Shia Iranian sincerely and deeply, albeit morbidly-beating themselves with bicycle chains and whips on their heads and backs- mourned the martyrdom of their holiest, Ali and Hossein, incensed the conservative old folk whose dislike and distrust of Americans grew more than they had ever felt for the

Arabs, the Turks, the Mongols or the Russians who had invaded their country before. To them the US was not only more powerful than the former invaders had been; the US seemed to have the Shah by the short hairs for some reason they could not fathom. Worst of all, the suppression of the people, via SAVAK, the dreaded secret police of the Shah was becoming more severe and more pervasive.

These final little details neither Jordan nor her mother had heard of. All they knew was that the Americans were sustaining democracy in the land of the Peacock Throne, and that everything American was well-loved by the handsome Shah, his adorable wife and people.

Chapter 3

August 25, 1977.

There's nothing to worry about. I'm going to have a great time here, mused Jordan recounting the chat she had had with Renee, before she left New York. In addition to her knowledge of the mundane history, she revealed the more racy details, which she had saved for the last. The Shah has an eye for the girls. His present wife is his third," she had told Jordan. "His first was Fawziya, sister of Egypt's King Farouk." Renee did not mention, nor did she know, that this had been an inauspicious and injudicious marriage from the Iranian point of view. Farouk and the Egyptians are Sunnis while Iranians are ardent Shia Moslems. The insensitivity to Shia sentiment by choosing a Sunni as first lady rankled and appeared to have doomed the marriage to failure right from the beginning, when at the wedding ceremony, a huge argument had taken place between the bride's mother and the bridegroom as to whether the dowry should remain in Iran or be kept in Egypt. The bridegroom's will had prevailed and everything pointed to a happy alliance. However, when Fawziya failed to bring forth a male heir, the marriage began to flounder, and finally ended in divorce. "Then he married Soraya, a great beauty, who many believe, was the love of his life," said Renee.

Again, Renee did not know that Soraya Esfandiari was the daughter of a Bakhtiari chief, and the marriage held the additional promise of increasing the stability of the Pahlavi dynasty building connections to the powerful Bakthiyari clan. "But unluckily, she couldn't produce a male heir either, and then she married Farah, who obliged within a year," chuckled Renee.

Renee was also unaware of the circumstances under which the third marriage had taken place. Actually, by the time he divorced Soraya, the Shah was getting cantankerous, and having temper tantrums at the ignominy of being unable to produce a male heir, as well as the political necessity of divorcing Soraya. The absence of a male heir was a visible threat to the preservation of the Pahlavi dynasty, which might well revert to the Quajars through matrimonial blood lines unless he fathered a son and quick.

Farah Diba, daughter of a wealthy, aristocratic Iranian family was studying architecture in Paris when she was brought into Reza's orbit more by human rather than heavenly design as traditional Iranians liked to imagine. The real architect was Shahnaz, daughter of the Shah by his first marriage, who arranged for the two to meet during one of the Shah's many visits to gay Paris. Before long, the Shah proposed and they were married at the Marble Palace in December, 1959.

Jordan had been well informed by her mother on these details, but there were many things she knew nothing about, and one may conclude that if she had known these things, she probably would not have so readily decided to go to Iran.

For instance, she did not know that the University of Tehran had been the symbol of modernization in the vision of the Shah, who regularly lavished grants and donations towards its progress. On the contrary, the conservative clerics viewed it as a hotbed of decadence, and infamy- where Shia-Iranian culture and tradition were being gradually being eroded, where the legitimacy of the position of the woman in traditional society was being weakened. The clerics watched with smoldering resentment young Iranian women doing what young Iranian women had been doing ever since time began, though without inhibition or guilt, in the company of young men, and that, too, without the chador safeguarding their modesty.

In January, 1960, barely a year after the wedding, the long awaited male heir to the Pahlavi throne was born.

It was the event of the century and was celebrated with indescribable pomp and jubilation. Helicopters showered Niavaran Palace with roses for Farah, and herbs and potions for the protection of the young prince against any harm. Fireworks displays and grand parties across the length and breadth of the country were ordered and financed by the Shah. The new hope for the Pahlavi dynasty had arrived.

The Shah was beside himself and lulled into a sense of euphoria and self-importance, which blinded him even further to the aspirations of the people. The people, who first rejoiced with the king, began to protest when they found themselves getting entrenched deeper and deeper in poverty, and the rich-poor divide kept getting wider.

The expected social justice, compassion and equality seemed to be getting further and further away from the people. In the meantime, the extended royal family, along with their friends and favorites, were making hay while the golden sands gushed out the liquid black gold. While the poor battled the hot summers and the frigid winters in their little tenements, the rich cavorted in their villas, or enjoyed lavish holidays abroad.

Not surprisingly, the people began to protest, inter alia, the high cost of living.

The Shah, far from seeing the protests as an index of the mood of the people, viewed the people's demands as a threat to the stability of his dynastic ambitions. He called upon his trusted Head of SAVAK, the dreaded, merciless Nematollah Nasiri to bring the dissidents under control.

The organizers and leaders of the protests were arrested, taken to the dungeons, and were never heard of again. SAVAK terror ruled the streets, manned by sycophants and hired snitches who carried all tales great and small to SAVAK.

And the people moved away from the Shah and closer to the clergy, seeking the elusive social justice and equality that Ali and Hussein had symbolized, and sacrificed their lives for.

Prince Ali Reza had hardly reached his second birthday when the University of Tehran, the Shah's bastion of social progress, became the scene of student demonstrations demanding social justice, and a change of the Shah's policies. Student groups of different political hues joined forces demonstrating and rioting in and around the campus, damaging university property. What followed shocked even the most moderate critics of the Shah. The demonstrators were hounded out and brutalized in the most atrocious and bestial ways. The more fortunate ones ended up in hospital. Most of the leaders ended up in the dungeons and were never heard of again. Female students were criminally attacked by club and knife wielding men in military uniform.

Many Americans who had been in Iran at the time and knew what had happened had returned to the US. The few who still remained had forgotten. Nobody had the wish or the inclination to recall those turbulent times and events. So Jordan was blissfully ignorant about the protests and the unrest before she arrived in Tehran. Like her mother, she thought that Iran was a place of peace and stability, ruled by a sage and wise monarch, loved and respected by all.

"I read somewhere that he has a holiday palace in California," said Jordan.

"Yes, and another in St. Moritz, and wherever else his romantic adventures take him. He's had a few liaisons in Hollywood, too, first an Italian actress, Sylvana Mangano, then Jean Tierney and later Yvonne de Carlo, who plays Herman's wife in the Munsters now. Those are the known ones. So you'd better be careful," she admonished Jordan facetiously. "But seriously, I'm sure you're going to have a wonderful time in Iran, darling," she had tried to assure Jordan, "and you'll make a lot of money."

But at my back I always hear some alarm bells, thought Jordan, recalling the words of Marvell to his Coy Mistress with apologies to the poet. Well, this is my first time out of home, and I'm going to make the most of it. But the tiny dark cloud of concern was difficult to get rid of.

Chapter 4

March, 1977

"I'm home," Jordan trilled as she walked into the apartment she shared with Josh, her boyfriend of two years. The Jackson Five were dishing out their brand of Rock 'n Roll on TV.

"How was your day?" enquired Josh, from the only bedroom on their second-floor apartment in downtown Albany.

Jordan and Josh had gone to school together at the State University of New York. They had started dating in the middle of their junior year. Graduating together, Jordan decided to teach school, and had had no difficulty in finding a job at Duanesburg middle school, thirty minutes out of downtown Albany. Jordan's mother had herself been a teacher, and had imbued in her daughter the love for English literature. Jordan loved to see the faces of her students light up as she took them through stories, poems and drama, making it all come alive with her own passion for the great writers. She made sure that she got the students fully involved in whatever she dealt with in her class. She wore a grotesque raven's head as she read

Poe's classic poem in class, and the fear in the eyes of her students and the deathly silence that prevailed convinced her that she had what it took to be a good teacher. She had overheard one of her students say, "I love Miss Moore's class. She brings all those characters in the stories to life." She had pretended not to hear what they were saying, but quietly patted herself on her back, and knew that teaching was going to be her lifelong career.

"It was great, darling. We read 'The Gift of The Magi' and 'The Last Leaf' in class today, and even some of the boys had lumps in their throats when we got through them." recounted Jordan.

"What are those?" asked Josh, a business major, on whom the charms of English literature had the sticking power of water on a duck's back.

"They are two of O' Henry's great short stories depicting the great sacrifices people make for those they love," she explained patiently. Not that I would expect you to do anything like that, she thought.

"I was watching Archie Bunker after you went to sleep last night. I love that guy, don't you? And what he's saying is true, you know. Most of our problems are due to the blacks. See that family downstairs, always yelling and fighting. I wish we could move to a better neighborhood." Jordan knew what a better neighborhood meant for Josh-a place where there were no blacks or browns or Jews! She wanted to tell him that America was, as Kennedy wrote, 'a Nation of Immigrants,' where everyone from the far corners of the earth had the right to live peacefully. She also wanted to tell him that the writers of the show were actually making fun of people's bigotry and small-mindedness through

Archie's speech and behavior. But she checked herself. After a long day at school, she was pretty tired, and didn't want to start the evening with an argument.

Her mind suddenly went back to how she had come to be 'shacked up' with Josh. They had met in the Ratskellar pub on campus one sultry Friday evening in June 1975. She was attending summer school because she wanted to graduate as soon as she could. She was impatient to launch out on a career-to make money and begin an independent life. I want to live it up, she said to herself and for that I need to make some real money.

She worked part-time in the school library to earn her living expenses; her mother paid for her tuition. She had not been dating anyone at the time because she felt she just didn't have the time or the patience to deal with a boyfriend. It was the time of women's lib, and the ERA, and she felt that she had to make some contribution to the cause of womanpower by being independent. It was also the era when gay sex was becoming an acceptable way of life. She was not herself a lesbian, although she had many friends who were, and they were not afraid to talk about it. The age of permissiveness had branched out in many ways. She recalled an incident in the school cafeteria, when some of her friends who happened to be lesbian were discussing a party they were organizing over the weekend. One of their mutual acquaintances, Richard Rheinheimmer, a self-assured Catholic from upstate New York, was listening to their discussion, and facetiously asked Nicole, the most voluble in the group, "Am I invited to the party?"

"No, Richard, it's only for girls," explained Nicole, patiently.

"Oh? And what is it that you do at these parties that you can't do when guys are around?" insisted Richard mockingly.

"We have girl sex!" growled Nicole, so loud that a few heads at the other tables turned around to look at them. Richard, completely abashed and very red in the face, excused himself and made a hasty retreat.

That Friday evening, Jordan and Patricia had been sitting around in the Ratskellar pub on Campus, enjoying a beer and sharing a joint. The Stylistics' "God bless you, you make me feel brand new," played on the enormous stereo speakers. The atmosphere was thick and heavy with tobacco and marijuana smoke dimming the lights to near darkness. Out of the haze and the cacophony of voices and music, Jordan sensed more than saw a towering figure rising out of a chair at the next table. "Hey Jordan," she heard, and the towering figure transformed itself into Josh, a guy she knew from one of her classes.

"Hey, yourself," responded Jordan as she watched Josh ease himself into the chair next to hers.

'How's it going?"

She knew Josh was on the football team, and with his tall gangly frame, curly brown hair, slate-grey eyes and boyish looks, was being pursued by at least two girls she knew. She did not know if the feelings were mutual, or whom he pursued, or even if he was gay, which would probably not have surprised her. It did not seem to matter to her anyway, for the euphoria of the youthful atmosphere, the alcohol and the pot were all having a benign influence on her. She wanted nothing else. It's good to be alive, she mused.

They had a few more beers, and after Jordan had introduced Josh to Patricia, a couple more joints had been passed around the group, now made up of three. Small talk and music dominated the rest of the evening. "Hey, I'm feeling pretty good," giggled Patricia, leaning on Josh, singing "Lady Marmalade" as they stood up to leave. As they walked towards Brubacher Hall, the co-ed dorm they all lived in, Josh volunteered to see Patricia to her room, and Jordan walked on to hers.

On Monday morning, Jordan was rushing down one of the corridors to her nine o'clock class when she bumped into Josh again. "Hi, Jordan," he greeted her exuberantly, and she wondered what had happened between him and Patricia after they had walked arm in arm to her door. It was the era of the new permissiveness. Anything could have happened, she thought.

"Hey, I'm having a game Friday night, and I was wondering if you'd be free to have dinner with me afterwards," he invited.

"Oh, I don't know," she countered. The invitation came as a big surprise, and she was totally unprepared for it.

"Aw, come on," he cajoled, "I promise I'll see you back to your room without letting you get sloshed," he teased.

"OK," she said on impulse, and there seemed to be a sparkle in his eye as he said, "I'll pick you up at 7.30."

They had dinner at a Japanese restaurant downtown. The hibachi cook was a great performer, and the Japanese food was delicious. They had lots of shrimp and lobster with steamed rice and sushi. The wine Josh ordered went well with the meal. Josh was a great talker, and kept not only Jordan, but the four other guests who shared their table, and the chef entertained with his anecdotes and jokes about college life and football.

Driving back to the campus, Josh was his ebullient self, but when he saw her off at the entrance to her room, he suddenly seemed shy and uncomfortable. "Goodnight, Jordan. Thanks for a wonderful evening!"

"Likewise, Josh," she replied, and they had parted.

Monday evening, and Josh called Jordan. "Hey, there's a Woody Allen movie in town-*Love and Death*. Would you like to see it? Diane Keaton's in it, too."

They had been talking movies, and Jordan had told Josh that she liked Woody Allen, who she thought was brilliantly funny. They had talked about his budding romance with Diane Keaton. She was a little surprised and quite touched when she realized that he had remembered. "Not tonight, Josh," she said, remembering the paper she had to write for Dr. Blackburn's applied linguistics class on Tuesday, "Maybe tomorrow."

"Good things are worth waiting for," laughed Josh.

They both enjoyed the movie, and had Chinese food at a downtown restaurant. When she saw him off at the dorm, Jordan reached up and kissed him briefly on the lips. "Thanks Josh," she murmured, "I had a great time."

"Likewise," murmured Josh, and Jordan was a little surprised to see him blush from ear to ear. God, he's a virgin, Jordan thought, amused.

From then on, their meetings became regular, and Jordan found herself liking Josh. But as far as their physical relationship was concerned, Josh had been almost shy. Belying his seeming confidence and bravado with the opposite sex, it was after their fourth date that he had even tried to kiss her. And when he did, she had had to give him some encouragement. Probably his catholic upbringing, she thought amusedly. "Thank God I wasn't born a catholic," she said out aloud, without realizing that Josh could hear her.

"What did you say?" he asked.

"Nothing," she laughed, as she directed his attention to more delectable exertions.

Before long they were lovers. As time passed, Josh graduated sexually from a novice to relative competence. He was caring and considerate at all times, and always tried to please her in every way he could. She on her part cared for him very much. He was fun to be with, and was sensitive to her physical and emotional needs, but she realized that there was nothing spontaneous about what he did. He was like a good businessman, always trying to please in order to hang on to the customer base. Whenever she showed that she needed something by word or deed, he spared no pains in getting it for her, but deep inside her, she wanted something more. She couldn't say exactly what it was. Maybe it was not just what she wanted from him or of him. It was what she wanted out of life. Talking to Jill about her relationship with Josh, she said, "He's very dependable, and I know that he wants to please me, but everything he does is becoming so familiar."

"So why are you complaining? There's comfort in the familiar, right? I'm sure he'll always be faithful to you, and you can depend on him to be a caring husband."

"Hey, take it easy woman. I'm only twenty-four, and marriage is the last thing on my mind right now. I need to live it up, a bit. Besides, the familiar can get pretty boring sometimes," she mock whined.

But seriously, she thought, I want to play in a bigger arena. I don't want to end up in suburbia with a two-car garage, and two kids in the nursery, and that's exactly where I seem to be heading with Josh, unless I do something about it. What she was going to do or how she was going to do it she had no clue about.

Soon after they graduated, they moved in together into an apartment on Spring Street off Washington Avenue. It seemed like the normal thing to do. And here they were, living a life of domestic ease-at least for Josh, it was. Jordan would leave early for work, but Josh would sleep late since he didn't have to get to his job until eight. He worked as an administrative secretary in the Department of Labor, and his office was right by the Capitol building about three blocks from their apartment on the corner of Spring Street and Washington Avenue. Jordan would return home around four, and cook dinner. She wasn't much of a cook, but the recipe books her mother had thoughtfully given her when she left home in Schenectady to move in with Josh came in handy. She tried to cook something different each evening, especially in the first few months, but the novelty of keeping house and cooking for the man she loved was gradually wearing thin. Thinking back, she was beginning to wonder if she actually loved him or vice versa.

They did go out to the movies, to visit a few friends that had settled in and around Albany, and to eat at some of the fancy restaurants in the neighborhood. They drove to the Big Apple whenever they felt like it-it was a leisurely two-hour drive from Albany- and when they did, they really had great fun. The twin towers of the World Trade Center were the latest addition to Manhattan's skyline, and they made it a point to visit all of the splendid landmarks in the city. They had skated in the Rockefeller Center, ridden up to the top of the Empire State Building, and caught up on the history of the music scene at the Radio City Music Hall. But it was the museums that had really fascinated Jordan. The museums opened her mind to what was out there- out beyond New York City, both in terms of time and space. Many people, especially native New Yorkers considered New York a world all on its own. The people, the places, the things to do-the variety, the magnificence of it all did not have a small impression on her. However, now that she had experienced the greatness, the enormity, the diversity and the beauty of the Big Apple, it all began to look so familiar. Just like her relationship with Josh, she thought, she wanted to move on.

Chapter 5

Josh and Jordan were sitting in their living room one evening when the phone rang. "I'll get it," said Jordan. It was her friend Jill Mc Shane, who taught at the middle school where Jordan worked. Both Jill and Jordan taught language arts at school.

"Hey Jordan, how y' doing?"

"OK, Jill. Just watching the tube," replied Jordan, trying hard to keep the listlessness out of her voice. They engaged in small talk for a while, when Jill said, "Know what? Just heard from a friend in New York that some job openings are coming up in Iran. Would you like to go?"

"What are you talking about? Iran? In the Middle East?"

"Yeah, Iran y'know Persia. Tehran University."

"OK. I know that. Just get to the point, will you."

"Tehran University has posted some English teaching jobs, and I want to apply for one. A friend of mine told me that there are quite a few vacancies for English teachers in Iran. The Shah, that is the king, is very keen on taking the country out of the camel and the donkey era to the jet age. He's encouraging Iranians to learn English, and the universities are offering scholarships to students who want to study English. Hey, how about it? Would you like to go to Tehran? The money's great you know."

"You bet I would!" said Jordan, surprised by her sudden impulse. "I think that's just what I need-to get away from it all for a while," looking furtively at Josh to see if he had overheard, but he was completely mesmerized by Walter Cronkite, dishing out the evening news in his 'immaculate all-American accent' as her linguistics professor had called it.

"Let me know the details tomorrow," she whispered, almost guiltily, since she had never talked to Josh about her pent up desire for change, which she knew had been bottled up for a while.

She felt even worse when, a commercial break interrupted Cronkite, and Josh asked her what Jill had said, "Nothing, really," she lied, "she's having a bad evening, and needed to chat a bit. Hey, do you want to watch *Tony Orlando and Dawn*? It'll be on in a few minutes."

"No, but you go ahead. I brought in some work from the office."

Oh, sorry, thought Jordan, two black women and a half Puerto Rican- not your idea of entertainment, I guess. Well, I'm going to watch it and afterwards, I'm going to watch Freddie Prinze, a Hispanic mechanic and his quirky white boss in *Chico and the Man* she thought, annoyed at Josh's apparent conservative taste in entertainment.

Jordan and Jill got their applications ready and mailed them before the week was out.

Jordan's feeling of boredom with the familiar and the comfortable, smoldering initially, increased progressively, especially after she had done the deed of turning in her application to go abroad. I must tell Josh about it soon, she thought, with a sense of guilt, almost as if she had been unfaithful to him. Yikes, she thought, I'm already thinking like a married woman. That's terrible!

But the opportunity did not present itself, until about a month later, until after she had received a letter from the employment agency in New York. She was invited to attend an interview in the Agency's office at Broadway and 35th street.

When Jordan got home, Josh was watching Walter Cronkite's evening news broadcast.

Jordan prepared a great-looking dinner, which had turned out to be particularly delicious- a succulent filet mignon with fresh roasted vegetables and mashed potatoes from scratch, just as Josh liked. A full bodied California wine, chilled and served 'with beaded bubbles winking at the brim' thought Jordan, resisting the temptation to say out loud Keats' famous line which, regretfully, would have been lost on Josh, who probably had not even heard of John Keats. On the other hand, Josh seemed particularly happy with the meal, and praised Jordan many times for her culinary accomplishments as he savored the delicious food. He tried, with little success, to disguise the belch that rose from his sated innards.

"Hey, you're a great cook," he beamed, "the food is way out!"

With rising trepidation, Jordan decided to broach the subject. "Honey, I have to attend an interview in the Big Apple on Monday," she began, trying to sound as casual as possible.

"Interview? What for?" Josh asked, confusion written all over his face.

"I applied for this job in Tehran," she said.

"Tehran? Where's that- in New Jersey?" he asked.

"No, in Iran, you know Persia, in the Middle East" she replied patiently, "an English teaching position at the University of Tehran." And she added spitefully, "That's the capital of Iran."

"You're going to Persia? When? Why? What about your job here? What about me?" he babbled, annoyance, confusion crimson-darkening his face.

"Well, if I get the job, we can go together if you like. I can ask the university to include you in my visa," she said, and immediately realized that she had put her foot in her mouth. Josh was very nice to her and appeared to respect her as an equal, but she knew tagging along 'on her visa' as she had thoughtlessly called it would be anathema to his male ego. "It'll be great darling. I'm sure you can find a job there, too. They pay very good salaries, and they love us Americans," she added flippantly.

Despite the frivolous tone she assumed, Jordan knew this information would not go down well with Josh. A conservative to the core, Josh, could think of no other place where he would be happier than in his hometown or some place near it-certainly not out of New York State. Only U.S. troops should go outside the US of A, and tourists, he had once remarked in all seriousness when they were discussing the idea of going abroad for a spell. Jordan waited with bated breath for the inevitable outburst that she knew would come.

"You want me to leave my job here? I can't do that. I have very good prospects of advancing in the career I have chosen, and suddenly you want me to leave it all and chaperone you to some god-forsaken country in Africa?" He spoke as if he were addressing, with subdued impatience, a little girl who had done something wrong. She half expected him to say, now let's stop this nonsense and get to bed.

"Not Africa, the Middle East," she said, a note of frustration creeping into her voice.

"Wherever. I don't think I want to do that. You're being very unreasonable, Jordan. I never expected this. You know, I …"

Something snapped inside Jordan. "It's all about you, isn't it, Josh?" she burst out, unable to hide the annoyance at his selfishness. "It's all about what you did in office, and what you're hoping and planning to do – never about me. You never even ask me what kind of day I've had at school. We sit down to eat, and you say how great the food is. I might as well be your housemaid."

"Well, I …"

"Well, this is about me, Josh," she interrupted him, unable to suppress the pent-up emotion she had kept bottled up, "I've reached a higher level in Maslow's hierarchy."

"Maslow? Who?"

"Never mind, Josh. The fact is that I'd like to travel out of here, for a while at least. I'd like a change. Life is getting to be too familiar." She'd have preferred to say boring, she thought.

"What about us?"

"I really don't know, Josh. I feel like our lives are going nowhere. You seem to have it all planned out for yourself, and you want me to string along any way I can."

"Come on! That's not fair. It's just that I want our lives to be secure. If I continue for a few years, I will get promoted in my job, and our lives will be more comfortable. That's what I want from life, and I thought you did, too."

Comfort and security, that's all you need to build your life on, mused Jordan.

"Yes, but the spark seems to have died already. We hardly have anything in common anymore. And we are not even married."

"Oh, is that what this is all about? Marriage?"

And Jordan thought, Oh, Josh, that's the last thing on my mind, and the first thing you could have thought of. But that's just the way you are.

"It's not about marriage Josh. I want things to be different, more exciting. I just don't know what I want. What I do know is that I want a change from the routine."

"I don't know either. I don't know what you're talking about. I'm going to bed," and he stormed into the bedroom.

That night, for the first time since they had moved into the apartment, Jordan slept on the couch.

In the days that followed, their relationship became first formal, and gradually strained and uncomfortable. Jordan knew that their relationship had reached its first obstacle. It would probably be their last she thought whimsically. Yet, she had no regrets.

Judged in the present light, it was inevitable, she said to herself. As a college relationship, It had gone well. And as a college relationship, it has to go, she thought wryly, surprised at her ability to dismiss it so lightly. It had been good while it lasted. She, at least, had been able to examine their relationship, albeit subconsciously, and the present situation did not cause her much surprise. She would move on, and so would Josh, with little more than pleasant memories of the way they were.

Jordan attended the interview, and she knew she would get the job.

Three weeks later, she received a letter from Tehran University that she had got the job.

"We welcome you and hope to see you soon," the Western Union telegram read.

When she told Josh about it, he said, "Congratulations!" The tone of resignation and acceptance in his voice was unmistakable. He's not even fighting back, she thought. I guess it's for the best.

Jill called her that evening to say that she had got a letter, too. Tehran, here I come, said Jordan to herself.

Chapter 6

August 25, 1977.

Two tall, good-looking men whom Jordan guessed were Iranian, one holding a board with her name in giant letters, welcomed her at the airport. They were dressed in expensive suits and were very well groomed, and Jordan thought they were administrative officers of the university. She said, "I'm Jordan. Thank you for coming to meet me!"

Grinning sheepishly, the men replied, "Salam Aleiyqum, Khanum," and picked up her luggage. "We take you hotel," one of them added haltingly.

They did not venture to speak again, and Jordan decided not to add to their woe, for they obviously had fully drawn on their English lexicon already.

They drove for about forty minutes in silence, until the car pulled up at a hotel.

The men escorted her to the reception desk, and one of them said a few words to the receptionist. "Welcome to Hotel Pars, Madam. We have a room reserved for you. I will call Miss Faride Rafsanjani and inform her that you have arrived. She is the administrative secretary of the English Department at the University," she said.

After she had settled in her room, Jordan called Faride, who spoke flawless English with a lilting accent, "Welcome to Iran, Miss Moore. I hope you had a pleasant flight."

"Yes, the flight was great. I'm just a little tired, but I'll be fine after a good night's sleep," she replied.

"That's wonderful to hear, Miss Moore. I hope you're comfortable in the hotel. We will talk about your permanent accommodation, and other matters when we meet tomorrow. Have a good night's rest. The driver and the peon who met you today will bring you to the university in the morning. What time do you think you will be ready?" she asked in a business like tone.

"What time do you come in," asked Jordan.

"Around 9.00,"

"Can they pick me up by 8.30, then?"

"Sure, that's no problem," she assured Jordan, "Oh, Miss Moore, you can order anything you like at the hotel; that includes anything you want from the mini bar. It's all paid for," she added. And Jordan thought, hey that's nice. Maybe I should get sloshed my first night in Tehran exotica.

Jordan's room, on the third floor of the hotel, was large and very tastefully decorated. The huge double bed was covered with lilac satin sheets. Large photographs of the Shah and his wife, in ornate gold colored frames took up one wall of the sitting area, furnished with a large sofa and two chairs.

A coffee table with a crystal glass bowl of red roses, and another of fresh fruit stood in the sitting area with an enormous sofa and two plush chairs. Pity I won't be having any visitors, thought Jordan, ruefully.

The mini bar was stocked with beer and soft drinks and a variety of liquors. An enormous basket was filled with packs of pistachios, cashews, peanuts and several varieties of American crackers and snacks.

Jordan wasn't hungry, for she had eaten almost all of the curried lamb and lemon rice served on the plane. I could do with a drink, though, she thought and made herself a vodka tonic. She drank it slowly, munching on some pistachios, which she had never tasted before, but found very much to her liking. Here I am, she mused, in the historic land of Persia. Tomorrow is a new beginning, she whispered to herself, as she got into bed. She had confused dreams of Josh and her mother, while the vodka she had imbibed induced a deep slumber.

Jordan walked down to the reception desk at 8.30 the next morning, and there were Laurel and Hardy, who had met her at the airport, with their big grins and a tad more familiar "Salam Alciykum." They were dressed in coat and tie, and their suits looked even more impressive in the morning light, Jordan noted. For a driver and a peon, they sure dress to kill, she thought. One of them opened the door of an enormous gun-metal grey BMW saying "Befarmoidh," and she sank into the comfortable rear seat. He got into the passenger seat in front and said, "We go," for her benefit, and the car started rolling through the dust and the fumes of Tehran's morning gridlock.

Tehran's streets were intensely overwhelming to Jordan, who had seen nothing like it in the quiet backstreets of Albany or Schenectady, where everybody's head turned when a car horn sounded. Here, everybody seemed to be in a great hurry, thought Jordan, if the constant blasts of the car horns were anything to go by, but nobody could get out of the almost anarchic tangle of cars, buses vans and trucks, each driver trying to steal a march over everyone else. Orange hued taxis dominated the roads, not only in number but in the devil-may-care manner in which they were driven. They would creep into the tiniest of spaces available between vehicles, and suddenly change direction heading for the curb to pick up a fare. It was vehicular frenzy at its highest, and Jordan resolved that she wouldn't be driving in Tehran traffic anytime soon.

Gridlock or no, Hardy rose to the occasion; he, too, had no regard for any other vehicles, taxis included, and made fast, though manic progress toward their destination. They arrived at the gates of the Tehran University campus at ten minutes to nine.

A huge sprawl of very traditional drab looking buildings, Tehran University was located flush on the tumultuous Ferdowsi Street. Everybody was honking, trying to get through where there was no way of doing so. It seemed to her that the drivers didn't need a reason for honking. A little different from the sedate drivers in the environs of Albany!

A row of tall, old palm trees and a four-foot parapet wall separated the buildings from the street. Little green bushes dotted the grounds adding some greenery and acting as a buffer against the dust from the street.

Inside, the buildings were cool and comfortable although the sound of cars honking kept ringing in Jordan's ears as she walked into the building that was the

English Department office. The furniture and the decor were comparable to that of any American college, she thought. In fact, they could be exact replicas. Enormous images of the Shah and Farah, in ornate frames dominated one of the walls of the foyer.

Faride Rafsnajani, slim and a head shorter than Jordan, left the security of her desk to walk across the hall to greet her. Jordan was convinced that the clothes the young and efficient looking secretary wore had pretty high-end designer labels. Her pleasant features seemed to light up as she smiled radiantly at Jordan, a smile that seemed to start in the depths of her beautiful brown eyes. Her face was made up to perfection, and the subtle perfume she wore must have cost her a pretty penny.

"Befarmoidh; Welcome Miss Moore," she said as she led her to a sofa. "Please sit down. Would you like some tea?" she invited, glancing at the huge shiny samovar bubbling in a corner of the room. Jordan declined and sat down under the benign gaze of the Shah and his pleasantly regal looking wife.

"Dr Firooznia will be here shortly," she assured Jordan, "in the meantime, we can work on your residence and work permits. May I have your passport, please? I will get your papers ready so you can take them in to Dr. Firooznia for him to sign." And Jordan obliged.

Soon she was sitting in the office of the Chairman of the English department, Dr. Seyyed Firooznia. Standing nearly six feet tall, he looked almost bony. He was clean-shaven, and had a pale, narrow face. A sharp aquiline nose dominated his features. His slate-grey eyes seemed to peer right through Jordan. A merry twinkle in his eyes, and a faint smile on his lips, he rose to greet her proffering his well-manicured hand. A pepper and salt beard almost hiding his handsome looks, Firooznia made an imposing figure in his exquisitely tailored charcoal grey suit. Despite his obvious charm, and the deep resonating voice that seemed to dominate the room, Jordan couldn't help noticing an avuncular disposition about him, and immediately felt at ease in his presence. "I hope you had a good flight, Miss Moore. I know it's a pretty tedious flight from New York to Tehran."

"It was a little tiring, but I had a great traveling companion on the second leg, so it went by easily. We made friends, and she promised to look me up some time," Jordan felt herself gushing, having already made up her mind that this was a man she would have no trouble working with. So far, so good, she thought.

"I'm glad to hear that. We're very happy you are here Miss Moore. I hope you will be very comfortable and enjoy your stay in Iran."

"Thank you, Sir" replied Jordan deferentially.

"Please call me Seyyed. I won't feel so old that way," he joked, "we have ten other Americans, three Britons, an Indian and a Sri Lankan in our little department. I'm sure you'll like them all and enjoy working with them. I believe you know Jill Mason, don't you?"

"Yes, we taught at the same school in Albany."

"That's good. Since this is your first time away from home, it will be nice for you to have someone around that you've known before."

Jordan was impressed by his sensitivity and was comforted that her first impression of him as a caring, sincere individual was very probably right. His voice and his words, and his cultured tone of voice confirmed her thoughts further. He said, "Faride will look after all of your needs as far as settling down is concerned. Dr Brad Foreman is the Head of the teaching unit, and you will be meeting with him later in the day. If there is anything I can do to make your stay more comfortable, please don't hesitate to talk to me. I will meet you with Brad this afternoon to discuss your schedule. We have departmental meetings once in two weeks. I look forward to working with you."

That went very well, short and sweet, thought Jordan, who had never met an Iranian before, except for Soraya on the plane, much less an Iranian Head of Department.

Chapter 7

Later in the morning she met Jill and the other members of the English Department staff. Everyone was very welcoming. Ed, the coordinator of the English program, was another friendly individual. Samad and Muzzafer seemed quiet compared to the Americans and the Briton. Bernard, the Sri Lankan, sounded very sincere and friendly as he made some helpful suggestions about settling in Tehran. Jill, who had arrived two weeks before Jordan, had rented an apartment with Carole, a friend of hers from New York. "Pat Mallory is looking for a roommate. She has rented a two-bedroom not far from the campus. I told her about you, but you have to wait a few days while the ministry of foreign affairs processes your residence and work visas. Without these documents, a foreigner is persona non grata here," she explained.

Dr. Patricia Mallory, (everybody calls me Pat), a very sharp looking thirtyish blonde from Wyoming, immediately caught Jordan's attention. The most quick-witted of the group by far, Pat epitomized the new liberated American woman who brooked no nonsense from anybody, least of all from Bob, the military type who emanated an air of chauvinistic arrogance, bordering on the intolerable. Jordan took an immediate liking for Pat, and thought she would be a great roommate.

Pat and Jordan leased an apartment on Khuresh street, about fifteen minutes away from Tehran University. It had two large, comfortable bedrooms and came fully furnished. The next day, they went to the Grand Bazaar in downtown Tehran to get a few things for the apartment.

Chapter 8

If there was any place that could fit Jordan's image of Alladin's cave, the Grand Bazaar in Tehran was it. Spread out over an area of over a square mile, it was a myriad of dimly lit domed passages stacked to the roof with a variety of merchandize ranging from household goods and furniture to clothes, and jewelry from all parts of the world.

At the beginning, it was all very confusing and Jordan thought the entire population of Tehran was crowded into it. The cacophony of buyers and sellers haggling over prices was overwhelming. The smell of spices and sandalwood, Arabian perfumes, and human sweat and carpets seemed to fill every nook and cranny, but they merged harmoniously into something close to the magic of the East, the myrrh and the frankincense, and the jasmine and cinnamon taking her mind back to the tales of Scheherazade of the Arabian nights.

A samovar, with a teapot boiling away on it was a regular fixture in every shop. Beside it were several containers with different types of sugar cubes, some brown and others white, some soft and melting easily in the mouth, others hard crystal. An Iranian would drink from ten to fifteen cups of the brew each day.

People jostled against each other with never an 'excuse me.' No offense was taken, although Jordan noticed that the women tried hard to avoid bumping into the men, some of whom seemed to get a bit of quirky pleasure out of it. Jordan was reminded of the rush at a clothing store in New York during a sale.

Jordan's early confusion was because she did not know the geography of the place. After she had been there a couple of times, she realized that it was a very systematically organized shopping place-an enormous supermarket-with everything arranged for the convenience of the many customers who thronged the place everyday. She would later learn that some of the nondescript, ragged looking merchants who sat dreamily as if they were not concerned about what they sold or how much were actually architects of huge international financial deals transacted not through computers and ledgers, but little pieces of paper which changed hands surreptitiously, but with deep and branching roots in absolute trust; the bazaar was the nerve center of a financial center interconnected with the financial centers of London and New York, Beirut and Baghdad. It was the kind of financial organization of a primeval past, an anachronism to the western mind, yet working with exquisite efficiency. Million dollar deals were made through the little scraps of paper that changed hands in the Bazaar in Tehran. And there the Bazaari sat looking inept-even destitute- yet wielding infinite influence both locally and abroad.

In addition to the hundreds of shopping kiosks, there was a mosque, baths and little restaurants, where both Iranian food as well as American food such as hamburgers and hotdogs were sold. There were different areas for different types of products. The spice shops dominated the air with the strong aroma of ginger, cinnamon garlic and other spices. The entire area was covered by huge domes, typical of Middle Eastern architecture, which served to keep those under them pleasantly cool in the summer and warm in the cold winter.

An enormous area was taken up by little dress boutiques stocked with the most glamorous apparel from the biggest fashion houses in Europe and the USA, but unlike the neatly arranged displays in the West, the clothes were just hanging in disarray from nails in the walls and strings drawn across the little stalls.

Another area was full of household goods. The best from the East, and the West – clothing, electronics, furniture, women's fashion products, and jewelry they were all there. All one needed to know was where to find them.

And one day Jordan stumbled into the carpet area, literally the heart of the bazaar. Persian carpets rate among the best in the world, and are mostly hand-made. Historically one of the oldest cottage industries in Iran, carpet making is an occupation that the Iranians talk about with great pride and joy. The skill and the materials that go into production, combined with the traditional designs and magnificent colors bring forth exquisite works of art. Jordan saw a particularly beautiful carpet three feet by two feet in one of the shops.

"How much?" asked Jordan and the shopkeeper replied in Farsi. Faride, who had gone shopping with her that day, interpreted for Jordan. "It's about two thousand dollars," she said, and Jordan thought she was joking.

"I'm serious," explained Faride, "It's made of pure silk yarn, and the design is so intricate, it took three people working over a month to weave it. There are carpets here that are worth a king's ransom. In Iran a man's standing and prestige are gauged by the carpets that adorn his house."

The ways of the East, thought Jordan.

Chapter 9

Work at the university was quite pleasant. Jordan taught two classes, each having twenty students. The first thing that she noticed was that both the male and female students showed great deference to the teacher. The girls were also somewhat shy in the class, and at the beginning she had to use all of her skills to get them to actually participate in the lessons; they tended to sit quietly and listen. However, as time went by, they gradually shook off their inhibitions and Jordan was greatly impressed by the pace at which they picked up the language. The great motivator was their desire to be like Americans, and hopefully go to the USA in the future. The boys, too, showed great promise and Jordan found it very easy to hold their interest in the language learning situations she simulated in class. The students were very conscientious, and tried very hard to cultivate the American way of speaking. They often spoke about tourist spots in New York and Chicago. The boys were eager to visit the Statue of Liberty and the Radio City Music Hall, and the girls to shop on Fifth Avenue and the Magnificent Mile! I haven't done that much myself, she said to herself, but perhaps when I go back.

About ten days after she had arrived, Jordan received a call from Soraya, her traveling companion from London. "Hey, Professor, how are things?" she chortled.

"I'm fine, Soraya. How are you? And how are those adorable little guys I saw on the plane?'

"Oh, they're running wild. When they come home, they're uncontrollable. Having a young brother and grandparents who dote on them doesn't help either," she complained mock seriously. "Listen, Jordan, I want you to come to my house. My parents and –I have two sisters and a younger brother- they all want to see my American friend."

"Thank you Soraya. That would be wonderful. I'd love meet your family."

"Great! That's settled then. I'll pick you up on Thursday. Everyone will be home then."

"Thursday?" exclaimed Jordan, "but I'm working."

"No, you're not, silly. It's the weekend, don't you know?" And then Jordan remembered that Thursday was Saturday in Iran.

"I'll come by around ten to pick you up. Will that be all right?"

"Sure, that would be great. But you're putting yourself into so much trouble. I can take a taxi if you give me directions," said Jordan.

"Oh no," giggled Soraya, "this is Iran, Jordan. We don't expect our guests to take taxis."

Soraya was at Jordan's apartment at five to ten. She drove a dark blue Volvo. Beside her sat her brother, a smart curly haired eighteen year old, smiling from ear to ear, ogling Jordan, mesmerized by her blonde hair and blue eyes. "OK, Naser, sit in the back with the brats," she laughed pushing him by the shoulder, and Naser sheepishly withdrew his gaze from Jordan and joined his nephews, who pounced on him as soon as he sat down.

Although it was ten in the morning, the already hot sun beat relentlessly down as their car sped through the dry and dusty streets of Tehran. Most of the streets had open drains-the *jubes*- with water tinkling down-not dirty sewer water, but reasonably clear water which people had actually used a few decades ago, before the city had pipe-borne water. Now the jubes carried water to the many trees that lined the streets of the northern part of the city. In the southern part, some people still used jube water for washing, the ones who could not afford to install pipes in their homes. The sight of the water made the heat outside seem easier to bear.

They drove steadily for about twenty minutes through the Tehran traffic, when the car slowed down and turned into a short driveway. A tap on the horn, and the black metal gate swung open inwards into the grounds of a villa.

Jordan could not help but marvel at the beauty of the garden they had entered. Several colossal trees shut away the stifling heat of the sun, but a few bright rays which managed to creep in through the thick foliage were enough to provide the sunlight for the numerous flowering shrubs and miniature fruit trees that adorned every nook and cranny with a myriad of colors and subtle perfumes which took Jordan's breath away. She wanted to just sit and savor the splendor of this little wonderland, thinking this is how Alice must have felt when she tumbled down into her magical world. "It's gorgeous out here, Soraya," was all she could say.

Soraya's mother, smiling expansively greeted them at the door. A statuesque fifty something beauty, Razieh beamed, "Befarmoidh, Khanum! Welcome! Come. You sit." And she guided Jordan into the enormous living room.

A gigantic bowl of fruit, bright, and fresh stood on the ornate brass coffee table in the center of the room. Plush sofas invited the visitor to feel at ease in the delicious cool air of the room made pleasant by summer fresh fragrance of oranges and apples, and the liberal application of jasmine air freshener. Jordan sank into the soft comfort of the plush sofa, and Razieh beckoned to Jordan, "Eat. Orenji, apple, is good." Soraya, watching amusedly from across the room cautioned Jordan, "You'd better eat some fruit, or you'll never hear the end of it from my Mom. It's a Persian tradition that the guest that does not partake of the fruit offered by the host has no respect for the host!"

"Oh, I certainly must not give your mother that impression. And I do love your tradition of offering fruit before anything else," said Jordan, reaching for a little sprig of grapes.

"Yes, we Persians believe that fruit is the food of the gods. It improves one's skin complexion and puts one in a good humor. We can eat fruit anytime of the day, and we usually do," she chuckled.

"Oh, I now see where you guys get your beautiful skin," remarked Jordan.

After a delicious meal of lamb kebob, chicken cooked in wine, and sabs-e-pullau, an aromatic dish of rice cooked with an assortment of spiced vegetables and olive oil, Jordan and Soraya sat in the living room looking at old family pictures. As they thumbed through the albums, Daniel suddenly rushed into the room with an album, shouting, "Pedar. Father." And suddenly it dawned on Jordan that Soraya's husband was not in any of the albums she had seen. Soraya looked sharply at Daniel, but let him show the album to Jordan. A tall, handsome man of about forty-five, in impeccable European dress leaped off the pages. Charmingly pleasant looking, the man seemed to have a permanent smile adorning his sharp Persian features, and Jordan could not help asking Soraya, "What happened?"

"It's a long story, Jordan. Yes, he's cute and pleasant, and always behaved the gentleman-to everyone else but me," she added sardonically. "He saved all his unpleasant side for me. At the beginning of our marriage he was the epitome of romance, love and caring. I thought I could never be happier for I had everything a woman could want-a loving husband, two adorable kids and all the creature comforts money could buy. He used to shower me with gifts and love. But suddenly, everything began to change. First, it was as if he transferred all the love he had for me to the children. I didn't mind that, but as time passed, he began to keep the children away from me. He didn't want me to have any influence on the children."

"How did that happen? I thought he loved you."

"Yes, that's what I thought, too. And then I found out that he was seeing someone else- a Swedish woman who worked with him. When she first called the house and asked for him, he explained that the call was job-related. As time went by, and the calls became longer and more regular, I confronted him. The next weekend he left the house saying that he was going to Esfahan for a business meeting. I knew he was lying."

"What did you do?'

"Actually, before I broached the subject, he told me that he was planning to take a second wife. He said that he needed his sons to have Western influence, and that he was going to marry the Swedish woman. She had agreed to be his second wife. I was pretty amazed. He was, of course, within his rights according to Iranian law."

"But why did he want to have a second wife? Didn't you ask him? Did he give you a reason?"

"No, he doesn't have to give a reason. He could say anything- like the sex was not satisfying, for instance. Usually an Iranian wife does not ask that question for the obvious reason that the man can say anything."

"So the woman has no say in the matter, is what you're saying," asked Jordan, a note of incredulity creeping into her voice.

"The only thing a woman can do is opt for divorce, which is what I did."

"Oh, that's good. So he was reasonable, and let you go with the children, huh?"

"No Jordan, that was not it at all. I had to really fight for the divorce. Fortunately, my father is pretty close to Prime Minister Hoveyda's family. The Hoveydas have considerable influence on my husband's family. The Prime Minister himself had to persuade him to allow me the divorce. According to our law, a man is within his right to have a second wife. The first wife does not have the right to object."

"What about the children?"

"The children he would not let go. Again, according to Iranian law, the father has full rights over the children over the children."

"So how do you have them?"

"After my husband got married, he had full custody of them. The newly-weds moved to Shiraz, where the company has business interests. It was the worst time of my life. I had to travel all the way to Shiraz to see them-and it was just about once a month-for a few hours on Saturday and Sunday that I could do that. And the kids were not enjoying it either. They hated the Swedish woman."

"Oh, you poor guys! That must have been terrible."

"It was Jordan. I didn't know what to do. I thought my life was over. But then, luckily, I discovered that the Swedish woman didn't like the idea of looking after my kids. That's the one thing I'm thankful to her for."

"What do you mean?"

"I think she made this obvious to Irfan - that's my husband's name," she added as if she were talking about an archaic object from another life.

"So I had my benefactors, the Hoveydas, talk to him. He very reluctantly allowed me to keep the children. But he set down one condition- that I should not take them outside Iran without his approval. I agreed. I was in such a state I would have agreed to anything. There, too, he has rights. The mother is not allowed to take the children out of the country without the father's approval."

"So what happened?"

"Naturally I wanted to make a clean break. I applied for a work visa in England, and without telling him, moved to London, all this in the utmost secrecy. It's a year now since we moved, and I can tell you it's not easy. I have to hide the fact from him and his family. Luckily, everybody in his family lives in Tabriz, and after the divorce, they haven't even tried to visit us. My poor father has to do all kinds of things to keep up appearances that we are in Tehran. My little brother, too, the poor guy."

"You mean Irfan doesn't know?"

"That's right. I had to forge his signature. And you know what? He seems to be so taken up with his Swedish bombshell that he has never bothered to check us out."

"Doesn't he come to see the children?"

"He does-at *No Ruz*-that's our traditional new year. So I make sure they're here during that time. I come home twice a year."

"Wow. What will happen if he finds out?"

"He can inform immigration and bar them from traveling out of the country. That means I wouldn't be able to go either. I can't leave them here, even with my parents, because they mean so much to me. He knows that, and would love to see me squirm. I'm walking a tightrope here. It's tough on the kids, too. They cannot talk to him about what they're doing in London. The last time he saw them, he noticed that they were speaking with a British accent. I told him that it was because they went to the

British School in Tehran. He was quite happy about that. He wants his sons to be WOGS," she giggled.

"What's that?"

"Western-Oriented Gentlemen! It's a derogatory term that was coined in China, I think, for men who were so taken up by Western ways that they forgot their roots. The irony is that he doesn't realize a very important thing. If they turn into WOGS, they will probably shun the crazy marital laws that prevail here. Good for them, of course, but I'm scared, Jordan. I'm terrified that he will find out what I'm doing. I have nightmares. I pray that we can keep up the charade going until the boys are eighteen. Then they can act on their own."

Jordan placed a comforting arm on Soraya's arm. "I'm sure you'll be fine, Soraya. But be very careful." And Jordan thought, she's a really brave woman. It took real courage to do what she was doing, and she offered a silent wish that nothing would go wrong for her friend. Unconsciously, Jordan was caught up in the intrigue and the danger, and she knew it would always be there. It was as if she was a willing conspirator with Soraya, but she did not regret it. The one thing that gave her some solace was the fact that Soraya had a powerful ally in the Hoveydas, and she would be able to get their help if things got bad.

Jordan also knew that she would always be Soraya's friend, and remain in a bond of friendship and sympathetic understanding-almost like partners in crime- which she entered without the slightest hesitation. "I hope everything works out well for you and your wonderful children," she whispered, as if she felt that saying it out loud would jinx her wish.

That night Jordan had a terrible nightmare. She dreamed of Soraya and her children. They were bound and gagged, and Irfan was standing over them, and he kept saying, "They're my WOGS. Don't you try to take them away from me." Jordan woke up in a cold sweat. When she realized it had been only a dream, she burst out laughing in great relief. But the utterly unreasonable position Soraya was in continued to bother her, as she tumbled into a fitful slumber.

During the rest of her stay in Tehran, Soraya invited Jordan to her house on several occasions, and Jordan began to feel herself part of the Tehrani family. The feeling was reciprocated by the Tehranis. Soraya's mother affectionately looked forward to seeing Jordan and referred to her as her 'Amerikai Doktar'- her American daughter.

Chapter 10

The fortnightly staff meetings were presided over by Brad Foreman. Dr. Firooznia sat as observer, and contributed his thoughts and opinions, and sometimes judgments and decisions when protocol demanded it. On the whole though, he preferred to let the expat staff do the work in the way they thought best. And as Brad Foreman rationalized, when Dr. Firooznia was not around, "He does not like to interfere. He wants us to do the job the way we think fit. We are the specialists, after all, and we are paid for whatever originality and enterprise we bring into our work. Considering the salaries they pay us, I would do the same if I were in his place"

"Probably doesn't want to show his ignorance," opined Bob Rogers, the eternal cynic of the group.

"That's not fair, Bob," admonished Brad, "You know he got his Ph. D at Cornell."

"Ha, those Ivy-League Universities will grant their degrees as long as they get their money."

"Don't badmouth the Ivy-League schools just because you couldn't afford to go to one," growled Pat, a graduate of Stanford. There was little love lost between Pat and Bob, and Pat, particularly didn't take the trouble to hide it. In fact she used every opportunity she could to 'cut him down to size' as she admitted to Jordan in private. "He's a malingerer and an upstart, and would do anything to get a free ride."

"Bigmouth Bob," as Pat secretly called him, was tall and good-looking in a rough, military kind of way with a carefully tended Mark Twain like mustache. "Probably grew it to impress us as a literary man," said Pat. Bob was mostly full of himself recounting stories he told about his tour of duty in Vietnam. He loved to describe the skirmishes his company had had with the Vietcong, and his romantic encounters in Saigon.

"He probably couldn't get it up when he was there, and I don't mean just his machine gun!" Pat said to Jordan when they were gossiping about the staff in a downtown pub, and Jordan giggled in agreement.

Despite his cynicism toward the world in general, and the Iranians in particular, Bob tried hard to make the best of his stay in Tehran. 'The self-proclaimed carpetbagger' was what Leon called him. He made friends with the staff in other universities, and kept constant contact with them, and availed himself of every opportunity in the social round there. "Always looking to get laid, but sadly with little success," said Pat.

He made sure he was invited to all the parties, and even managed to get invitations for his colleagues at the university. One Thursday afternoon, he came to the office and announced, "Laura Baines is having a party at her house on Friday. All of you guys are invited, but don't forget to bring a bottle of your favorite poison."

"Who's Laura Baines?" asked Brad.

"Oh, she works for the Free University. You know, it's the equivalent of the Open University in Britain. The Ministry of Higher Education wants to take education to the rural areas, especially teacher education. The Free University works through what is called distance education. Most of the teaching is done through audio-visual media."

And Bob was about to launch out on a commentary on how the Open University system worked, when Ron interrupted him, "We know, Bob."

"It seems that Bob first heard about distance learning from Laura Baines. So much for his literary accomplishments," observed Pat, when the beer group was gossiping at the pub.

All expatriates in Tehran looked forward to the Wednesday night parties, for they provided everybody the opportunity to really let down their hair. Often attended by everyone who was lucky enough to hear about one, the parties brought the most incongruous people together, for the Wednesday night party was the high point of the social round. College teachers, engineers, businessmen, and journalists, men and women, straight and gay, from all the continents were there. What all of the invitees had in common was that they were expatriates looking for a good time away from home. Drinking and dancing, and some pot were the normal attractions, and the opportunity to get laid was always in the air. Iranian WOGS who were close friends were also invited, but for the most part, the partygoers were expatriates.

The parties were usually held in an apartment building where one or all of the organizers lived. It was their responsibility to make sure that two or three apartments in one of the floors of the building were available. They were also responsible for the food. The revelers could sit around, drink and dance all night long, and the next day and the next night in the main area where the music played, and move to another of the open apartments when they needed rest or privacy. A good party would last till the wee hours of Friday morning. All invitees were expected to bring at least a couple of bottles of their favorite booze, so the liquor never ran out, and even if it did, there was a liquor shop down every street in Tehran, so the liquor never ran out.

Brad Foreman, Jim Vickers and Leon Davis showed interest in Laura Baines' party, and Bob said, "Hey, how about you ladies? Don't you want to go? Hey Jordan, would you like to be my date Wednesday?" he asked facetiously.

Jordan gave Bob a non-commital shrug, but said nothing.

Pat, who had been watching the exchange bemused, whispered to Jordan, "Hey, you know what? Remember that young Columbian guy I told you about- you remember? Jose? He invited me, too, so maybe we should go."

"Oh, I don't know. I've got loads of papers to grade. Besides, I'm not in the mood to drink, and that's all that happens at those parties."

"Come on Jordan! They do coke and hash, too, you know. Hey, but seriously, maybe you'll meet someone interesting there."

"Just look at the people we've been meeting here. Bob, and Samad the shy Injun, and Ron is gay. Leon and the others are involved. The only sensitive and interesting guy is Bernard-and he's married."

"That's exactly the point. We need to widen our horizons, spread our wings a little bit. It's unhealthy to mope around on a weekend. It's bad for your mental health! Let's go, girl. I'll help you grade your papers later. I promise"

"Oh all right, Pat. I know you're more interested in trying things out with Jose than in my psychological or sexual health. But we'll go anyway. If it's dull, I can always come back to my papers."

That was the first Wednesday party they attended, and both Pat and Jordan had a good time. Jose was there to liven things up for Pat, while Jordan got sloshed, experimenting on the unending supply of liquor. It became an almost weekly feature, and Jordan was surprised that she seemed to look forward to them as the weekend drew near.

Jordan met some interesting people, but none of them was anything to write home about, she thought wryly. Pat, on the other hand, was building up a steady relationship with Jose. "He is so caring and sensitive. Nothing like the drug barons you see on TV. I think I'm smitten, honey," she confessed to Jordan.

"That's great, Pat. I'm so glad for you."

And a few weeks later Pat told Jordan that she was planning to move in with Jose. "But we'll go to the Wednesday parties together," she consoled Jordan, "or else you will have to ask Bob to take you!"

God forbid, thought Jordan.

Chapter 11

Madonna, the rage in Tehran, was wailing *Don't cry for me Argentina,* as Jordan and Pat walked into the marijuana-smoke filled house on Pahlavi Avenue in the northern section of Tehran. The twenty or so couples that swayed in slow rhythm to the music looked either very high or very much in love as they held on to each other in different levels of embrace. They're already high, thought Jordan, as she walked toward the makeshift bar, a huge table covered with a smorgasbord of liquors, and deposited the bottles she and Pat had bought at the foreign liquor shop a few yards from the entrance to their apartment block. Liquor was so cheap in Tehran, Jordan and Pat often had to hold back their urge to buy more than they could carry. The alcohol never ran out, but Jordan and Pat often wanted to make sure they always had their favorite brand to drink throughout the night.

Jordan poured herself a glass of wine and walked towards the seating area, while Pat immediately got lost in the throng of dancing couples in the arms of Jose.

Jordan had just settled down on a gaudy sofa that seemed to have been borrowed from a nineteenth century French brothel, and was pondering on the fact that the sofa was, nevertheless very comfortable, when her reverie was suddenly broken by the loud, hail-fellow-well-met voice of Bob, "Hello, Jordan. It's nice to see ya. Are you enjoying yourself?"

His mocking tone annoyed Jordan, and she nearly screamed-do I have to tolerate you on weekends, too- but she remained calm and said, "Oh! Hi Bob. Having a good time?"

"Can't complain. I just met this great local chick, and have great plans for her and me. She's gone to powder her nose. Would you like to dance until she comes back?"

She lied, "Thanks, Bob, but no. I just want to get plastered a bit before I dance. That way I will have an excuse when I tread on my partner's toes."

"Ho, ho," guffawed Bob, as if it was the best joke he'd heard, and Jordan thought he was on cloud nine. Just then, a dowdy middle-aged Iranian woman suddenly waltzed up to them, "Baab, shall we dance?" she whinnied, grabbing Bob by the arm, and the couple joined the revelers.

So much for his 'great local chick,' mused Jordan, and was toying with the idea of quietly leaving the party, her eyes roaming across the room looking for Pat whom she wanted to tell before she left, when her thoughts were interrupted by a deep, cultured voice, "As-salaam-aleykuem, Khanum! Hale shoma kube?" Hello Madam. How are you?

Impressed by the Persian greeting, given in a friendly tone, Jordan looked up to see a tall man, probably in his early thirties, standing before her. He stood as if he were in a military parade, albeit with a relaxed, easy grace. He had the aristocratic looks of traditional Persian lineage, and Jordan was drawn to the boyish glint in his eyes. Dressed in a short-sleeved dark blue shirt and cream-colored slacks, with a thick gold rope around his neck, he fitted in well with the relaxed atmosphere of the room. Jordan couldn't help thinking that he was a handsome man. "Aren't you enjoying the party?" and Jordan was again struck by the richness of his tone, and the quality of his English pronunciation which hinted at a British-English education, certainly not American.

"Kheille-mothshekkaram" –Thank you very much- "Oh, yes. I'm having a great time," lied Jordan almost guiltily, realizing that she looked out of place in a setting so filled with total abandon, "I'm just taking a break."

"Well, I guess I need a break, too. May I sit down?" he asked, and didn't wait for her reply before he sat down beside her. "Actually, I came here because I had to drive my aunt-that's her," and he pointed to Bob's dancing partner, and Jordan chuckled inwardly.

"I'm Captain Ahmed Khosravi," he said winking at her, looking around guardedly, for reasons Jordan failed to understand. "I'm a member of the Imperial Guard." he added, holding out his hand which Jordan was obliged to shake.

"Pleased to meet you," returned Jordan. She was impressed by his presence, and the fact that he was a member of the Imperial Guard.

The Imperial Guard was a specially chosen, and carefully trained group of men whose primary responsibility was to protect the Shah. They worked closely with SAVAK-Sazman-e-ettelat va -e- eshkevar- (Intelligence and Security Organization of the Nation) comprising the army, the gendarmerie and police, which had, over the years come to be greatly feared and hated by the people for their ruthlessness and cruelty. Many a family in Tehran and other cities such as Isfahan, Shiraz, and Ghom- especially Ghom, hometown of Ruhollah Khomeini, had lost a father, brother or son to SAVAK, which had no compunctions about arresting any young man, or woman, on the flimsiest of evidence of conspiring against the Shah. "I am from Ghom," he added. "Do you know Ghom?" he asked after a pause.

"Yes, isn't it the hometown of Khomeini?" she asked, and Khosravi put a finger on his lips, "Shh! You shouldn't mention that name in public. It's quite dangerous. The walls around you have SAVAK ears built into the bricks," he confided, and Jordan found it strange that he would mention SAVAK in that tone, considering that he was an officer of the Imperial Guard with its strong connections with the fearsome group. However, she decided not to question him on that, for something told her that she would find out eventually. How, eventually, she wondered, when I leave this party, I don't think I will meet this guy again.

"Would you like to dance?" he invited, and Jordan was piqued by the casual tone of his voice. Well, a dance or two won't matter, thought Jordan, "I don't dance too well, and I'm sure I'll be stepping on your toes," she laughed.

"I don't dance very well myself," he said, "but I guess we can console each other on our failure, and find something better to do later."

The man is a consummate liar, thought Jordan, as she let herself be led masterfully through the first few bars of the slow waltz playing softly, to which not more than a dozen couples were moving in the enormous room. There was a grace in his step and a commanding authority in his arms, not threatening but reassuring. Jordan couldn't help feeling that he was a caring and sensitive individual. She was also gratified that she was able to rise to the occasion, and match him step for step. "Liar!" she said laughing out loud.

"The same to you," he replied, with a guffaw that jolted a couple dancing in a world of romantic slumber beside them, and Jordan blushed, warming to the youthful abandon in his voice.

Suddenly, he seemed even more relaxed in his movements, and Jordan felt that she had crossed the barrier of tension and anxiety that had loomed over her for most of the evening.

When the waltz ended, the music was turned up for Mamma Mia, and the dance floor began to get crowded with wildly gyrating couples. Ahmed led Jordan back to the sofa; it was as if that's what they both wanted to do.

Jordan tried to say something, but ABBA drowned her out, and Ahmad had to shout, "Shall we go some place quiet, where we can talk," and Jordan felt a sense of relief as he led her out of the noise to his car parked a couple of blocks away. The sound of their shoes was the only thing that interrupted the stillness of the cool and dry Tehran night. The trees, grimy with dust during the day looked clean and bright at night as the moonlight bounced off their leaves. No wonder they look so clean, mused Jordan, municipal workers washed the dust off the trees with high-pressure hoses every evening or else they would all shrivel up. The bright street lights played tricks with their shadows, lengthening, and shortening as if on a constantly changing whim as they walked. A bright orange Persian cat darted out of the corner and vanished into an alcove. A night bird screeched shrilly in the distance and Jordan shivered. What am I getting myself into? wondered Jordan when Ahmed, as if sensing her thoughts, took her hand protectively in his. And surprisingly, Jordan felt a great sense of confidence in this enigmatic man whom she had met just a few minutes before.

They drove to the Intercontinental Hotel on Jamshidabadh Avenue, and as he was parking the car, Ahmed ventured, "This hotel has one of the finest wine cellars in Tehran. I read somewhere that it is worth a few million dollars. That is something for a hotel in this part of the world," and added humorously, "Oh I'm sure there are much bigger ones in Texas."

"I hope you're not planning to make too much of a dent in it tonight," joked Jordan matching his jocular mood.

They sat in a quiet corner of the French restaurant, and Ahmed ordered a bottle of Chianti. As they waited for the wine, Ahmed said, "Tell me about yourself." It was a request, Jordan noted, and a humble one at that, and she couldn't help noticing the note of sincere interest. Jordan responded with a sincerity to match his. She felt no self-consciousness as she would have usually felt on a 'first date' with a man she had met barely a couple of hours before, and a man from a world which she knew very little about. Their meeting itself had been accidental, not a date in the strict sense of the word, yet she spoke with the greatest of ease. She told him about her high school days, and her life in college, her mother and her boyfriends, including Josh, and how she had parted with him to follow a dream. She had no regrets, she said, but she wondered whether she had done the right thing. Here she was in Iran, not knowing what would happen in the months ahead, she confessed.

"You're going to be fine, Jordan. I'm pretty sure about that."

"What do you think about the political situation here?" she asked, for she had been hearing whispered comments about trouble brewing for the Shah, of which she had never talked about with anyone else. It seemed to her not only that Ahmad would know what was really going on, but also that she could trust him to tell her the truth. Again she was amazed by this very quickly evolving belief in a man whom she had known nothing about a couple of hours before.

It was like an instinct that she was just discovering within herself, an instinct that had been lying dormant until this moment, surfacing to her consciousness like the most natural thing in the world. For a moment she wondered if it was the romance of the moment, in the presence of this exotic man, a man she knew so little about, but at the same time seemed so familiar, so close, as if she had known him since her life began. She involuntary shuddered at the mystery of it, the wonder, and her rational mind seemed to say, no that is not possible. Tread softly, Jordan, and for a moment her mother crossed her mind, and Ahmad seemed to have sensed her reaction rather than seen it. "Are you OK, Jordan?" he asked, a note of unmistakable concern taking over his voice. And at that moment she knew that it was all right to trust him, that in spite of the humungous chasm that seemed to divide them socially, culturally and in every other way possible, that deep down, they were kindred souls, a man and a woman seeking understanding, even solace in each other's company. "I'm fine, Ahmad, thank you. It must be the air-conditioning."

It was the first time she had addressed him by name, and although it came out a little different from the way he had said it when he introduced himself, it rolled easily off her tongue.

"The Shah is in power, but Khomeini is trying hard to gain influence among the people. Naturally, we are all concerned about the seeming turmoil in the political situation, but we will see it through."

"So you think the Shah will weather the storm?" she asked.

"I'm sure he will. If he plays his cards right, the Pahlavi line is here to stay."

As though reassured by his words, Jordan continued to talk about herself, her father, who had died when she was a barely ten years old, her mother, who doted on her; Jordan wanted him to know everything about her. Ahmed let her talk. He listened with great interest, and Jordan continued to prattle on like a teenager out on her first date. They had gone through the first bottle, and started on the second when Jordan said, "There. Now you know everything about me. It's your turn to tell me about yourself."

"I wish I could tell you everything about myself," confessed Ahmed, "But I'll tell you what I can. Like I told you, I'm a trusted member of the Imperial Guard, and like everyone else in our elite group, I'm sworn to guard the Shah with my life. I received my military training in Sandhurst in Britain, and there is little I do not know about arms and ammunition, and military strategy. My father was a trusted, and decorated officer of the Iranian navy, and I considered it a great privilege when my father told me that I had been recruited to the Imperial Guard. That's how recruitments to the Imperial Guard are made-through family connections. The four years I spent in Britain were four of the best years of my life so far. Today I hold a position that is envied by thousands of officers in the Iranian army, navy and air force. My job gives me everything I desire-a great salary, and benefits, and wonderful times when I travel in the Shah's entourage to various countries on official business and holidays. Holidays for him and his family are holidays for us, too. I shouldn't be opening my heart out to you like this, Jordan, but I can't help myself. When I saw you sitting forlorn on the sofa, a wall-flower, my heart went out to you."

Jordan blushed, and was about to retort angrily that she didn't need his sympathy, when she saw the teasing glint in his eyes. "I was only joking, my friend," And Jordan relented.

"You spoke of your father in the past tense. Why?" she asked with a genuine concern that moved him.

A steely far away look came into his eyes. "Actually, Jordan, I don't want to talk about him except to say that he is no longer among the living. We buried him about a year ago. May his soul enter the kingdom of Allah." and the steely look gave way to one of great sadness, and uncertainty, a kind of conflict in him that Jordan could not fathom.

"I hope you will be my friend for a long time, and if you do, some day I will tell you more about it."

Ahmed's sincerity engulfed Jordan in an infinitely comforting way and she decided not to pursue the matter.

"I know you have come to Iran at one of the most turbulent times of its history, Jordan. But ours is a great country. We are a peace-loving people, friendly and hospitable. We are easily satisfied, and are not very ambitious. Maybe that is why many foreign countries have been very successful in exploiting us. The Germans, the British, the Russians-they have all made good use of our country. Our rulers have allowed this just to achieve their selfish desires. Even today, we do not know what will happen. On the one hand, there is the Shah, the Shahanshahi- the king of kings. He is trying to bring the country from the age of the donkey and the camel to the age of the jumbo jet in an incredibly short time-so short that it is causing a great deal of uncertainty in the minds of many. The population of Iran, too, is very complex. There are those of us who trace our lineage back to the great age of Persia, of Cyrus the Great, Xerxes and Darius, when our armies could take on the best the West could throw at us. But there are also other groups. Reza Pahlavi has been trying very hard to revive the glorious past of Persia, a Persia which existed before our Prophet was born in Mecca. The Shah has been trying hard to emancipate the women, to bring democratic rule to the country-at least his own brand of democracy."

"What do you mean by his own brand? Isn't there only the one kind?"

"Don't get me wrong, Jordan, but you Americans-well at least some of you- are naïve. In Iran today, you can be arrested on the flimsiest of excuses, especially if you speak against the Shah, or his rule. The SAVAK is so powerful, and Naziri, the Head of SAVAK, is nothing but a ruthless sadist who could put the infamous Nazi, Dr. Mengele of Auschwitz to shame by the techniques of torture and persecution he uses on all those who has had the misfortune of being taken to his chambers of horror. The press is censored, political meetings are banned. Is this democracy?"

"Doesn't the Shah know what SAVAK is doing?"

"Well, when I first joined the elite corps to protect the Shah I thought he could do no wrong. If someone had told me the things I'm telling you now, I would have informed SAVAK and had him arrested for a traitor. But now, I have a great deal of doubt. I really don't know what to do. I am sworn to loyalty to my king, but my conscience bothers me when I see the terrible things Naziri and his goons are doing to the people."

And the tone of despondency in his voice brought much sadness to Jordan. She didn't know what to say.

"I cant believe I'm saying all this to you. I have never confided this way to any one, not even to my mother. Maybe I've had too much wine," he laughed, but Jordan knew what he meant. He was baring his soul to her, and she knew that her trust in him was equally reciprocated.

"Actually, it's been weighing on my mind for a very long time. When I saw you seated by yourself, I couldn't help feeling that you were unlike many of the Americans and most of the other foreigners here, who are here mainly because Iran is a rich country. They are here for the money. Yes, they do perform a service to the country, and we need many people who are doing jobs that the Iranians won't or can't do," he continued, "but when I saw you, I somehow got the feeling that you were different. I got the feeling that I could talk to you without fear."

And Jordan felt a sense of apprehension at the unburdening of his soul to her. She felt it a great responsibility, responsibility fraught with danger, and an inexplicable fear gripped her. As if he had sensed her fear, he said, "I think we should go back. Are you tired?"

Jordan smiled at him with empathy, and he took her hand in his. "Forget all the things I told you, Jordan. I'm sorry if I spoiled your evening by telling you all these things. I didn't mean to bother you with all my problems."

"It's all right Ahmed. I understand. You can tell me anything you want, and your secrets are safe with me."

"Thank you very much, Jordan. But we must go now. My aunt must be looking for her ride back home."

They drove back engaging in small talk until they were back at the party. As they entered the hall, Nizreen, Ahmed's aunt rushed up to him, "Where have you been Ahmed? I thought you had forgotten about me." And she gave Jordan a strange look that Jordan couldn't fathom. Jordan shivered, and a sense of foreboding seemed to occupy her, but when she looked at Ahmed, she saw a tenderness in his eyes, which easily dispelled her apprehension. "Can I call you some time, Jordan? I don't really know when we can meet, but Id love to see you again."

"Of course, you can," she said.

Back at work the next two weeks, Jordan often thought of what Ahmed had told her. She could not talk about it to anybody. Although Ahmed had not specifically told her not to talk about it to anyone, she knew first that he did not expect her to do so, and secondly, she just could not do so because it would be dangerous not only for Ahmed, but to her as well. So she did not even tell Pat, whom she trusted with all of her other secrets.

Chapter 12

Hardly three months had passed since Jordan's arrival in Tehran. Work was going smoothly, and Jordan was really enjoying teaching the young Iranian students, many of whom were making impressive progress in the use of the English language. Many of them built up an easy relationship with her, and the girls, especially came to her for advice not only academic, but personal as well. They would ask her about life in the USA, about boy girl relationships, and food and a variety of other topics. Some of them brought her Iranian food, which she sat and ate with them in the school cafeteria. Teacher-pupil relationship between herself and her students couldn't be better. One day, Soheila, one of the more outgoing students in her class said, "Miss Jordan, I want you to come to my house for lunch on Thursday. My Mom is preparing some special dishes for you. Will you come?"

"I'd love that Soheila, but can I bring a friend along?"

"Yes, Miss Jordan. Of course, you can bring your boyfriend. I'm happy for you." And Jordan blushed, involuntarily thinking of Ahmad. "No, Soheila. It's my roommate, Pat, I'm talking about. We usually go out

Thursdays, so if I go to your house by myself, she will be alone. Is that OK?"

"Of course, Miss. But you have no boyfriend? You like Iranian boyfriend? I find one for you," she giggled. "I have many cousins, good guys. I can, how you say, er introduce?"

"Thank you for your concern, Soheila, but I have no time for boyfriends. You guys are keeping me busy enough," she laughed.

"I must tell my mother that my teacher needs boyfriend. She works in foreign ministry and has many foreign friends, Americans, British, Germans. She find good man for teacher."

"Take it easy, girl. A boyfriend is the last thing on my mind. Besides, I have a boyfriend in New York, and he's waiting for me to come back," she lied.

"Oh, how romantical! You have picture?"

"No, but his picture is in my head, and my heart," she claimed, and Soheila was gratified.

"That's wonderful. I am very happy. I wish you and your boyfriend good luck."

"Thank you," said Jordan with a little curtsy.

Jordan enjoyed this kind of easy relationship she had with her students, and knew that they liked and trusted her. She also knew that this helped her make good progress in her work. They hung on her every word, and most of them enjoyed her classes as well as the assignments she gave them, which they all did with great interest. There were, however, a couple of students, both males, with whom Jordan thought she was not making much headway, for they always seemed to be preoccupied and far away from the task at hand. The other students generally gave them a wide berth, and Jordan wondered why. She had intended to have a heart to heart with them for some time, but had not been able to schedule a conference hour with them.

Chapter 13

It was October ninth, Jordan remembered later, because it was the day before her mother's birthday. Jordan's class was scheduled for the afternoon, so she decided not to leave for the campus until after the lunch break, which would give her time to call her Mom to wish her a happy birthday. She called Renee, and had a long chat with her, but did not tell her anything about Ahmad even when Renee pointedly asked, "Haven't you met any interesting people there, yet?"

She hailed a passing 'orange crush' going in the right direction for her, got in and said "Daneshga Tehran," and the driver replied "Bale, Khanoum."

Her taxi was a few hundred yards from the campus gates when she heard the blare of police sirens and saw several squad cars and army jeeps racing past. The taxi screeched to a halt, and as Jordan watched, she saw the squad cars and jeeps drive in through the campus gates. The driver signaled to her to remain in the taxi, and hesitantly walked up to the gates. He returned a few minutes later, and made her understand that there was some trouble in the campus grounds, and it would be dangerous to go in; it would be safer to go back home.

Jordan was persuaded, and she reluctantly had herself dropped off at her apartment. Pat had already gone to work, so she called her and found out what was going on. Pat sounded pretty scared as she filled her in. Around twenty masked young men had suddenly appeared from nowhere and demonstrated in and around the campus, smashing windows, and destroying campus vehicles and other school property. They chanted anti-Shah slogans, and called for the segregation of women in the campus. The staff and the students had remained in their classrooms in a state of complete shock.

The police had arrived about fifteen minutes later, but by that time the demonstrators had vanished. The efforts of the army and the police to apprehend the suspects had come to nothing. They had vanished as if into thin air. "All classes have been canceled, so you'd better stay put. I'm about to head home now"

The next day in class, Soheila whispered to Jordan when they were alone, "The silent ones were not in class yesterday," and Jordan realized what she meant. She knew why the demonstrators could not be found. They had all been students of the campus. All they had to do to hide from the police was to get rid of their masks. Jordan also knew that the "silent ones" were two of the masked demonstrators.

Even though Jordan had not seen the disturbance, she, as were many others in the campus, visibly shaken by it. It was the first such incident in many years, whispered some. They had been hearing about demonstrations in other parts of the city and the country, but never in the campus. The presence of armed policemen on the campus, and the reassuring speech of the Vice Chancellor at a hurriedly called up meeting of staff and students did little to relieve the nervous tension that seemed to have descended over them like a huge gray cloud. Though few realized it at the time, it signaled the entry of university students into the anti-Shah campaign, which hitherto had been limited to the leftist and other radical elements in the country.

At lunch in the school cafeteria, Pat observed, "If university students get involved, it's going to spread very quickly."

Faride, who was a diehard Shah loyalist, and staunchly anti-mullah, shot back, "Don't worry Pat. Things will settle down. The Shah can handle it."

"SAVAK must be really annoyed that they haven't been able to apprehend the perpetrators yet," whispered Bernard glancing furtively around, "Pity the poor guys if they get caught!"

"But they're asking for trouble," countered Faride.

And Jordan felt nervous, knowing that she probably could identify two of them. It filled her with a sense of dread to have to carry such information, the kind of dread that filled her with a sense of guilt like that of Raskolinikov in Dostoevsky's *Crime and Punishment*. She tried to reassure herself that she had nothing to do with it, and she was not obliged to say anything to any one. It was just an observation she'd made. But what if she was questioned? She had heard stories of how persuasive SAVAK could be. She knew Soheila, the observant one, would never betray them, but the nagging sense of guilt remained at the back of her mind. Well, I wasn't even there to notice their absence and unless Soheila had pointed it out, I would never have known, she argued in her defense.

The investigators had returned, but made no headway and were no closer to finding out who the perpetrators had been. However, when they finally left, she felt greatly relieved that no one had questioned her. The two young men did not attend her class again.

The Kayhan, the national English daily published in Tehran, and NIRT, the government sponsored TV station reported nothing about what was happening in the country. The only news they got came through the grapevine, and the many clandestine newspapers published in Farsi. The Iranians were mortally afraid to talk about the political situation, and gossiped behind closed doors. It was said that every office and other public building in Iran had at least one SAVAK agent who reported what people said. When she first came to Tehran, Jordan had been warned not to talk about the Shah or politics. Any foreigner found guilty of saying anything against the Shah would be summarily deported. Iranians would face a much worse fate. They would be arrested and taken to SAVAK headquarters, and what happened there would be anybody's guess, but one thing was certain: he or she would never be heard of again. Jordan had begun to feel the pressure of what Ahmed had told her, but she could tell nobody about it.

Chapter 14

When the first semester at the university ended, Jordan was pretty familiar with Iran and Iranian ways. Jordan met Ahmad off and on, but their meetings were often very brief. Ahmad was very busy with his work and although he tried hard to find time to meet Jordan, it was as if some sadistic hand was intervening to keep them apart, or so Jordan thought. Jordan found Ahmad very attractive and in some ways mysterious. It probably is his job, she thought. It was as if he was always guarded in what he said. "It's for your own protection, Jordan," he had confided. "There are some things that are too dangerous for you to know." And Jordan knew that he was being very honest with her.

During the three week Christmas vacation, Jordan saw Ahmad just twice. Pat and Jose, Jill, Jordan, Ron, Samad, and Bernard met regularly in the evenings in one or another of the pubs in mid-town Tehran. The Irish pub was their favorite watering hole, being frequented by the avant garde in Tehran. The food was excellent, too, although Jordan steered clear of the shepherd's pie, which Ron described as 'a hash of 'cows' entrails.' It was Samad's favorite dish, however, and he enjoyed regaling everyone at the table about its nutritional value, and delicious taste every time he ordered it.

It was at the Irish pub that they had first met Donne. Certainly no relative of the poet, Donne had chosen to spell his name that way 'because D-O-N is so common, darling.'

And Donne was certainly not common-not in contemporary Tehran, for his penchant for attending all the evening parties in drag. While most Iranian and expatriate gays tried their best to hide their sexual preference, Donne flaunted it with a flamboyance that made the conservatives cringe and avert their eyes while the liberals were tickled to death. The gays themselves were pretty embarrassed and even nervous, for they did not want any undue attention to be drawn to them. Nonetheless, everybody loved Donne for his frankness, sincerity and sharp wit. Portly as a British dowager, he literally rolled into the parties like the queen he was, with a retinue of young handsome Iranian men. His generosity knew no bounds, and the phenomenal expenses he ran up wherever he went kept everyone wondering where the money was coming from. The salary he earned teaching English at a private English teaching institute could hardly take him through a couple of nights in the bars he frequented-often with his 'boy concubines' as he liked to call them. He criticized Iranian politics. He praised and insulted the Shah as his mood dictated. Nobody was spared his acid tongue. "The mullahs are a bunch of dark and evil dervishes," he would chant. Even SAVAK was not spared. "Nasiri is a pervert. You know what he does as his final act of indignity to the young men and women that cross him?" he asked one day, and everyone perked up, expecting to hear about some exotic sexual perversion.

"He gets his goons to hold them down and shits on them!" he said.

Despite his crudity and acid tongue, Donne was very popular among the Irish Pub fraternity, and the alcoholic bar flies as he called everyone coming there loved to have him share their table. He was a raconteur in the mold of the best known, and always had an audaciously racy yarn to spin in his raucous voice which often grabbed the attention of everyone present. Often it was about people in Tehran-politicians, businessmen, religious leaders and other important people. His imagined or real, no one knew for sure, tales spared no one, and always kept the listeners roaring with laughter. He was the Queen with her consorts, the one everybody felt they had to listen to.

And then one day, the unthinkable happened; the tragic news reached the pub that Donne was dead. His body had been found in a dimly-lit cul-de-sac in downtown Tehran. His throat had been cut from ear to ear. It was rumored that a conservative Islamic group, which Donne had chosen to castigate a few days before was responsible for the gruesome act. The shock and the horror of Donne's murder rattled Jordan and her friends very badly. For two or three weeks after that they did not go to the pub, but would get together at Jordan's or Ron's apartment for their evening drink. But memories are short, and before long, one by one, they all trickled back to their old familiar watering hole. Donne and the horror of his departing was soon forgotten, and only Ron, being gay himself, and so having a closer kinship with the late storyteller, would sometimes recall one of Donne's tales, which were still amusing enough to send everyone into paroxysms of laughter.

Chapter 15

Ruholla Khomeini, the exiled cleric based in Iraq, was hardly known to the foreign community in Tehran when Jordan first arrived. Now, hardly four months into her tour, he was becoming the red-hot topic on the grapevine. Many Iranians were now beginning to talk bout him in admiration, others in awe, and still others with undisguised fear. During the lunch hour, when Iranians as well as expatriates sat down to break bread, interesting viewpoints came to be expressed, some in admiration of the Shah, others pure tribute to Khomeini. Some spoke about the absolute insensitivity of the Shah to the needs of the people. In crowded downtown Tehran, they said, people died of cold in the winter months, and heat exhaustion in the summer. This despite the fact that Iran was the second largest producer of oil in the world, whose oil revenue even, after the foreign companies managing the oil companies had taken their share of the profits, was staggering. Every member of the Pahlavi family, their near and distant relatives, and a legion of individuals who claimed inheritance as extended family lived a life of decadent opulence. His lackeys and political supporters, his ministers and other shadowy characters who acted as his spies and loyalists, all gratefully accepted his generosity. Little of the real wealth generated in the oil fields found its way down to the large numbers among the populace that bordered on poverty, the poor flagrantly exposed to an exhibition of wealth and luxury which they could not lay claim to even in their wildest dreams. It was the perfect breeding ground for revolution, and Islamic militancy.

While adhering to the basics of Islam, and practicing the religion in his own way, the Shah was convinced that Islamic culture would do nothing but take the country back to the sixteenth century. His Persian lineage which had roots in the Indo-Aryan background of the major ethnic group, namely the Farsi speaking Persians, did not allow him to acknowledge any serious affinity with the Arabs, notwithstanding the fact that they surrounded his country, along with the Turks and other tribes that had invaded and made their home in his empire. He desired to bring back the past glory of the kingdom of Persia of Cyrus and Darius, and to do this, all Iranians had to adopt a European lifestyle, backed by Western education. It was with this intention that he had organized, in the backdrop of the ancient city of Persepolis, a magnificent celebration of the 2500th anniversary of the Persian monarchy, where he declared himself Shahanshahi-king of kings. This despite the fact that his own dynasty had begun with a military revolt by his father, a commoner to all intents and purposes in terms of Persian dynasty.

Khomeini was the expected Messiah, the savior who would defeat the Shah and restore Iran to Islamic culture and mores, which the Shah, and his father before him, had tried very hard to wean the population away from. And now in mid 1977, it seemed Khomeini's star was on the ascendant. It seemed that despite the wholehearted backing he had from the US, the Shah was about to meet his Nemesis yet again.

Chapter 16

Two months to the day after their meeting at the party, Jordan received a call from Ahmed. "Hi, Jordan! Remember me?" he asked humorously, and Jordan, recognizing Ahmed's voice immediately, pretended not to do so. "Is it Mr. Ali, the wine merchant from the Intercontinental?" she joked.

"Yeah, I was out of town the last ten days, and returned to Tehran this morning. Can I see you some time?"

Jordan was happy to hear his voice. Although she hadn't seen or heard from him, her mind had often wandered back in time to the things he had said. She was filled with a sense of empathy for him and his unenviable situation. She, too, wanted very much to see him again.

Face to face with him again the next evening, Jordan had a thousand questions she wanted to ask Ahmed, but most of all, she wanted to ask him why he didn't give it all up and go away like many Iranians were doing, buying new places to roost out in the West.

She sensed the conflicting burden of guilt and responsibility struggling within him. The simplest solution would be to give it all up, leave the country, and start life somewhere else. To her it seemed the easiest thing to do-just as she had done with Josh, she thought ruefully. But she knew also that he had in him something that would make such a step impossible. Neither his sense of loyalty to what he had sworn to do, nor his sense of guilt at supporting a system in which innocent people were being sacrificed on the whims of a sadist, a maniac driven by bloodlust, would allow him to turn off his conscience which kept resounding in his ears like his nephew's new tape recorder which kept blaring out the popular American music in the record stores all over downtown Tehran. "Iran is going through one of the most difficult periods in her history," he told Jordan.

"But your country has gone through more difficult phases, and come out of them well," said Jordan, as if to comfort him.

"I don't know. Our past rulers have hardly been model rulers. The Sasanids, the Arabs, the Turks and the Safavids, as well as the Qajars- they all had their own agendas. Many of them couldn't care less for the people and were only interested in their own welfare. Many of them were pawns of foreign powers, which were mainly interested in exploiting our wealth. The coming of Islam actually helped the rulers because it made the people more submissive and easier to rule than they would otherwise have been.

"Do you think the Shah is not interested in his people?" ventured Jordan.

"Not really. He wants to do well by his people. When Reza came back from exile, he had good intentions. But the road to destruction is often paved with good intentions. The majority of our people are still under educated. Worse still, they don't seem to be interested in any education other than the religious; that's what the mullahs tell them." he said, and continued, "The present Shah has been trying to change their mindset. He wants all Iranians to be educated. He wants to liberate Iranian women-to educate them, and get them to take on a more active role in society. He wants them to shed the Chador, and wear Western dress, drive cars, and become doctors and businesswomen."

"So what's wrong with that?" ventured Jordan, "Is it wrong for women to be treated equally as men?"

"No, I don't mean that. It is just that Reza is moving too fast. I would like to see an Iran where men and women can work together as equals. But there are a lot of elements in this country that would like to put the clock back. They want all the women to cover themselves with the chador, and confine their lives to the bedroom and the kitchen as they do in many other countries in the Middle East. It is partly due to loyalty to the Islamic culture, and partly due to the inherent nature of the male psyche. Many Iranian men, like their Arab counterparts, want subservience from their women. You'd be surprised by some of the old cultural practices that practically keep women in thrall. For instance, if a woman's husband dies, the husband's older brother gets complete control over her. She cannot leave the house, or marry again. The best she can do is to submit to being the second –or third- wife of the brother-in-law. It's worse than the old Indian practice of having to leap into the husband's funeral pyre."

"How so?"

"It would be a living-death," he said sardonically.

"This is the age of women's liberation, and even American women are still fighting for complete equality. Don't forget that women in the US, too, had to fight for their rights. It is only about a hundred and fifty years ago that they won the right to vote," observed Jordan.

"Yes, but ironically, here in Iran, some women believe that society is better off with women playing a subservient role, wearing the chador, and being obedient to their husbands in every way. They think that the Shah does not know the importance of the conservative role for women. They don't realize how much more terrible their lives would be if the mullahs replaced the Shah. Women would be no better off than they are in Afghanistan, where they have no human rights!"

"Don't you think that is because of the lack of education?"

"That's precisely the point. The Shah wants to make education available to everybody. He has established many new colleges and universities in different parts of the country. He has even established an open university for those who are unable to attend traditional universities."

"Don't the people want that?"

"Yes, but he believes that it is only Western education that can lead to the progress of our people. There are others, goaded by the clerics, who see Western education as the path to moral and spiritual decadence-even destruction."

"Do you think that the people can be swayed by the clerics? Will the majority of the women give up their right to equality?"

"That's left to be seen. I sincerely hope not. But the clerics in this country are a tough and persistent bunch. Ever since Khomeini was forced into exile, the clerics have been like embers beneath the ashes, waiting for the day when they could burst into flame once more. All they need is some fuel if you will forgive the pun. And the people are unsuspecting. They don't realize that the mullahs want to create a situation where they can be kingpins. The Shah has kept them at bay so far."

"Do you think that an entire population can be swayed so easily? Are they so naïve as to give up their freedom to the clerics?"

"I don't know. What I do know is that they are really wonderful people. They are friendly, hospitable, and trusting. They do not have the suspicious nature of their neighbors; that's simply because they are not of the typical desert culture."

"What do you mean by a desert culture?"

"In desert cultures, people don't trust anybody outside their clan. In some countries, even today, a man will not invite another into his house. Fear and suspicion rule. A man's home is his fortress, to be jealously guarded lest another take away what's his. Of course it is changing now as people are becoming more educated and a little more liberal."

"Yes, I know Iranian are not like that. They are not suspicious or afraid of foreigners."

"No. If you visit their homes, they will invite you inside with a hearty "Befarmoidh!" and make you feel comfortable and welcome, and insist on sharing their tea and their fruit. Hospitality is a tradition among Iranians.

To leave a home you have visited without partaking of a fruit or a cup of tea is an insult to the host," he said smilingly, and Jordan thought how true he was. Her visit to Soraya's house had taught her that. She also remembered a day during her first week in Tehran.

Jordan and Pat had been out apartment hunting with Pat. A realtor had called her and given the address of an apartment that he thought she would really like. "Go see it today. I have told them you would be coming to see it this evening," he pleaded. "It's a wonderful place. You'll love it."

Jordan and Pat had got into a local taxi, an "Orange Crush," as the expatriates liked to refer to them. The taxis worked like little buses, and were more public than taxis in the US, for with one fare already in the taxi, the driver would stop for whoever else hailed it on route to its destination. Consequently, a taxi starting out with one passenger would soon fill up with others going in the same direction.

Reaching what they thought was their destination, Jordan rang the doorbell, which was answered by a pretty teenaged girl, who smiled sweetly and invited them inside with a flourish and a pleasant "Befarmoidh Khanoum" which could mean a variety of things such as "Welcome," "Come in," "Go ahead," or "Try one,"-like "Aloha" in Hawaii, it evoked sentiments of bonhomie. Soon they were sitting in a plush living room, and were soon joined by an equally pleasant, but older woman, obviously the mother of the girl. Conversation was minimal, but momentarily their appeared a huge bowl of fruit before them. The girl who spoke falteringly in English interpreted for the mother, who smiled benignly at them. After thirty minutes or so had elapsed Jordan asked the girl, "Can we see the apartment, please?" causing a great deal of confusion to their hosts. When the smoke cleared, they realized that they were at the wrong address! They had been treated to typical Iranian hospitality!

Jordan reflected on many other instances of Iranian generosity and hospitality. During her first week in Tehran, Jordan had complimented Parveen, whose office was on the same floor as Jordan's, on the beautiful gold necklace she had worn to the office that day. Parveen had immediately taken it off and offered it to Jordan, "Take it. It is yours."

Jordan was amazed to see that Parveen was not joking. "You must take it Jordan. I want you to have it. I can get another one."

Jordan had had a tough time declining the gift as courteously as she could. Ever since then she had been very careful about how she complimented her Iranian friends on their usually fabulous clothes and jewelry.

"I guess that is why we have been exploited by foreigners on so many occasions. Actually, if you look back at Iranian history, we have lost many wars and given way to many invasions because we are hospitable and friendly. But we can be proud of the fact that our strengths have never been diluted by the invaders," declared Ahmed, and Jordan couldn't help but notice the pride in his voice.

"Yes, your policy seems to have been able to conquer your enemies in a different way. You have bestowed on your visitors your culture and way of life," said Jordan.

"There is no doubt that your culture has always been superior to that of your invaders."

"Yes, but today the Islamic culture is the dominant one. Before the advent of Islam, our people lived a much different kind of life. Our values were different, and so was our thinking. Pre Islamic Persia had its own problems, but when the Arabs invaded this country, it is they who were influenced by us, not the other way around as it usually happens. The only good thing they brought us was the religion of Islam. The Shah rightly believed that we Persians had contributed much to the glory of Islam through our own art and architecture, for example. The Iranians are a very creative and sophisticated people. Our literature has always overshadowed anything that the Arabs have produced."

And Jordan, who had studied a little bit about the great Persian poets after she arrived in Iran, agreed. Before that she had heard only about Omar Khayyam's Rubaiyyat, thanks to Fitzgerald's splendid translation. She now knew about about the eleventh century Persian poet, Ferdowsi, whose great epic, the Shah Nameh or the Book of Kings, brilliantly recorded the glory of pre-Islamic Iran. Hafez, the greatest of all, painted exquisite pictures with his poetry. His themes and their treatment, using the nuances of old Persian before it came under the influence of Arabic, could be compared to the poetry of Keats or Byron, she thought.

"The Shah is not ready to acknowledge the fact that the Islamic way of life is integral to and quintessential to Iranian society. He wants to change everything back. When he came back to Iran, having experienced everything there is to be experienced in the West," he said very somberly, "he made it his sole objective to change things back to pre-Islamic times-or maybe, change it forward." There was no humor in his voice as he continued, "The main thing is he realizes that Iran would face a terrible fate if the clergy gained control of the country."

"What do you think?" asked Jordan.

"I believe so, too. The clerics should remain in the mosque, and guide the spiritual lives of the people, not rule the country, for they know nothing about international politics or the way the world works today. I think this is true for all clergy, everywhere in the world. Their concern should be with the after life. They are complicating matters by sticking their fingers into politics, and governance," he continued humorously. "But they will not stop. Look at Khomeini. He's in Najaf- that's in Iraq" he explained seeing the confused look on Jordan's face, "but his influence here today is greater than it was when he was here. The Shah made a big mistake by sending him into exile. If he had let him stay here, his wings would have been clipped."

"Do you think he will come back?"

"That's what I fear. And if he does, I can't imagine what would happen here. I really am concerned, Jordan."

They had dinner at the Xanadu, and went dancing at a popular disco in central Tehran. Jordan had never been to a local disco before, and so was a little apprehensive, but Ahmad's presence was so reassuring. As they danced among a throng of couples, mainly Iranian, her trepidation was dissipated by Ahmad's quiet confidence and strength. She had never felt happier, nor more comfortable as his strong arms guided her in the frenzied exuberance of youth, in a magical new world of their own. After a few dances, they decided they'd had enough physical exertion, and Ahmad drove her back to her apartment. He stood outside while she opened the main door to the building, and her own apartment door and was safely inside. She waved to him through the window, and he acknowledged it with a tap on his car horn.

Chapter 17

At the next weekly Departmental meeting in the office, Brad Foreman sounded very somber. "It seems that our days here are numbered," he said. "I was talking to Dr. Firooznia this morning, and he told me that demonstrations have started in downtown Tehran as in other cities like Esfahan, Shiraz, Ghom and Abadan. You are all advised not to travel out of Tehran until we know what direction these happenings are taking. And don't go walking by yourselves in downtown Tehran." he warned. "The Red Light area is definitely out of bounds," he added facetiously, looking pointedly at Bill Rogers.

From that day forward, Jordan became more and more anxious about the situation in Iran. Ahmed called her often and saw her on a regular basis. They were deeply attracted to each other, and the mutual burden which hung over Ahmad like Damocles' sword seemed also to have pinned them together in a kind of invisible bond.

Jordan called Renee at least once a week. They talked about family and friends, and Renee would always report on the weather in upstate New York. "The winter is milder than it was in the last two years. Remember last year when we got snowed in on Christmas day? There's not much snow this year and the temperatures are not hitting any records."

"It's getting a little cold here, too, normal for November in Tehran I'm told. There's not much snow except in northern Tehran," reported Jordan.

They sometimes talked about Ahmad. "I'm dying to see him," said Renee, joyful anticipation in her voice. "Can't you make a flying visit for Christmas?"

"I wish we could, Mom, but he's very busy right now. Maybe things will ease up a bit next year. And in any case we don't get leave of absence until we have worked for a year."

"Oh, I read in the newspapers that the Shah is visiting the US this month, "I'm waiting to see him, too" she said, levity in her voice, "but I guess it will have to be just on TV."

"I'll tell Farah to invite you to the banquet at the White House," joked Jordan.

When the royal couple did visit the US, Renee avidly followed their every movement in the media. She was particularly interested in Farah-what she wore, how she walked and talked, and she was enamored of the empress' grace and beauty. She was anxiously looking forward to talking about her with Jordan. Ironically, though, Renee missed the live broadcast of the welcome ceremony of the Royals at the White House.

Had she seen it, she would have been very alarmed indeed.

President and Mrs. Carter, Shah Mohammed Reza Pahlavi and Empress Farah stood on the dais on the White

House lawn as the US Marine Band played the national anthems of Iran and the US. As President Carter stepped up to the podium to speak, all hell seemed to break loose on Lafayette Square, as a thousand or so Iranians, mainly students studying in US colleges, began screaming at the Shah: Fascist Murderer, Death to the Shah, Puppet of the USA. Their faces covered in white masks to avoid being identified by SAVAK agents, the students stole the thunder as TV cameras swept over them. The police, totally surprised by the belligerence of the mob, and fearing that the protestors would try to scale the railings of the White House, tossed canisters of tear gas at the demonstrators in an effort to control them. The wind carried the pungent fumes right across the South Lawn, causing great visible discomfort to the distinguished guests, who were seen dabbing their eyes and coughing. President Carter remained calm, and praised the Shah for his admirable leadership in his country and in the region.

Jordan, on the other hand, saw the welcome ceremony for the Carters when they visited Iran a month later. The grandeur, the opulence and the decorum of the occasion impressed her so much, and the words used by Carter in praise of the Shah seemed so sincere that Jordan had no inkling of what he and the country were in for in the year that followed.

In fact, both Jordan and Renee were in for a rude awakening as events began to unfold.

Chapter 18

Jordan and Pat were sipping coffee in the faculty room, when Bernard joined them. Sitting next to Jordan, and looking around to make sure he was not overheard, he asked in a conspiratorial tone, "Do you know what happened in Qum yesterday?"

Curiosity bristled on the face of Pat, and a look of consternation clouded Jordan's face, as they both demanded in a whisper, "What? What?"

Bernard, nicknamed 'Reuters' in the office, savored the moment. He was the omnipresent news gatherer, and the one person whom everyone in the office trusted with their secrets, and came to for advice of all sorts. He had friends in high places and low, among the Iranians and the Americans, the Pakistanis and the Brits in the huge expatriate community in Tehran. He attended all the parties, and the news just gushed into his grapevine. Yet, he was as inscrutable as the sphinx, and gave news out only when it would serve a good purpose. He did not favor the pastime of groups of expatriates sitting around and gossiping about others. He knew all, but would not tell all, especially if he thought the news would be damaging to anyone. Today, he obviously knew something which his colleagues did not, and was dying to share it with them. "There was a huge demonstration in Qum yesterday, and the police opened fire on the demonstrators killing some of them."

"Why?" asked Jordan in anguish, her thoughts flowing out to Ahmad, who she knew would be affected by the event. Bernard elaborated. "Last week an article appeared in the Farsi newspaper 'Ettelat.' It had been written by the Information Minister, and accused Khomeini of homosexuality and other 'unislamic' practices. The people in Qom, that's Khomeini's town, think gold is dust of Khomeini. When they read the article, they were outraged. They were even more outraged when they found out that the minister had written the article on the orders of the Shah. The people of Qum, the Qumites-does that sound right, Pat, or should they be called Qumies. Well, whatever, they saw the article as blasphemous, for Khomeini to them is the new messiah, and over 5000 men women and children took to the streets swearing blue murder at the Shah and his friends. The Shah loyalist police would have none of it, and opened fire. They estimate that over one hundred people are dead."

"What will happen now?" asked Jordan, plaintively, rhetorically.

"Nothing good, obviously." intoned Pat, stressing the obvious.

That evening Jordan called Ahmad's house and was told that he was away on business. Jordan knew where he would be. She glanced at the calendar and noted that it was January tenth. She would later recall that this day began the most tumultuous and most tragic year of her life.

And in Iran itself, it would be the most catastrophic year for Mohammed Reza Pahlavi, and his dynasty.

Rumor was rife in Tehran. Some believed that the Shah had everything under control, and would ride the little ripples that were rising in his ocean of power. Others swore that Khomeini was gaining control over more and more people, and that soon things would come to a head. The Shah himself was brimming with confidence, for he had seven hundred thousand troops, one of the best arsenals in the world, and as he often boasted, the support of all the workers and most of the people.

Jordan would ask Ahmad, but he would always tactfully divert the conversation in a different direction, to more interesting and pleasant things. One day he said," Dear Jordan, the less you know of what is going on the better. Don't worry. Everything's going to be fine." They didn't talk much about the politics in the country. Ahmad was often called away on his official duties, and Jordan didn't ask him about what he was doing. On rare occasions, he would confide in her about things that he saw and experienced. Mostly they were neither very mysterious nor ominous. He talked about the leaders of the anti- Shah forces. One day he said, "I feel frightened sometimes, Jordan-not for myself, but for my people. They have suffered greatly in the past-under the various powers that ruled over them. Right now, the country is going through a critical stage. I only hope it will come out of it without too much suffering and destruction."

Jordan heard the strain in his voice. Her heart reached out to him, but she felt so impotent. She did not ask him for explanation or description. Yet she knew that for him, too, it was a critical period, and wished with all her being that it would not take too much of a toll on him.

It was a Wednesday afternoon at the end of January, about three months after they had first met. Ahmad called to invite Jordan to dinner, and she gladly accepted.

Around five in the evening, the door-buzzer rang, and it was Ahmad. Jordan hurriedly picked up her purse and ran downstairs. Ahmad was standing there, looking as relaxed as ever, a huge bunch of roses in his hand. "Thirty six roses," he said, "a dozen for each month I've known you."

"Oh Ahmad, they're beautiful. Thank you very much." And as she reached out for them, she wanted to hug him, but this was Tehran, where anybody could be watching. She was conscious of his status in Iranian society, and she did not want to embarrass him, so she said, "Let me put these in a vase." And they both walked up to her apartment. Once inside, she said, "Thank you for remembering darling." And they kissed.

They were sitting in their rooftop restaurant at the Intercontinental, savoring their favorite wine. The political situation in the country was far from their mind, the cool evening, the starry skies and a Viennese waltz playing softly in the background creating a magical environment for them which nothing else could intrude. Ahmad took her hands gently in his. "I have to make a trip to Shiraz next weekend," he announced, "It's a business trip, but the business will only take a couple of hours on Thursday morning, and I will be free the rest of the weekend. Would you like to go with me?"

Jordan felt a kind of warmth radiate from her hands, which he still held firmly in his, to every part of her body. An imperceptible tremor ran through her, "I'd love to Ahmad. That would be wonderful."

The spontaneity of her response did not surprise her in the least. It was like the most natural thing in the world for a school teacher from suburban America to connect with an officer of the Imperial Guard of Iran with all of his background of power and mystery- and now intrigue and danger. Momentarily, a picture of her mother flashed across her mind. She was smiling happily at her, "Go for it Jody! Have a wonderful time."

Chapter 19

It was a weekend from the Arabian nights. They stayed in an enormous hotel, a Moghul palace built a few centuries before, renovated with the kind of luxurious comfort that only the splendorous East, with its ancient culture of opulence could offer.

The floors were covered with the most beautiful Persian carpets that Jordan had ever seen. "Most of these carpets were laid when this palace was first built around the end of the fourteenth century-that is the Turko-Moghul period. Nader Shah and Karim Khan Zand, both of whom ruled in the Safavid period are said to have stayed here in the late eighteenth century. Karim Khan Zand, who loved nature, extended the palace gardens, and kept many exotic animals in and around the palace. The exquisite chandeliers you see in every room were imported from France in a later era."

"Someone told me that certain carpets, like good wine, improve with age," said Jordan

"Yes, the more you walk on them the more beautiful they become."

And the more I see you, the more I like you, thought Jordan. "Seeing these carpets, I certainly believe that now, and I thank you for bringing me here dear Captain of the Imperial Guard," intoned Jordan, effecting a somber tone and facial expression.

"Anything for you sweet American teacher who has come to help my people," said Ahmed with equal seriousness, and they both laughed. But deep inside of her, she knew that he had meant what he said. She felt happy and satisfied in his company, and hoped that nothing would ever come between them, but there always was that sense of foreboding that seemed to take hold of her, of some impending danger.

That night they made love for the first time.

In the few months they had known each other, Ahmed had always treated her with great sensitivity and delicacy. It was as if he was afraid of something, something fragile that held them together in companionship. He appeared to look at her as if she was an image in a pool of water, and he was afraid that something would disturb the water and fragment that image. The physical side of their relationship had been confined to holding hands, and he held them so tenderly, as if he was afraid of his own strength- a strength so great that could overpower her both physically and psychologically.

She on the other hand did not think of this as strange or unnatural. She didn't even, as most women would, wonder whether she was not physically attractive to him. She simply accepted it as part of their relationship-not just Platonic or beyond the physical realm, for that would have not lasted as long as it had. She was, after all, a normal, American girl with a healthy sexual appetite! Yet, she did nothing to encourage or discourage him. He seemed to have exerted on her a kind of control, of discipline both intentional and purposeful. It seemed to her that he was building up to the perfect moment, a moment that would transcend them to a perfect point in their relationship when their physical union would take them beyond the dangers, the problems and the turmoil they faced, into the transcendental world of their own.

The next day, they had visited the ruins of Persepolis. Ahmad's voice was filled with pride and joy as he described Takht-e-Jamshid the throne of Persia.

Built around 500 B.C., Persepolis had been the ceremonial capital of the Achaemenid dynasty which had ruled the Persian Empire from 550-330 B.C. It had been the Golden Age of the Persians, and modern day Iranians looked back to the period with immense pride and joy.

Ahmad led Jordan walked up the more than six meter wide main stairway consisting of one hundred and eleven steps which led to the north eastern side of the terrace. They visited the Apadana Palace built by Darius the Great andd served as the audience hall for the kings. Built mainly of grey limestone, the walls of the Apadana Palace were decorated with figures of two-headed bulls, lions and floral designs.

From the Apadana, they went into the Throne hall which had served as the Imperial Army's hall of honor. "If we had lived during the time of Darius and Xerxes, I would have invited you to this hall, to celebrate our victories in battle," he said humorously, but with a kind of seriousness that revealed the great respect and adoration he had for her. Jordan seemed to hear a note of sad regret in his voice that they were not in another time, another place.

Later they visited the tomb of Ferdowsi, the great 12th century Persian poet, author of the Shah Nameh, the book of kings.

"Hafez perfected the Ghazal as a poetic form which is used by poets in many countries in the East even today." he explained. "The Ghazal is used by lovers in the same way as Westerners used love letters in years gone by," he added. "I'll recite one for you," and he sang, "agar an tork-e shirazi be dast arad del-e, mara /be-khal-e henduyesh bakhsham samrkand o bokharara."

"Wow, that sounds so melodic," she exclaimed, "Can you translate it? And he recited, looking deep into her eyes:

Sweet maid if thou would charm my sight
And bid these arms thy neck infold;
That rosy cheek, that lily hand,
Would give thy poem more delight,
Than all Bocara's vaunted gold,
Than all the gems of Samarkand

And what Jordan saw in his eyes overwhelmed her, and terrified her though she couldn't think why. "I love you, Jordan," he said and she knew he had made a commitment, no matter what.

She fiercely hoped that she could match that commitment as she whispered, "I love you, too."

They had dinner at a little restaurant, which specialized in classical Iranian cuisine. Jordan ordered kebab hosseini, which consisted of lamb, grilled on skewers to succulent perfection with onions tomatoes and green peppers served with rice and raw vegetables. Ahmad suggested Dolme felfel as an appetizer, and for himself, Dolme Barg Mow, Wine leaves wrapped around a mix of ground meat, rice and herbs.

Jordan had learned something about Iranian cooking and recalled that the lamb was marinated in the best spices of the East; the spices were an adjunct to the natural pastoral taste of the lamb, and the taste stayed on long after the food had left for less sensitive areas of the digestive system. The rice, soft and flaky, not thick and heavy as in other ethnic preparations had the aroma of rosemary and jasmine, incense and rose petals, speckled with red and gold strands the delectably flavored saffron added to the rice in the last stages of cooking. She had been told that the Iranian housewife went through fourteen steps in cooking rice, and she fully believed what she had heard. The rice was so good. For dessert, they had Shir Berenj, made with rice, sugar rose water milk and cream, and sipped hot tea afterwards.

As they entered their room, Jordan let out something between a whoop and a shriek of delight as she took in the flowers that adorned the room. The roses, ranging from red to scarlet, were tastefully arranged in crystal vases and bowls which occupied every table, shelf and corner of the room. The scent of roses suggested a quiet romantic splendor befitting the royal heritage of the palace.

"It's amazing, Ahmed," she cried, "Thank you so very much."

"I'm glad you approve," he replied gravely as he took her in his arms, "My love is like a red, red rose!" And Jordan wasn't surprised at his familiarity with the poetry of Keats, and Shakespeare, Byron, and Marvell. His knowledge of English literature was astounding, and their mutual love for it had brought them a little closer to each other.

Like Jordan, he, too, loved Keats, especially the incomparable odes to the nightingale, to Autumn and To a Grecian Urn. Heard melodies and those unheard had been sweet for her thought Jordan.

Chapter 20

The somber atmosphere prevailing in the office when Jordan walked in to work on Saturday was palpable. Even Bani, the spirited office boy, who usually greeted Jordan with a cheery "Salaam Aleykum, Khanum e Jodaan," seemed worried. Before she could sit down at her desk, Pat and Gregg walked in. "Hey Jordan, where have you been," Pat asked incredulously.

Many things had happened in Tehran in their absence.

The city had been rocked by demonstrations over the weekend. "Marg ba Shah- death to the Shah," from tens of thousands of lips and throats had reverberated in central and southern Tehran as rampaging mobs had attacked shops and other business establishments, and set fire to cars and buses. Things were getting pretty hot, and Jordan shuddered as she thought what this would mean to Ahmad. Macbeth's witches refrain 'Double, double toil and trouble' kept reverberating through her head. Ahmad would be very upset, she thought, for he knew nothing. They had spent most of the time in their rooms, and had not even turned on the TV to watch the news broadcasts.

Ahmad had given strict instructions to the hotel that they were not to be disturbed for any reason.

"This weekend is for you, sweet maid. And for me," he had said gleefully, like a little boy out on a glorious adventure. She knew how terrible he must feel now-not knowing anything about what had happened. Jordan felt a terrible sense of guilt, because she was indirectly responsible.

After Gregg had left, Pat asked, "So where were you anyway? How come you didn't see what happened on TV?"

They had had no time for TV, thought Jordan again and, felt personally responsible that their tryst had kept Ahmad ignorant of what was going on. On the other hand, she thought, he would have had to cut short their trip if he had known, and that would have been the unkindest cut of all. She felt a thrill of residual pleasure as she savored the memory. As if in answer to her thoughts, Ahmad called her during the lunch break to tell her that everything was OK. He had not been missed during the tumult because his cousin had covered up for him. Before leaving for Esfahan with Jordan, Ahmad had told his cousin Firooz, who was also his best friend and confidante about his plans, so when Ahmad's boss had asked for him on Saturday, when Ahmad was officially due back from his mission, Firooz had told him that Ahmad had called in sick with a bad case of the flu. Ahmad's boss, who knew Ahmad's conscientiousness and sense of duty, had accepted it. He knew that Ahmad could not have done anything in the face of the sudden upsurge in the people's mood. It had given everybody, including himself, a nasty surprise. There was nothing to be gained by chewing Ahmad up for his absence, he thought.

"Right now, matters are out of our hands," said Ahmad, "'The Shahanshahi'–the king of kings was the respectful term he always used to refer to the Shah- "has made certain decisions which no one could have influenced, so my absence did not matter," he explained. "Thank you Babe, for the best weekend of my life-so far," he said in a bantering tone, and then, seriously, "The demonstrators are crying for vengeance for their martyrs in Esfahan. It's too early to stay how things will gel, but don't worry Jordan. We'll see how things go. I don't want you to worry about anything. We will see it through."

And again Jordan had the urge to tell him, let's give it all up and go, Ahmed. She wanted to plead with him, yet knew that he would never agree. "It's not that I love you less, dear Jordan," he had said as if reading her thoughts. "It's just that I have to live up to the oath I have taken. I just cannot forget that. It's not that I haven't thought about it either. Sometimes I think I should forget the honor, the traditions in which I have been brought up. I wish my father were alive. I could at least ask him what to do although I already know what he would say."

Jordan felt helpless, but loved him the more for his loyalty to his oath, and his sincere consideration for her fears. "Oh, Ahmad. I hope things will get better," she said tremulously.

Chapter 21

Reuters' Bernard and Pat joined her in her office. "I was downtown with some of my friends on Friday afternoon," began Bernard. "Nobody was expecting trouble on the streets because up until last Friday, the demonstrators were carrying on their screaming and shouting in the mosques. But suddenly, all hell broke loose. Multitudes of mullah inspired men, women and children poured on to the streets from the mosques and houses. The noise was frightening-like an earthquake."

"Were you walking the streets when this happened?" Jordan asked Bernard.

"How else would I garner all this info that I bring you?" asked Bernard seriously.

"Aren't you afraid to be out on the streets?"

"Well' yes, but then I think my color is a definite advantage here, so I'm safe. I wouldn't say the same for you white guys, though," he declared assuming a tone of comical solemness.

In the last month or so, the demonstrators in Tehran and other cities had changed their tactics. The reason for this was that Khomeini's rooftop announcements were becoming more incendiary than they had been. He literally screamed at the people to come back on the streets and show their strength. "Do everything you can to show Reza"-Khomeini's form of address for the Shah- "that you are serious."

The rooftop announcements were the ingenious communication system adopted by the Shah's opponents to carry Khomeini's words to the people in Tehran and other major cities. Audio tape players with powerful amplifiers and duffels were set up on the rooftops of buildings in vantage positions. Everyday, an audiotape carrying a sermon and instructions from Khomeini was smuggled into the country from Iraq. Several copies were made and sent to the various towns, including Tehran, where they were aired at full volume. Men, women and children listened in awe-it was the voice of the messiah, virtually from heaven, and a resounding "Allahu Akbar" reverberated in the southern part of the city when the signal for the Khomeini broadcast was heard. "Last Thursday's rooftop serenade must have been especially effective," added Bernard.

"How so?" asked Pat.

"Remember I told you about Shariatmadari? He's one of the least radical of the Mullahs, and is highly respected by the people. Some time ago, he appealed to the people to protest in the confines of the mosques, and not to come out on the streets. He wants to avoid anuy confrontation with the armed forces, which could lead to violence and bloodshed. And his appeal of was respected until last Friday. Khomeini himself seems to have bowed to Sharitmadari's view. However, last Saturday all hell broke loose. Khomeini's speech had been quite a rant."

Khomeini used the recent massacre in Esfahan to add force to his invective. He was obviously losing his patience, the people had reciprocated by showing that they meant business. The Shah, realizing that he had to make some amends, promised to have free elections by June, but this had fallen on deaf ears. Over three hundred thousand people had marched in Tehran alone. Many other cities had exhibited similar strength. "Marg ba Shah," thundered and boomed across the land. It seemed that an unprecedented storm was imminent. Jamshid Amouzegar, the recently appointed Prime Minister, panicked, and declared martial law. Tanks and artillery rumbled on to the streets. Thousands of heavily armed commandos took up positions at every street corner. Tehran and other cities took on the appearance of a war zone. Khomeini thundered from the rooftop, "Reza is at war with his own people!"

"And it certainly looks like that," said Pat. "Now tell me what you were up to," she said after Bernard had left the room.

"I took a trip to heaven," she told Pat, and went on to describe her idyll.

"I'm so glad for you, Jordan. For a while there I thought you were going to end up a cantankerous old maid, spending the rest of your life in libraries and classrooms! You really had me worried, you know," she joked.

"Oh, you know what? Remember that shrew we met at the party where you met Ahmad?

Nisreen, I think her name is. Well, our great friend Bill has shacked up with her. He moved into her apartment last week. That gigolo. He's walking around on cloud nine."

Jordan gasped. Nisreen was Ahmad's aunt. "How do you know?"

"Well, Bani, our friendly office boy brought me the news. Apparently he helped Bill move his stuff to Nisreen's house. And you know Bani loves to bring me the office gossip. Another thing. Remember we noticed a lot of shredded paper outside Parveen's office yesterday? It seems Parveen found a letter in her husband, Ali's, pants pocket when she was doing the laundry. The letter was from Ali's girlfriend in the US. It seems that Ali had fathered a bonny Irano-American boy while he was a grad student at UCLA. The proud mother had sent the glad tidings to Ali, asking him when he was returning to California."

"Is he planning to go back?"

"I doubt it very much. It seems there's going to be one more single parent in California," she giggled.

Jordan didn't see the humor in it. "What's that got to do with the shredded paper?"

"Oh, Iranian women have a habit of shredding paper when they are distressed. Parveen had been doing just that while telling the story to her friend, Lali."

Jordan's thoughts went back to Nisreen. She knew Nisreen doted on Ahmed, and Ahmed on his part was very loyal to his aunt even though he did not seem to approve of how she behaved. She was his mother's sister, and he felt that her behavior was frivolous.

Chapter 22

So much had happened in the month of January, mostly good, but some bad. You got to give a little, take a little, thought Jordan sanguinely, recalling the theme song of Guess Who's Coming to Dinner which she had watched with Ahmad a few days before.

As Arbayeen, the fortieth day after the massacre of the protestors in Qum approached, hushed and ominous sounding rumors hissed and slithered in the hallways and closed rooms, at private tables in restaurants and cafeterias. Something's going to happen, they said. Some pooh poohed them, while others lived their lives in great fear. Others were quietly making arrangements to leave the country. Still others glowered with great expectations.

And as expected, things did happen. The protestors had efficiently organized a rash of protests in several cities, including Tehran. Ahmad had told Jordan not to leave her house that day, except to go to work, "And please tell your friends, too."

"Where will you be?" she asked, a note of near desperation in her voice.

"I'll be in Tehran, darling. Don't worry. I'll be OK. I'm not leaving Tehran because I want to make sure that nothing bad happens here. If it does, it will give a lot of exposure for the terrorists in the international press. That's what the protesters are hoping for."

"Can't the police avoid clashing with the people?" asked Jordan.

"Actually, Jordan, some of our cops and commandos are pretty dumb. They are very easily provoked, and have itchy trigger fingers. I was at a meting with the Chief of Police and the Army's Commanding Officer for Tehran, and we agreed that there should be no violence, whatever the protestors say or do."

It seemed that Ahmad's presence in Tehran had paid off, or so Jordan liked to think, for no serious incidents were reported anywhere. The protestors-thousands of men, women and children had marched the streets of the capital screaming invective against the Shah and his loyalists. "We allowed the citizens of Tehran their First Amendment Rights," quipped Ahmad.

However, another psychological tactic was being used by the protestors. The young women among them carried bunches of red roses under their chadors and offered one to every soldier and policeman they encountered, entreating them not to kill their own people. "Iranian men are essentially very sensitive to this kind of gesture. The protestors tactics are becoming more and more refined. It must have a very damaging effect on the morale of our security forces," Ahmad told Jordan, when they were discussing the events later.

Again matters turned bad, however, for the police in Tabriz had not had the strength to curb their trigger fingers. By noon that day, over two dozen men, women and children had been mowed down on the streets there. The protestors were gaining on several fronts. Cameramen, who had been on the ready, captured the scenes on video with all of the gory details of death and destruction. Some bodies were stage-managed for maximum effect. Bucket-fulls of chicken blood from slaughterhouses had been brought to dress up the dramatics. Volunteers to play dead were easy to find. It was an easier martyrdom than actually getting shot to death. Anything to help the cause!

"This means there will be another Arbayeen in March," lamented Ahmad. "Khomeini is playing his cards well," he added grimly. "There will be more martyrs before that day is done."

And just as Ahmad had predicted, on the fortieth day after the Tabriz killings, on the 29th of March, demonstrations were held in several cities to mourn for the dead. This time it was in Yazd, a little town located almost in the exact center of Iran, near the border of Dasht-e-lut, (the Great Sand Desert). The police had lost their patience when the demonstrators taunted and cajoled them in turn asking them to shed their uniforms and join the protestors. When one of them opened fire, others had followed, leaving many dead on the street. Actors covered in chicken blood and offal from butcher shops had added to the numbers of the 'dead and injured.' Still photographs and videos were made and distributed throughout the country.

The arbayeen of the Yazd martyrs, held in May, proved to be even more damaging to the image of the Shah.

Chapter 23

Ayatollah Kazem Shariyatmadari was a moderate and a pacifist, and although he had often voiced protest against the policies of the Shah, he had been willing to work with the Shah as Head of State. He had made many attempts to advise the Shah, and if there was one Ayatollah the Shah trusted, it was Shariatmadari. Shariatmadari was working very hard to lead the demonstarators towards non-violent protest in the hope that Iran would continue to remin a monarchy at peace with the clergy. He had advised the Shah to replace Namatollah Nasiri, the dreaded and hated Chief of Savak, reviled as "the Butcher of Tehran" with a more moderate civil servant.

Nasiri was said to have been responsible for the deaths or disappearance of thousands of young Iranian men and women, often arrested on the flimsiest of excuses, and charged for treason. Shariatmadari was an ally the Shah desperately needed, but that was not to be.

That day in May, military commandos entered the house of Ayatollah Shariatmadari, and shot to death a young and ardent follower of the cleric before his own eyes. Nobody knew the reason for this attack, but it was enough to persuade Shariatmadari to align himself with Khomeini, at least temporarily. A rumor engineered by Shah loyalists, that the dead man was one of Shariyatmadari's gay partners did not carry much weight, even among the Shah loyalists, and was seen as a weak attempt to vilify a holy and powerful man for political expediency.

Bernard was on his way to the campus when he noticed an unusual regularity in the honking of vehicular horns. Turning to his taxi driver, he asked, "Chera, Agha?"(Why?)

The larger than life driver turned his cherubic face, and grinning from ear to ear, announced, "Nasiri raft!" (Nasiri's gone)

The joy in his voice was palpable.

Momentarily confused, Bernard asked, "Nasiri?"

"Bale, agha. Namatollah Nasiri, SAVAK boss," he gushed, grinning and chuckling.

"Oh, Khob, Kheili Khob.(Good, very good) agreed Bernard, matching the driver's enthusiasm as best he could.

Later in the faculty room, Brad Foreman, ever the optimist declared joyfully, "Well, that should satisfy the demonstrators. Now we can expect some sanity and get back to work."

Bernard, who had a better perspective of the situation said, "Don't be so naïve, Brad.

To me it seems like it's too little, too late. The shah should have done this a long time ago, and followed it up by giving in to more of their demands."

"Oh, I don't know," complained Brad in disgust.

In fact, the decision to sack Nasiri at this time made things worse for the Shah; his supporters saw the move as a sign of weakness, while for his enemies it was a sign of victory. Many started counting the days until what they saw as his inevitable departure from the country. It Besides, it would not be a new thing, for he had done it before, when things got rough.

As if to coincide with the fall of Nasiri, the number of deaths among the opposition groups was falling considerably. Supporters and loyalists of the Shah attributed the lower incidence of death and destruction to the success of the newly introduced economic policies. They argued that the resulting decrease in the cost of living would take the minds of the people off revolution. In fact, however, the reason was that Shariatmadari, who now had the ear of the revolutionaries, had been able to persuade them, yet again, to confine their protests to the mosques and their immediate environs, which the police or the army would not dare enter with arms. The sermons within the mosques became more and more intense, filled with invective against the Shah, and it seemed that no one who attended Friday prayers would side with the Shah again.

Ahmed and Jordan continued to meet as often as they could. His work, to which he was very much devoted, took a great deal of his time, but he always found time to see her even if it was for a few minutes. They would meet in the Intercontinental, which was very close to Jordan's apartment, or some other place where his work took him. He would tell her all the details of what the security forces of the Shah were doing. They were on their toes most of the time, for the revolutionary forces were slowly but surely gaining ground in the country. "The Mullahs are creating havoc. The mosques are becoming the hotbed of political plotting and intrigue. They are inciting the people to revolt against the Shah. They organize demonstrations in different parts of the country. In Tehran alone, there were more than fifteen demonstrations last week. The police have been ordered to come down hard on the demonstrators."

"What are their demands?"

"They want the country to revert to Islamic law. They want the liquor shops closed down, and the chador to be made compulsory for women in public. In fact they want to remove everything the Shah stands for. And they blame the West in general, and the USA in particular for all the problems the country is facing."

"But there are so many women taking part in these demonstrations. Do they all want to be encumbered by this anachronistic mode of dress?"

"You'd be surprised how much influence these clerics have on the people. Both the men and the women believe that they will all burn in hell unless the women dress appropriately. Right now there are some women who are against the chador. They are the ones who have had some education and seen what's going on in the rest of the world. You see, Jordan, many of our women are uneducated. But this doesn't mean that all educated women are against the chador. Anyway there are many who are trying to change traditional thinking. So they, too, are organizing demonstrations against the chador. Those who are still loyal to the Shah are helping them. We are doing the same."

"What do you think is going to happen," Jordan asked.

"I wish I could tell you, darling. I really wish I could tell you." He rarely used words of endearment when he talked to her, probably because it was not in his nature to do so, she thought, but she knew that he loved her fiercely, and would do anything to protect her. His rare use of the word now seemed to indicate to Jordan a sense of the seriousness of the situation, which he did not want to frighten her with by putting into words. But it had escaped out of his lips involuntarily, and Jordan was again filled with that all familiar sense of foreboding.

The demonstrations in Tehran were increasing by the day. The only silver lining in the pallid cloud that loomed over them was that there were counter-demonstrations, too, by people who knew what clerical rule in the country would amount to. It seemed there were still many people who were loyal to the Shah, in spite of the mistakes he had made.

"It's not so much the loyalty to the Shah as the fear of autocratic clerical rule. Many people who live in the cities, at least, want the freedom to live the way they want, and not be told what to wear, what to drink and what to watch on TV," said Brad.

"That's right," agreed Leon. "The ethnic Persians are not Arabs, and their thinking is way different from those who have descended from their Arab invaders. And even they have been greatly influenced by the Persian culture."

Bob, who was usually silent on such matters, suddenly piped in, "Yes, they like their blue jeans and T shirts, their records and movies from Gandhi Street, and the vodka and wine."

"A loaf of bread, a flask of wine and thou," quoted Brad. "Well, that goes for some of us here, too, right Bob?"

Bob fell silent, probably feeling worried about what the Islamic supporters would feel about him, thought Jordan.

Chapter 24

Manafi, a devout Muslim, who did not hide the fact that he disapproved of the way the foreign staff conducted themselves-he often spoke against the weekend parties-sometimes ribbing, sometimes admonishing Bob and the others who went to them regularly. "You are going to suffer the same fate as the citizens of Sodom and Gomorrah,' he had said facetiously one day. And now, out of the blue, he angrily broke out, "The Shah has corrupted the minds of the people. He is trying to destroy Islam in Iran. He should listen to our religious leaders. Only they can save this country from utter destruction. Look at our women. They are walking on our streets half-naked. It's an insult to Islam."

His outbreak was so sudden and unexpected that no one said a word; a heavy, deafening silence descended upon the room. Manafi had always been a very quiet person, speaking only when spoken to. Now, it was as if he had been waiting a long time to say what he did. His face was flushed, and he averted the gaze of everyone else in the room. Lali, an administrative officer known for her candor and sharp tongue, burst out, "Manafi, you can wear the chador when you go out. I am not. Iran is a free country, and we don't want anyone to tell us how to live.'

Manafi glowered at Lali menacingly, but deciding not to test Lali's tongue any further, got up and left the room.

"These people are mad," Lali continued, "I am a good Muslim. I believe in Allah, but I don't think He wants us to be second class citizens. These mullahs want to keep the women in total subjugation. People like Manafi don't know that once the mullahs get power, they will go extreme. We will have to dance to their tune in every way. He doesn't care because he's not married, he's an only child, and his mother's dead," she joked. But the silence continued.

Jordan couldn't help thinking about how much the situation had changed since she first came. Then nobody dared to speak against the Shah. Later when Pat, Brad and Bernard were in the room by themselves, Brad noted, "That was a big surprise coming from Manafi. I didn't think he had it in him."

"I'm not surprised," said Bernard, "Some of these guys even think of us as infidels, and an obstacle to their way of life. They really believe they will have a better life under Shariar law."

"They think the Shah is more interested in the image he portrays outside the country-as a democratic liberal, as an upholder of Iranian culture and civilization than the Islamic- than doing what's best for his country," opined Brad, "It's an idea that has been gaining force in recent times, especially with Khomeini and his supporters adding strength to it."

"The Shah has not done much to check those sentiments," said Jordan, he has given SAVAK a free hand under the mistaken assumption that any budding revolution can be stifled by force."

"What else can he do?"

"Too much blood has been spilled, too many lives lost. Maybe it will stop now with the dismissal of Nasiri, but I doubt it. I agree with what you said, Bernard; it's too little, too late."

"What do you suggest?" asked Leon.

"He should go to the people; he must show them that he is not against Islam in any way," said the moderate, soft-spoken Dr Hosseini. He should probably give a little power to the Mullahs. He can choose some of the less conservative members of the clergy to work out some reforms in the country. That way he can pacify the moderates, who are still in the majority. He needs to keep them on his side, or they will join up with the conservatives."

"How about the demonstrators?" asked Jordan.

"They should be allowed to demonstrate. There's nothing like a little show of liberalism to turn attention away from extreme conservatism."

And Jordan thought, but how can he change the grim realities of what has already happened? What about all the other repressive acts of the police? And her mind was occupied with Ahmad. She hadn't seen him in over a week. He had called several times, and they had chatted for long hours. But each time he had very apologetically told her that he couldn't see her. Work was taking him to various parts of the country, following all kinds of leads.

"We need to stay on top of things. The Shah's enemies are trying very hard to get things organized all over the country."

Dear Ahmad, she thought, you are in the middle of such an awful situation. Why is it that you had to be caught up in this? Can't you leave it all and go away?

But she knew, even as she asked the question that he would never do that. He had too much character, too much integrity and loyalty to the cause he had chosen-to defend his king, even at the cost of his own life.

"We were in Fars last week," he said, "You know Fars is the real center of Persian culture. That's where the real Persians still live. In most of the other provinces, invaders-the Arabs, the Moghuls, the Turks and even the Russians and the British- have left their influence." She knew he was trying to steer the conversation to a lighter mode. He didn't want her worrying too much. She felt grateful for his concern, but couldn't steer her mind away from the present. He had many enemies, and he was walking a tightrope, hoping to get to the other side. Not wishing to add more turmoil to an already troubled mind, Jordan did not pursue the matter further.

Chapter 25

Ahmad was driving to work amidst the din and dust of Tehran's frenetic rush hour traffic when his thoughts suddenly went back to the events of the previous week. His immediate boss, Colonel Aliakbari had called him into his office at a rather unusual time of the day, when everyone was getting ready to go home.

"Sit down, Ahmad," he invited gruffly as Ahamad entered, "I have an important assignment for you." The tone in which he spoke signaled Ahmad that this was not going to be an ordinary mission. "We have just received news that some of the top ranking agents of the Mujaheddin are planning a meeting in Esfahan next week. Actually they are meeting with some extreme elements from Iraq, who are bringing them a truck load of weapons. I need from you to intercept them."

"Am I to arrest them," ventured Ahmad.

"Do what it takes," said Alikbari grimly, "but the weapons must not fall into the hands of the Mujaheddin. Take them in or destroy them." And Ahmad didn't quite know whether he meant the men or the weapons, but he thought it would be imprudent to ask.

"Choose three or four of the best commandos you can think of," he continued after some thought, "and you must not tell anyone about this mission, not even the men who are going with you. Just tell them to be prepared to go, but don't give them any details."

And Ahmad wondered why it had to be so secret when it involved a treasonous plot. But again, he decided not to question his superior officer.

Now, he wondered if he should tell Jordan about the mission, and decided not to. It was too dangerous, and he had been told not to tell anyone, although he did not think of Jordan as "anyone."

They engaged in small talk for a while and he rang off promising to see her during the weekend.

When the intercom buzzed in her room, Jordan reached for it eagerly, her hand reaching out to open the gate for Ahmed, who she thought was at the gate. Thank goodness he's here, she thought. There was so much she wanted to know about how his work was going. Who would finally come out winner of the bitter struggle between the bearded ones, and the royals. She wished with all her being that the revolution would fizzle out, and the Shah would regain his stature in the Persian dynasty. A gruff, strained woman's voice on the intercom intruded on her reverie, "Khanume Jordan, can I see you for few minutes, please?" It was Nisreen, Ahmed's aunt, and Jordan knew at once that there was something amiss. She hastily unlatched the gate saying, "Befarmoidh, you are most welcome!"

Nisreen stumbled into Jordan's apartment like a steaming rhino, pushing open the door and forcing

Jordan to move out of her path. Jordan was astounded by the sudden appearance of the woman, who was not one of her favorite Iranians. She was polite to her during the few times they had met because of her relationship to the man she loved, but had never made any effort to cultivate a friendship with her. Nisreen was bossy and arrogant and didn't hide the fact that she did not care for any of these Americans, or any other foreigners for that matter, who had come to her country to take away their money. Except, of course, for Bob, whom she had literally 'shacked up with' as Pat liked to say. Nisreen made a great exhibition of her affection for Bob. Her hands were all over him when they were together and she made pointed displays of her affection especially when Jordan and Pat were around. "She thinks she has stolen him from us," shrieked Pat one day, "as if either of us would touch the jerk with a ten-foot pole!"

"He's probably told her that we are in love with him," said Jordan.

"You bet he has, the prick." Exploded Pat

Looking almost distraught, sans makeup Nisreen looked as if she was in great pain, and misery, and in spite of everything, Jordan's heart went out to her, one woman to another. Something awful has happened to her, she thought, and taking her hand, guided her toward the sofa. Jordan's tenderness was lost on her, however, as she snatched her hand away. The resentment and anger was unmistakable as she asked, "Do you know where is Bob?"

Jordan was startled by the question, and told her that she hadn't seen him since Wednesday.

"Why, what's the problem, Nisreen?"

"Is he at Pat's house?" she demanded, her eyes boring into the back of Jordan's head. And Jordan shivered in apprehension.

Oh my God, thought Jordan, she thinks Bob's with one of us. As ridiculous as it sounded, she couldn't laugh. The atmosphere was so charged with Nisreen's hostility. "I'm sure he's not," protested Jordan. "Why do you think so?"

"Bob left the house on Wednesday evening. He said he come back for dinner, but never come."

"Maybe he's with some other friends," suggested Jordan helpfully.

"OK, I find out." she fumed menacingly and stormed out of Jordan's apartment.

Despite the apparent hilarity of Nisreen's suspicions that Bob was secretly involved with Jordan or Pat, goose bumps began to rise all over Jordan's skin. An eerie feeling of impending doom overcame Jordan as she watched Nisreen leave, a marauding virago she thought. That and her fear for Ahmad's safety added to her misery; she crept into bed and lay in a fetal position, as worrisome thought took over.

Chapter 26

Ahmad had chosen three of the best commandos he could think of. Two of them, Firooz and Jamshid, were his cousins, and the third, Parvez was his neighbor from childhood; they had all been in the same class in middle school and later in high school. They were "the magnificent four," as they called themselves, and had gone through many adventurous boyhood experiences together. Their loyalty to each other was unquestionable, and though they had never said it out loud, there was not one among them who would not gladly lay down his life for the others. When Ahmad had told them that he wanted to go with them on this mission, he told them what their goal was-commander's orders or not, he argued.

Ahmad himself had handpicked the weapons they would carry. They would fly to Esfahan in a military helicopter, and drive a light, camouflaged military truck to the rendezvous in the desert.

The rendezvous point was about fifty feet away from a qanat shaft.

The qanat system was an ingenious underground waterway built many centuries before to irrigate the farms in the Esfahan region. It was necessary to keep the water underground and retrieve it close to the plants that needed irrigation. If allowed to flow on the surface the water would dry up in the unrelenting sun or seep into the sandy soil before it reached the crops. A shaft going down to the water level enabled the water to be drawn out of the shaft and fed to the crops. Each shaft was usually guarded by a muquani-a Qanat keeper, who was responsible for clearing blockages caused by debris floating on the water. A wooden stairway led from the ground to the bottom of each shaft.

In the last century or so, the qanats had fallen out of use, replaced by pipes. Now this far-reaching network of underground tunnels was abandoned, and provided a safe haven for bats, rodents and other small animals that inhabited the qanats in large numbers.

The sun was rapidly sinking into the horizon when Ahmad and his commandos arrived. It was a moonless night, cold and very dark, with a steady breeze blowing in a southwesterly direction. Little creatures of the desert scurried around, and occasionally the screech of an owl or the ruffling of its feathers was heard as it swooped down on an unsuspecting prey. Bats with their characteristic beeps darted in and out of the shafts. The rustle of little creatures going about their nightly business blended in well with the other quiet sounds of regional life. Other than these primeval nocturnal sounds of nature, the desert night was undisturbed.

The conspirators had chosen their night well, thought Ahmad.

The meeting was scheduled for midnight, so they had about four hours to spare. There were several date palms and huge boulders dotting the landscape. Ahmad chose a grove of palm trees for cover and settled down with his men. They were not going to take any chances, so there would be no fire, and Ahmad had instructed his men to maintain complete silence unless it was absolutely necessary to speak, and that too in whispers.

Ahmad's mind went back to the days of Cyrus and Darius. How many battles would have been fought on these plains as the ancient Persians stilled the advance of their enemies, until the young Alexander had done his magic, and sacked the Persian Empire. Sadness engulfed him as he thought of the bitter defeat of his forefathers.

"Shh," whispered Ali, with raised hand, as the stillness of the night was disturbed by the sound of an approaching vehicle moving towards in the distant sands.

"That's a small vehicle. It must be the Mujaheddin. The arms truck should be coming soon," said Ahmad, "We will stay hidden until it arrives and the carriers get out of their vehicle. Until then, nobody move."

The approaching vehicle stopped about three hundred yards from where they were hidden.

Their men got out, and started talking and laughing. Ahmad's group settled down to wait.

About three hours had elapsed when the silence was broken again, this time by the deep rumble of a heavy vehicle. "The weapons," whispered Ahmad.

The truck pulled up right by the small vehicle, and two men alighted from it. They heard the two groups greeting each other with typical Iranian camaraderie.

"Chetore, agha. Shoma Khube?"

"As Salam Aleikhum."

"There's five of them all together," whispered Ahmad, "I don't see any problems." The others nodded in assent. "Let's move!"

And they stood up in a crouch. They were sure they couldn't be seen in the darkness of the desert horizon.

They began to inch forward, making hardly a sound. Ahmad signaled to the others to spread out as they approached their quarry. It was going well, he thought. His men were skilled in this kind of action. They were now close enough to see three of the men in a huddle. In a few more seconds they would be close enough to have them covered with their weapons, and order them to surrender. Despite his commander's orders, he did not relish the idea of gunning them down. He wanted to arrest them and take them back to Tehran, where others would decide their fate. He stood up straight, his weapon aimed at the group, when suddenly all hell broke loose. A machine gun opened fire from behind them, and the three men in front opened fire in the general direction of Ahmad's group. The three commandos were instantly hit by machine gun fire, but Ahmad was miraculously unhurt, shielded by the men behind. He dropped to the ground, and began inching his way towards his friends and knew immediately that two of them were dead. The third, Firooz, tried to say something to him, blood gurgling out of his mouth, and Ahmad knew that he, too was beyond help.

"Come on, Firooz, let's creep towards the shaft."

"No, Ahmad. I'm done. Go. Save yourself," he rasped, and breathed his last.

Bitter rage and sadness almost overwhelmed him. He wanted to get up and start shooting at anything and everything that had brought such an ignominious end to the lives of his beloved brothers. He lay perfectly still, listening, trying to get a bearing on his adversaries. The desert replied with an eerie silence. And then, suddenly his commando training kicked in, as also did the words of Firooz, so urgent even in the throes of death. He had to save himself. He had to report back that the mission had failed. Reluctantly he began to scramble towards the Qanat shaft, which was his only escape route.

The five men in the truck reached the bodies of the commandos. He heard one of them ask, "Is Ahmad there?"

A few seconds later, "No, he's not here. Spread out. Look for him. He's the main target."

Realization dawned on Ahmad. He knew that it had been a setup. His boss had betrayed them for some unknown reason. He had to get back safely to Tehran. His friends' deaths had to be avenged. He had no time to think. With a new more purposeful sense of urgency he began to crawl as silently as he could toward the shaft.

Then one of them yelled, "He must be heading for the qanat shaft. Find him!"

And the powerful light of the truck lit up the area just as Ahmed dived into the shaft, bumping and rolling down the wooden stairs, some of them rotten with age, breaking under his weight. When he finally hit the water at the bottom, he knew that he was unhurt and the little creatures shrieked and squeaked in fear and indignation. Ahmad grabbed his weapon and started to move deep into the dark, evil-smelling cavern. Up on the surface, he heard a few more gunshots-they are making sure that no one will live to tell the tale, he thought, sadness and anger taking over, and giving him the strength to survive. He had to survive, he kept saying to himself. Holding his gun above his head, he began walking, going east in the dark cavern. Only the occasional sound of a bat disturbed the turbulent thoughts that kept running through his brain. He would probably have to spend the night underground and surface only at dawn. He chose the eastern fork of the qanat because he would meet the rising sun faster that way. He had to get out of this place and get to Tehran as soon as quickly ashe could. He had business to attend to. The deaths of his closest friends gave him the strength and determination. They shall not have died in vain, he said to himself.

Up on the ground, the plotters rushed towards the shaft opening. Flashlights were turned on as the men peered into the shaft, looking for their quarry. The leader barked orders. "One of you go down and try to find which way he's heading. The others move quickly, one to each shaft. He has to surface somewhere, and I want you to be ready to receive him when he comes out. Take a few grenades, too. He's a tough customer, and I don't want any slipups. Remember he's our main target. These other guys are small fry," he said, pointing derisively at the dead bodies of Ahmad's team.

Ahmad kept walking, making no noise at all. If they were waiting for him at the next shaft, they would be listening for the splashing sounds of water, so he moved hardly raising his legs. It was laborious and the dank and musty smell of the humid air trapped down there was overpowering, but he kept going, slowly and patiently. Suddenly the air began to become a little lighter, and he knew he was approaching a shaft. He slowed down, hardly breathing.

There was a man guarding the shaft entrance that Ahmad was approaching. A sixth sense in Ahmad became active. Firooze was beside him, whispering "Be very careful, Ahmad. He's waiting. He'll show you no mercy. He's carrying grenades, and if he hears you, he'll drop them in your path."

The man outside strained to listen, but all he heard was the steady ripple of the stream as the water had moved for centuries through the tunnels providing the lifeblood for the peasants. He settled down and lit a cigarette. The flare of the match was brilliant in the darkness, and confirmed the telepathic warning that he had received from his dead friend.

It was the most exhausting trek of his life. The death of his best friends weighed heavily on him. They had all given their life so that he would live, and this gave him an inner strength and determination to carry on. By now there were no bat noises in the tunnels. They were all out in the desert, looking for prey as they had done for hundreds of years.

The heat and the staleness of the air assailed him again. He was sweating and began to itch all over his body, but as he passed each shaft entrance, he smelled freshness in the air, which revived him.

At the tenth shaft, he heard whispers, so he stopped and waited. After fifteen minutes, he heard them moving away, and he continued cautiously. He would not try to come out for a long while yet, he thought. They could not cover every shaft entrance, and anyway they would be tired, too.

Ahmad's body ached. His feet were numb from the cold water, which had soaked his boots and made them as heavy as leg irons. The bats were coming back, grumbling in irritated screeches, jostling for places to roost until sunset and it was time to go foraging once more. They sounded sated, however, and Ahmad thought at least they are satisfied with their night's work. He trudged on quietly, exhaustion gnawing at his arms and legs and everywhere else, but he wouldn't give in. He had to carry on. So much depended on him, he thought. And suddenly he thought of Jordan. He had to be there for her, too.

Then, suddenly, he saw the faint light of breaking dawn, and decided to peek out of the shaft. A few broken wooden steps led halfway up to the opening. Very cautiously, Ahmad moved up the rickety steps, and raised himself to the level of the ledge. Bright sunlight hurt his eyes as he strained to look. Everything was a blur, and he thought what if they are waiting for me. And then gradually, his eyes began to clear. A cock crowed in the distance, and he turned in the direction from which it came. To him it was the sound of the phoenix, of life rising from the tragic ashes of his friends' demise. He thought of them lying in the desert, the temples of their beautiful lives desecrated, beyond cleansing, beyond recall. He knew that the men who had killed them would certainly give them an Islamic burial as best they could in the desert which left no traces, just memories of millennia into which his friends would merge without pomp and ceremony, yet with honor as those who had given up their lives for the one they loved. Yet, he would go back and trace their remains. He would make sure that their families would know when and where they had met their end, and why. But that would have to wait a while. First he had to avenge their deaths, for they had died for and because of their love and loyalty to him.

He saw smoke rising from a little house. And then he saw more houses. He was near a little village. Little figures moving about depicted life going on apace. No terror, no mendacity, no fear or suspicion; it was as life had gone on for many ages with no sign of fear or danger. Everything seemed so peaceful, idyllic. He pulled himself out of the shaft. No gunshots greeted him. All around him, the peace and quiet of the village in the desert welcomed him. The gradually rising sun, not yet hot and scorching as it would be in an hour or so, comforted him after his cramped, dank and stifled struggle for existence in the bowels of the earth. The fresh air of the desert revived and cleansed him. But the sad regret he felt for his friends, and the anger that welled in him at the thought of being betrayed invigorated him. He began to walk faster towards the village.

Chapter 27

Ahmad had told Jordan that he would be away for a couple of days on an important mission. He hadn't given any details, only because she didn't want to distress Jordan, who he knew would be deeply worried at the thought of the potential danger he would be facing. So, she was not worried when she had not heard from him in the last two days. However, Nizreen's visit, had unsettled her; she was getting anxious. She had to tell him about Nizreen most importantly because Nizreen was part of his family. He had the right to know, and Jordan knew that Ahmad would do what was necessary to help Nizreen if any one could. Still she didn't call him. She would wait until his important mission was over, and he was able to attend to what Jordan thought was a mundane, even frivolous matter, especially since she knew Nizreen's nature. Yet, his silence bothered her. She had dreamt of him driving down a road at high speed in a car that had no brakes. He was driving at great speed towards a huge wall of flame, and there was nothing she or any one else could do to stop him from hurtling into the raging inferno. Thinking of the dream sent a chill down her spine.

Mercifully, the phone rang a few minutes later. It was Ahmed. He sounded bright and cheerful.

"Hey, Jordan. I'm back in Tehran. Can I see you this evening?"

Please, dear God, yes she thought, and mumbled, "Of course. What time will you come?" It was almost a plea, and Ahmed must have noticed the despondence in her voice. "Is everything OK? And she told him about Nisreen's visit. "I don't know why, Ahmed, but I'm scared," she whimpered.

"Don't worry Jordan." he said. Jordan had told Ahmed about Nizreen's suspicions about Pat and her, so Jordan knew that Ahmad had a hold on the situation. So when he said, "I'll see Nisreen before I see you. I'll find out what's going on, and put things right. Nisreen can be very stupid sometimes, Jordan felt a great sense of relief, as if Atlas' burden hed been lifted off her shoulders. Of course, dear Ahmed, I know you'll make things all right with Nisreeen. But what about everything else? she mused.

That evening they sat in the French restaurant at the Intercontinental, sipping wine and nibbling on the world famous beluga caviar harvested from the Caspian Sea. Ahmed told her nothing about the near- death experience ha had had. When she asked him about how the mission had gone, he casually replied that it had gone off without a hitch. He did not tell her that when he returned to the office, he had heard that his boss had suddenly gone out of the country on an important military mission. Ahmad knew they would not hear from his boss again. He had probably been threatened, or was being blackmailed by a militant group into doing what he had done, and rather than stay and face the music now that Ahmad was still alive, he had taken the easy way out-life in the UK or the USA as a private citizen. His family had probably preceded him, so there was no point in trying to get any information from them. Ahmad decided to keep the matter secret from Jordan because he did not want Jordan to know that his life was now in jeopardy. Several important figures in the security forces had been assassinated in the last few months, but much of that information had been kept under wraps because the government wanted to save face. Assassinations of the Shah's recognized allies would give a moral victory to the insurgent forces, was the argument.

Ahmad sounded almost cheerful about the direction the conflict was taking. He told Jordan that the Shah was ready to come to terms with the revolutionaries in the sense that he was ready to make certain changes in government that would be acceptable to the insurgent forces. He was very optimistic that the Shah would be able to ride the storm. The Shah had refused to go with the more reactionary elements in the government, which were intent on total annihilation of the revolutionaries by sheer military force. He knew that this approach would lead to the massacre of thousands of people. He had argued that most of the protesters were innocents-not rabid revolutionaries. He had refused to be responsible for the deaths of thousands of his subjects. "The Shah is a good man, Jordan. He loves his people. He wants to protect them and look after them. He thinks that his loyalists will be able to show the people that he is a good and wise ruler that can be trusted."

"You think the people will be persuaded?" asked Jordan, tremulously. She now felt that she was so much part of the conflict, and wished very much that the Shah would come out unscathed.

"I sure hope so. They have to understand. The Shah has done so much to bring this country from the camel and the donkey to the Paykhan and the Mercedes. Everything rides on that."

"I hope so too, Ahmed."

"Oh, I forgot to tell you about Nisreen," he suddenly said, "It appears that her boyfriend has flown the coop."

"What do you mean?"

"Her dear Bob has left the country. He had told Nisreen that he was going to see a friend, and would be back in time for dinner. In fact he had gone to the airport and boarded a British Airways flight to New York."

Jordan was speechless. No one at the university knew anything about it. In fact, he had heard Bob, as he left the office on Wednesday evening tell the HOD, "See ya Saturday, Brad. Have a nice weekend."

"How is Nisreen taking it?" ventured Jordan.

"Oh, she's furious. She says all American men are bastards! But she'll be all right. She has known many men, and that's in the biblical sense," he winked, "just wait till she meets the next guy who pays her a compliment, and she'll be gushing full throttle again."

Jordan wished she could share Ahmed's optimism, but somehow she felt a sense of anxiety creeping up on her. She sensed that Nisreen's anger would not be limited to American men. Jordan and Pat would be in her direct line of fire if she ever held a gun in her hands, she thought.

But she said nothing for fear of sounding irrational. After all, you couldn't expect Ahmed to actually understand how the mind of a woman such as Nisreen would work. Hell hath no fury, she thought, and hoped that she and Pat would never be in Nisreen's line of fire.

"Let's talk about something else," said Ahmed, taking her hands in his.

"What do you have in mind?" she asked teasingly, as Ahmed took her in his arms. And then everything was mercifully and deliciously forgotten as they made passionate love. Every physical move that Ahmed made in bed was so intense and lingering that it was as if he wanted to prolong every moment for as long as he could, yet always worried that it would soon end. Something was bothering him very much, but he obviously did not want to talk about it. Knowing him, Jordan did not want to pry, but feeling that she was so much part of him, it ached not to know. She wanted so much to share his worries and concerns. The American woman in her was straining to ask him, to tell him that she had to know, that she had a right to know. She was angry and her mind rebelled against his Persian macho, if she could call it that, which kept it a secret. She knew it was because he did not want her to have to worry about all of his problems, and as Pat had told her when they were discussing a similar situation sometime before, that he would tell her when he felt it was absolutely necessary, 'All in good time, Jordan. That's the Persian way. And in the Persian way, he wouldn't want you to pry. So let it rest. In sha allah, as they say here, he will tell ya baby," she teased.

All right, she thought, but it was the hardest thing to do. And she might have unconsciously made him aware of her concern, for he suddenly said, "Jordan, I'm gonna tell you something, but you must promise not to worry about it. I promise you that everything's going to be all right for me and for you and for everybody else."

Jordan felt a cold and heavy hand tug at her heart, and pure dread engulfed her. His tone had that effect on her.

The warmth and comfort of their lovemaking a few minutes before seemed to vanish suddenly as she felt a chill run down her entire being. She knew that what he was going to tell her must be really terrible, or else she wouldn't even broach the subject. Fighting hard to keep the panic that was rising within her, she feigned a relaxed calm as he said, "I'm on the revolutionaries' hit list." The bed she lay on seemed to open up and swallow her as he continued, "They have deployed a group of their best to get me, because they know I'm very loyal to the Shah. They tried once, but I was very lucky to escape." And he told her about the Esfahan plot, and the death of his friends, but left out the harrowing details of his escape from the jaws of death.

Jordan was terrified, saddened in a way that she had never been in her life before-not even when her father had left them. Jordan had met his friends briefly, and knew what great guys they were-happy, without a care in the world, and so loving and lovable, sincere and loyal.

"Oh, Ahmad! What are you going to do?" it was almost a wail, and the terror in her voice and her face were unmistakable. "Let's leave it all and go away. Let's go to the USA," pleaded Jordan, but even as she said the words,

Jordan knew that it would never happen. Ahmad was certainly not going to run away. He was too honorable, too responsible to duty, and more than anything else, too brave and confident in himself, and his king and everything he stood for to run away with his tail between his legs. He looked at Jordan, and words were not necessary to communicate the same feelings that had come to Jordan's mind. He looked at her briefly, and drew her into his arms in a gesture of protection, forgetting, thought Jordan ruefully, that it was he who needed protection. He trembled for a moment, uncharacteristically for him, thought Jordan intensifying her fear of what she was going to hear. Ahmad deliberately pulled himself together, and in a voice without the slightest edge of worry or concern said, "Don't worry, darling. I can take care of myself and the ones I love. These fools and their hatchet men are not very smart, you know. I already know about the guys who have been given the job, and we are taking steps to neutralize them."

Jordan didn't ask him what those steps were, and Ahmad continued, "One of Ansari's closest aides told me about the plot. He is pretty reliable, and assured me that they will be taken in for questioning before the end of the week."

"But Ahmed," Jordan began, but Ahmad put his fingers on his lips. "Yes, dear, I know. I'm not taking it lightly. I am already making arrangements to send my parents and sisters to the US. We have a house in northern California, and they will be quite comfortable there until things blow over here. And Jordan, I want you, too, to start thinking about going back. Would you like to go and live in California with my family for a while? I've told them all about you, and I will take you to see them soon. They are looking forward to meeting you"

"Ahmad! Is this an indirect way of proposing?" laughed Jordan.

"Seriously, Jordan, I know I've not been very communicative these past weeks, but you know that's only because of everything that's going on. Please don't hold that against me.

I've been wanting to take you to a great place my family owns on the Caspian coast, in a quaint little town called Babolzar. You would love it there. It's cool and green, not like hot and dusty Tehran. We could buy Caviar on the beach as the fishermen bring in their catch. You could pick juicy oranges, not just in the orchards, but on the streets which are lined with trees. Yes, honey, we will go there when things get better. But for now, I would like you to leave Iran. I'm sure their spies have seen us together, and I can't take a chance on you. So let's call this the weirdest proposal on earth, for I'm asking you to marry me but I'm sending you away, but I am very serious."

Jordan was lost for words. All kinds of emotions assailed her. First, she was deliriously happy with the prospect of marrying Ahmad. She had actually hoped with all her being that he would propose to her one day, but had never expected it to come as it did. But at the same time, a feeling of apprehension engulfed her. A few moments before, she had been filled with dread at the news about the threat to Ahmed's life. Now it was the sheer delirium of the prospect of sharing her life with this wonderful man. He interrupted her reverie gently, yet urgently, "So, what do you say Jordan?"

"Of course, darling, but…."

"But me no buts," he joked. "I'm so thrilled, Jordan. I was so afraid you'd say no." he squealed as he took her in his arms. "Just leave the arrangements to me. Everything's going to be fine, I promise."

Chapter 28

The June Arbayeen of the martyrs passed with little incident; the exhortations of Shariatmadari to the protesters to confine their protests to the mosques, and to avoid confrontations with the armed forces seemed to be having a calming influence on everybody concerned.

"It clearly shows how much influence Shariatmadari in particular and the Ayatollahs in general have on the people," observed Dr Hosseini.

"Not as much as the 'Revered One' has," boasted Manafi, a diabolic grin on his face, obviously referring to Khomeini, 'when he calls them out, nothing will be able to stop them."

And nobody spoke. A cold chill seemed to pass through Jordan, who whispered to Pat, "And so spake the Prophet of Doom."

"He hates us Kharejis,"(the Iranian term for foreigners) quipped Pat, smiling evilly at Manafi.

"He thinks of us as infidels, right Manafi?" taunted Bernard loudly, and Manafi asked, "What's that?"

And Bernard, as politely as he could, asked Manafi, "Do you think of us as infidels?"

Manafi went red in the face, and saying "Excuse me," left the room hurriedly.

"You'd better not get in his crosshairs after that question," warned Pat.

For the rest of the month of June, and July, things did seem to be improving for the Shah.

His economic advisers appeared to be getting it right for once, for the inflation rate had stayed steady for a while, and then started falling. Food prices had come down considerably, and there were fewer complaints heard in the food stores and supermarkets. Although sporadic street demonstrations were seen, they were the acts of Tudeh party remnants and not of the majority who took heir orders from the mosque. Most of the faithful remained within the confines of the mosques, and discussed matters with a sense of decorum, and more importantly, with more refinement of purpose.

A pay hike was announced for all government employees. Shouts of jubilation were heard from government offices when the story was reported on the 12 O' clock news. Not wishing to be outdone, the private companies also made a similar announcement the very next day. It was later reported that the private companies had done so at the behest of the Shah. How the Shah had persuaded the private companies to suddenly become so magnanimous was expressed in many a joke circulating on the streets, pubs and workplaces. In one particularly funny story, the Shah had reportedly told the business community, "I've turned a blind eye to all the times you screwed the masses, now you'd better do something before they screw mine."

Things were calm. Were they too calm, wondered Jordan. Was it the calm before the storm that would blow them all away? And Jordan was not the only one who had such worrisome thoughts, for many believed that the lull in hostilities was too good to be true. Death and destruction, which had stalked the land these last months, seemed to be taking stock before a final assault.

There were some who rejoiced in the thought that the days of SAVAK, and whispered conversations were over. People could say what they liked in the open without the fear of being arrested or deported. Manafi was often heard rejoicing at the prospect of the return of the 'Revered One' at the top of his voice. "We can live in peace then, like Shia Muslims!" He didn't seem to care that the "Kharejis" could hear what he said. And Jordan felt goose pimples rise all over her body. But Pat quietly ridiculed him. "The mouse is roaring again! The fucking rat! I hope his wife strangles him in bed with her chador!"

"Keep your voice down," pleaded Jordan. "He will have us stoned to death." And they both had a good laugh.

Chapter 29

July

Khaled Jamal, a student of Tehran University, walked into a public telephone booth on Gandhi Street. Khaled was grotesquely skinny, but nearly six feet tall. A thick, black beard covered his face, and a snub nose rose out of the mass of hair giving his face an owlish appearance. He had narrow slits for eyes. His neck was long and thin and the face kept rowing around like the periscope of a submarine in a dark stormy night. He wore faded blue jeans and a black T-shirt with Berkley University in bold white letters printed right across his chest. He wore sneakers, and walked with a shuffling gait, but no sound was heard as he moved always looking for something as if his life depended on it. His tapering fingers which gave his hands an effeminate look, suddenly reached into a little slit in the belt around his waist, and eased out a tiny slip of paper with a list of telephone numbers. A Marlboro dangled from his lips; he studied his thin bearded face on the glass panel of the telephone booth, which he quickly entered looking up and down the road to see if he was being followed. Perspiration gleamed on his forehead. He looked like a man on a mission, a deadly mission, and determination seemed to take over his being as he pushed in a bunch of ten riyal coins into the slot and began to dial. Whoever it was at the other end picked up on the first ring.

"Salaam Aleiyi qum, Agha," he said with great deference.

For the next five minutes he listened intently, committing whatever was being said to memory, never failing to look through the glass paneling of the booth. Like a hunted animal, defending himself against the sudden attack of a predator; he was always en garde, ready to fight back, not just in defense, but in vicious counter-attack.

A click at the other end of the line signaled the end of the conversation. He replaced the receiver and looking around very furtively, left the booth, and walked briskly down the street entering a little shop at the corner which sold music cassettes and videos. Five minute later, he walked out with ten audio cassettes, neatly wrapped in brown paper. Anyone who had the opportunity of looking at the contents would have found it strange to see that the tapes all opened with "Allahu Akbar." The rest of the contents were anything but musical. They were all copies of a long diatribe by Ayatollah Ruholla Khomeini against the Pahlavi dynasty. Khaled continued to walk until he reached a six-storied apartment complex. He pressed the buzzer for one of the apartments, and the door was immediately opened. He walked up the stairs, and entered one of the apartments on the third floor.

A few minutes later, he walked out of the building, and his package was lighter by one cassette tape. An hour or so after he had started, all of the cassettes in his package were gone. He soon reached another telephone booth, pulled out the list again, and started dialing. This time he dialed six numbers. Each time someone picked up at the first ring. Obviously every one of the people who answered his call had been waiting for it.

Khaled spoke curtly and swiftly with no preamble, so uncharacteristic of Iranian speakers, on the phone or off. He was making a rendezvous with six others: Meet at the Shayyad Monument at 8.15 tonight, was the essence of his brief instruction to each of his listeners.

Chapter 30

The voice of the Lebanese singing sensation, Gugush, was blaring forth on the tape player in Nisreen's living room. Nisreen, draped in a flowing yellow dress was stretched on the red sofa that dominated the room. She had a tall glass of marguerita in her hand, and a camel cigarette in the other. The air-conditioner, buzzing furiously as if in protest, did nothing to cool down the occupant, sweating profusely, trying hard to dry her forehead with the skimpy handkerchief she held in her pudgy fingers. A pile of newspaper, torn to shreds, lay on the floor beside the sofa. The sudden and unexpected ring of the doorbell gave Nisreen a violent start; she evidently hadn't been expecting any visitors as evidenced by the alcohol and tobacco she was enjoying. She did not attempt to hide the irritation in her voice as she picked up the intercom and rasped into it, "Bale?"

"As Salam Aleyiqum, Khaneme Nisreen" announced the gruff male voice at the gate. "Hale shoma cetowre?"

The color drained from Nisreen's face, and a deathly palor took over her entire being as she recognized the voice of the speaker. Her lips began to quiver and she trembled as if the voice she heard had conjured a spirit from a past existence. Her voice came out in a hoarse whisper as she tried to respond to the greeting, but only for a moment. In an instant, she was in complete control of herself, a honey-dripping grin taking over her countenance. In a split second she seemed to have been transformed from the depths of despondency to the heights of passionate joy.

"Salaaaaam, Khaled. As tu?" beamed Nisreen. "As koja hast-where have you been Befarmoid. (Khaled, is it you? Where have you been) Oh it's nice to hear your voice. Come on up." She sang excitedly, releasing the catch on the gate. She rushed into the kitchen with her glass and poured its contents down the sink, and rinsed the glass. She put out the cigarette and dumped it in the trash bin. She hoped he wouldn't smell the tobacco smoke in the confined space of her not-very-large living room.

Nisreen's thoughts went back a few years. Khaled had been her high school sweetheart, and even after they had left school, their relationship had continued for a while. They would meet clandestinely, like many young Iranian couples did, take in a movie, sit on a secluded Park bench or visit the zoo, not to see the animals, but to sit and talk. They had never had sex, but held hands while Khaled looked deep into her eyes and spoke fervently about all kinds of things, but love. One day she had suggested they meet in a hotel which was a popular rendezvous for young couples, local and foreign, in downtown Tehran. They had met there, and while other couples sat and drank beer or wine as a preamble to sex in one of the many rooms in the hotel, Khaled ordered fruit juices and tea, and Iranian cookies to munch on. Many a couple had come and gone, but Khaled sat on talking about the most banal of topics. He even waxed eloquent on the virtues of fruit juice, when all she wanted was a beer and a roll in the hay. She was exasperated when he said, "Look at all these terrible people. Their behavior is totally against the Islamic culture. They should be punished."

He often spoke about American influence in Iran, and how Iranian youth had been corrupted by Western culture and mores. Nisreen, on the other hand, loved the company of the few young Americans she had met, although some of them did not seem much interested in her. She sometimes had the feeling that they just tolerated her, but she took it all without complaint, for she loved everything that was American: the movies, the music, the open relationships between young people, in fact she had longed to settle in America some day. She even wished for an American boyfriend, but nothing ever materialized for quite a while, until she met Richard, the son of an American oil worker stationed in Tehran. It had been a tumultuous relationship, and Nisreen had been transported to the very heights of her most passionate dreams. It was six months of unimaginable happiness, and unimaginable sex, as they traveled around, first the city of Tehran and then Isfahan and Shiraz, spending Arabian Nights in hotels and inns that dotted the country. Richard was a dare-devil in many ways, and this enamored her to him. His sexual prowess matched his other antics; he was an acrobatic lover. And he always had a stash of marijuana, Hashish or coke to add spice to their lovemaking. How different he was from Khaled, she used to think, and how awesome. At the beginning of her relationship with Richard, Nisreen had lied to Khaled about her whereabouts as they kept their trysts. Then, one day, Khaled had told her that he knew everything that was going on between her and Richard. The strange thing was that he never told her how he knew all the details, about where they went, where they stayed, and even the tourist sights they had seen. She was greatly relieved when Khaled said one day, "I have nothing against you Nisreen. It's just the fault of the Americans. They are the devil, and some day you will realize that."

Nisreen was amused, but she did not say anything, not even the fact that she was so bored with Khaled, and would pity the woman who married him. But all she said was, "I'm sorry Khaled. Please forgive me." And they had parted. In retrospect, Nizreen thought that he really loved her in his own convoluted way, but she was glad to be rid of him.

Three months later, Richard, who had returned to the US for a short vacation, had died in a skiing accident in Colorado. Nisreen was inconsolable. However, within six months, she had found another American boyfriend; he too, had returned to the States, and she had not heard from him again. She hadn't heard from or seen Khaled for a little over ten years, until she heard his voice on the buzzer.

Khaled's slit grey eyes looked even more steely than she remembered as he stared purposefully into her face. She shuddered imperceptibly, but gathered herself sufficiently to give him a vibrant smile of welcome. "Where have you been, Khaled. I haven't seen or heard from you in years. Come on in. Sit down." And she led him to the sofa. Khaled sat almost gingerly, on the edge of the enormous sofa, as if afraid to give in to its enormous softness. It was obvious he was not comfortable in her presence, and it was equally obvious he was hiding something from her, but she did not seem to care. Still smarting under the blow of Bob's desertion of her, she was happy for male company-any male, she thought, was better than none, even though she was hardly dancing with joy. But there had been a few good moments, and maybe other would come by, she thought fleetingly.

So tell me, Khaled. How are you? Are you married? How many children do you have?" she asked flirtatiously.

"No marriage for me. Not yet, anyway," he said cryptically. "How about you? Are you married? How's Richard?" and Nisreen could not contain herself any longer. "American men," she began, "I was never really serious about him, you know." She did not tell him that he had died, and how her loss had nearly driven her to suicide. She didn't tell him about the other Americans she had had relationships with. Not about Bob, and how he had flown the coop. "I am fine Khaled. I'm working very hard at my job, and I'm very happy with that. No romance. Just living an ordinary, humdrum life," she smiled.

"That's awful. Why would such a beautiful woman like you be hiding yourself away from the world?" he asked, half joking, half seriously. "I think I should do something about that," he chortled, and Nisreen warmed up to him. "Oh you say that now, but you'll probably be gone again come tomorrow, and I probably won't see you for another ten years."

"No, oh no, Nisreen. I'm here to stay. I'm involved in a very important project, and I badly need your help."

"You know I've always been there for you, Khaled, and always will be. Tell me. What can I do for you?"

"All in good time, my dear. But now, get dressed. We're going out. We're going to have dinner at the Xanadu." And Nisreen thought, he really has changed. This is going to be one way of getting out of my depression.

Chapter 31

Throughout the month of July, the government used positive and negative reinforcement techniques in dealing with the problem. It came down hard on the demonstrators arresting those who became violent, and letting the others demonstrate in peace. Those who were arrested were housed in the various prisons in and around the cities, and with Nasiri gone, torture and terrorization of the prisoners went out with him. The streets were relatively calm, but it was clear that the campaign to oust the Shah was far from over; rather, it had settled into the deeper recesses of the impending revolution, and lay smoldering beneath.

Significant political reforms were falling into place at least in theory. Free and fair elections were promised, and the government indicated its willingness to discuss the future political framework with the moderate reformists among the clergy. Not very surprisingly, neither the government, nor the clergy was willing to make the first move.

On the business and economic fronts, the government continued to blunder. In its hurry to please everybody, the government took certain decisions which added to the suffering of the masses.

The Shah suddenly issued an order that all racketeers and profiteers be released from detention; these worthies had been incarcerated on the express orders of the Shah in an effort to control prices of essentials. Thanking allah for their good fortune, they immediately went back to business as usual, and even the most ardent supporters began to suppose that the Shah had lost it. On the other hand, the Shah's detractors saw it as an indirect way of oppressing the people further.

On the phone from home, Renee gleefully announced to Jordan, "I read an interesting CIA report in the New York Times today. The CIA believes that the chances of a full-scale popular uprising against the Shah seem very remote. They predict that the present crisis will blow over in a few months, and the country will be back to normal come January."

While Jordan would have loved to believe that, she couldn't help being skeptical. "I don't know, Mom. I hope that is true, but there are some here who feel that what we are going through right now is the calm before the storm."

"Well, honey, you will just have to watch the situation very carefully. At the first sign of more trouble, you'd better get on a plane home. In any case, I'm sure Ahmad will know the best course of action. How's he?"

"He's fine," returned Jordan, and although she remembered the attempts on his life, he did not talk about it. There's no point giving her more reason to worry, she thought. Besides, she had great faith in Ahmad's ability to take care of himself, and her, too, if the necessity arose.

And yet, she worried, what if something does happen to Ahmad. The thought was too ridiculous to think about, and Jordan went to bed and dreamed dreams of peace and hope and love.

Chapter 32

When the telephone rang around six in the evening, Jordan knew it was not Ahmed because they had spoken earlier in the day, and he had told her that he was driving to Esfahan in the evening. "I'll call you when I get there, but it will be very late," he had warned.

"That's fine Ahmad. I will be up late grading papers," she had lied.

The call turned out to be from Soraya. Jordan was surprised and thrilled to hear Soraya's voice. "We flew in a few days ago, and I wanted to call you before, but had a lot of things to attend to. It's my Mom's birthday, and I wanted to give her a surprise. We are having a party for her on Thursday evening. Will you come?"

"Thank you Soraya; of course I will. How can I miss my Iranian Mom's birthday?" And they had a long chat about various things, but mainly about the political situation. Soraya, too, felt that things would blow over. I can't imagine what would happen to the country if Khomeini came into power. "I don't think I would ever want to return here if that happened," she said seriously.

Jordan told Soraya about Ahmad. "Oh that's wonderful, Jordan. I'm so happy for you and wish you every happiness. You must bring him to the party," she insisted.

The party turned out to be a modest one with Soraya's family and a few of their friends in attendance. When Jordan and Soraya arrived, they were warmly welcomed by the Tehrani family. Soraya's mother struck up a conversation with Ahmad, but Jordan had to look on as they spoke Farsi. Soraya, seeing Jordan's apparent discomfort, took Jordan by the hand and led her away from the two. "My Mom is giving Ahmad the third-degree, kind of," she explained. "She is grilling him to find out if he is worthy of you," she smiled, and Jordan blushed. "You must forgive her Jordan. My mother loves you very much, and wants to make sure that you have made the right choice. She has her way of finding out his background, his intentions, and whatever else she needs before she gives you her stamp of approval. You might think it's none of her business, but that's the Iranian way. We like to protect those we love. She will tell me what she thinks, and I will let you know," she said with a wink.

Jordan flushed, thinking I know him well enough to be sure that he's a wonderful guy who loves me very much, but she was touched by Mrs. Tehrani's concern for her. "That's really sweet of your Mom, Soraya, and I appreciate what she is doing very much. Please tell her that. I hope she'll go easy on him, though!"

After a several glasses of a heady wine with the sampling of the most incredibly delicious Iranian cuisine, Jordan and Ahmad were dancing to Donna Summer's 'Love to Love you Baby.' "Sorry you got a working over by Mrs. Tehrani," Jordan said in a whispered giggle.

"Oh yes, I enjoyed that. She will probably have me murdered if I treated you badly," he said, "but it worked out fine. It turns out that Mrs. Tehrani and my Mom have some mutual acquaintances. And I think I passed the test," he added, sounding as pleased as Punch.

"That you did, and with flying colors, too," said Jordan. Soraya told me about it a few minutes ago."

"And what would you have done if I hadn't," he asked, laughing.

"I'd have dropped you like a hot potato," she giggled.

"No, you wouldn't," he said, tightening his grip on her. "If you refused me, I'd build a willow cabin ……

"Oh Ahmad, you've brought so much happiness into my life that I wonder how I would exist without you."

"You won't have to, dear Jordan. In fact you will have a real hard time getting rid of me if you ever wanted to."

Jordan was about to reply when there was a visible disturbance on the dance floor. Soraya walked into the room in a state of great agitation. She looked pale and terrified, as if she had just seen the devil himself. She rushed to her mother, and whispered something in her ear. Mrs Tehrani remained calm and composed, but a cloud darkened her face.

Soraya had just received a telephone call from her estranged husband. A friend of his had spotted Soraya and the kids disembarking the flight from London the previous day, and had told him about it. He wanted to know where she had gone. Soraya had denied it, saying that his friend must have mistaken her for someone else. The husband, however, had been adamant, for his friend had sworn that it was Soraya he had seen. "I'm coming to

Tehran next week, and I want to know what is going on," he had said menacingly.

Soraya and her parents looked distraught, as Jordan and Ahmad joined them to discuss the matter. "I must leave Tehran before he comes," Soraya had cried. "He will find out that we returned from London, and will certainly use his right to curtail our future travel."

"How soon can you leave," asked Ahmad.

"I have booked a flight for Friday, a week from tomorrow," she explained, "but that will be too late. My agent told me that it was the earliest flight he could book for us. What shall we do?," she implored.

Jordan whispered to Ahmad, "Can you help her in any way," she asked.

"Let me make some telephone calls," he said somberly. The tension in the room was as thick as the smog in downtown Tehran during the workday evening gridlock.

Ahmad spent the next forty-five minutes in the study, with the telephone pressed to his ear. Jordan sat beside him. Ahmad's voice rose and fell as he spoke to various people, sometimes with authority, sometimes pleading and cajoling. At the end of it all, he squeezed Jordan's shoulder, saying, "They can leave on the noon flight the day after tomorrow. Let's go give them the good news. In the meantime, I will place two of my men to prevent her husband from coming to the house-just in case he decides to come sooner. I can have him arrested on suspicion of something or other, and release him after they've left."

"Oh, thank you, Ahmad. You're the best."

"I thought you knew that when we first made love," he joked, giving her gentle squeeze.

Ahmad and Jordan were at the airport to see them off, 'and just to make sure nothing goes wrong,' Ahmad explained.

Jordan was sad to see Soraya leave under such strain and strife. On the other hand, she was glad and relieved to see her go, to be free from any further control of her husband. Soraya knew that it would be a long time before she could return to her beloved country, but that was a sacrifice she had to make, not just for herself but for her children. As they parted, Jordan hugged Soraya, and her children. "Take care of yourselves. We will meet again, hopefully under better circumstances," she said.

"You too, Jordan. Maybe you need more care being here in Tehran," she quipped, "Ahmad, thank you very much for your kind help. I don't know what I would have done without you. My Mom told me yesterday, "I knew he was a wonderful man the moment I saw him!" And they all laughed, sharing the knowledge of Ahmad's 'grilling,' at the birthday party.

Chapter 33

Two days later, the fragile peace in the country was shattered yet again. This time it was in Esfahan, the beautiful historic city, southeast of Tehran. A few hundred demonstrators had been marching through the city, screaming invective against the shah and his government. As the marchers drew attention to increasing food prices, and other inconveniences, other joined to swell their ranks into the thousands. The marchers were screaming at the army and police to take off their uniforms, lay down their arms and join the protest. A few actually did. Then, out of the blue, someone set fire to a public bus, and a nervous soldier opened fire on the arsonist. Others followed, and before long, about a hundred men, women and children lay dead on the street. Amazingly, the protesters remained steely calm, picked up their fallen victims and setting up a monstrous wail to the heavens, marched on in dignified silence. In the face of such powerful collective emotion, the police and army fled.

Two days later, news of the massacre had reached the length and breadth of Iran. Violent riots erupted in all major cities in the country. The government was completely confused.

The new Prime Minister immediately declared martial law in the country.

Those who still supported the Shah were relieved when Martial law was declared.

"Now all this nonsense will stop," said Leon confidently during a staff meeting. Manafi glared at him, but didn't know quite what to say, and the others remained silent with their own thoughts.

It's time to hit the sack, thought Jordan, who had been checking student papers close to midnight. She was about to go into the bathroom to shower when the phone rang. Knowing it was only Ahmad who would call that late, she hurried to the kitchen to answer it.

Silence greeted her as she put the phone to her ear. Ahmad, who usually greeted her joyfully, remained silent at the other end, and Jordan knew that something was terribly wrong. She heard Ahmad's breath catch in his throat, and her voice rose shrilly, "Why Ahmad? What's happening?"

"Five hundred people were burnt to death," he whispered.

"What? Where? Tell me Ahmad"

"Can I come over?" It was almost a plea.

"Yes, Ahmad. Oh God, come right over."

Jordan' s heart went out to Ahmad as she saw the look of defeat and despair in his eyes; he looked battered and beaten. Jordan led him to the sofa and they sat down holding on to each other, and Jordan felt his body trembling with confusion and uncertainty. His voice sounded like a 78 RPM record playing at 45, Jordan thought. "A cinema burned down, and about 500 people trapped inside were burned to death. They believe the Shah was responsible for it."

"Where?" asked Jordan unnecessarily.

"In Abadan. It's a city near the Persian Gulf."

Jordan had read and heard much about the Nazis and the gassing of the Jews in the Auschwitz and Bergen Belsen death camps. That had been another time, another place, so far away. But this was here and now. Bile began to rise in her throat, and she could almost hear the screams of death and the smell of burning flesh.

Ahmad continued with a great effort. "Two well-known revolutionary leaders, trying to avoid being captured by the police, had crept into the cinema which was full of people watching a movie. The police, in their haste to apprehend them, had ordered the management to close and lock all the doors to stop their quarry from slipping out of their hands."

"And the police set fire to the building?" asked Jordon in horror.

"No, the two fugitives had started a fire in the building to cause a diversion, and slip out in the melee. However, when they tried to open the huge metal doors, the man who had the keys had vanished."

"But how?" Jordan interjected.

"I wish I knew Jordan. Anyway, when the fire department arrived, the fire had engulfed the whole building and everybody inside was dead."

"It's the revolutionaries' fault isn't it. They set the fire."

"But Jordan, see, they will turn this round somehow to vilify the Shah."

"I guess you're right. What about the people who died?"

"They have all been moved into nearby morgues, which cannot accommodate them. Some of them are being brought to Tehran. But the worst part of the tragedy is this. The film that was showing was an Iranian-made family film-The Deer- a film made for children, so eighty percent of the dead were children."

Horrific images she had seen of Nazi atrocities began to take hold of her once again. "Oh, Ahmad," she moaned and rested her head on his shoulder. Words stuck in her throat as the full implications of the tragedy seeped into her mind, making it incapable of any response. Totally enervated by the thought of the horrendous and tragic waste of human life, they held on to each other for support and fell into a fitful sleep, until the rays of the early morning sun brought them awake, and to reality. "I've got to go," he said gently disengaging himself from Jordan's embrace. I've got to see my new boss and find out how we can engage in some damage control."

Many different rumors began to circulate in the country; the two major versions of the tragic event were as follows: the first was that the police had set fire to the building on the orders of the Shah to kill the revolutionaries trapped inside, and put the blame on the revolutionaries who were generally against cinemas and movies. The second was that the revolutionaries had set the building alight to put the blame on the Shah, but the fire had got out of control.

Ironically, neither the keys to the cinema, nor the man in charge of them were ever found.

It wasn't surprising that the version that vilified the Shah spread faster and further, and became virtually the final nail in the Shah's coffin. His reputation as an evil king, devoid of any feelings of justice or love for his people got intensified in the in inferno that had raged at Rex Cinema taking with it five hundred innocent lives which would haunt even the staunchest supporters of the Shah, irrespective of who was actually to blame for the carnage. Chance had taken a strong hand against the Shah..

And the task of Ahmad, and others whose sworn duty it was to safeguard the life and reputation of the Shah was becoming exceedingly daunting by the day; even worse, they were being tainted in the public eye by the Shah's horrendous image. It is no wonder that even those who had long been staunch supporters of the king were now beginning to look at him with suspicion and distrust.

A week later, as if to make amends for what had happened in Abadan, the Shah replaced the tough talking, military oriented prime minister, Jamshid Amouzegar with Sharif Emami, who immediately disenfranchised the casinos which were indirectly owned by the Shah, through the queen's Pahlavi Foundation. Next, he proclaimed that all political parties were free to operate in Iran. The upshot of this was that several minor parties, which had been operating underground immediately surfaced, and began publicizing their manifestos. A number of new parties, too, joined in the fray in earnest. The majority knew that none of these had any chance against the Khomeini supporters, but in the spirit of democracy or in deference to the diversity of the population of Iran, they all had a hearing wherever they campaigned.

Chapter 34

At the English Department, Doug ribbed Muzaffer, whose penchant for the rolling dice was well-known. "No more gambling, huh Muz. Maybe now you can save some money to send to your wives back home."

Muzaffer, a happy bachelor, countered, "I'm inviting them to join me here to start a new political party in support of gambling. We'll campaign strongly for that, but not for the bars, so no more beer for you, Doug, old man."

"Speak softly, Muzaffer or they will close down the pubs and the liquor stores right away," warned Leon.

"There's no chance of that. There's many an Iranian, young and old, who swears by his booze and his hookah, so that's going to be a long time coming, thanks be to Allah!'

"But they are a little more circumspect when they go in and out of bars now," commented Doug. "They don't want to be noticed by the anti-alkies. I've actually seen guys covering their faces with whatever's at hand as they leave the bars now," he laughed.

"You guys better do the same," warned Manafi perversely.

"To hell with them," shot back Pat.

"Madam, it's you who will end up there," said Manafi in a deeply sepulchral tone.

"Oh, shut the fuck up, Manafi," said Pat, and Manafi did, casting a vicious look at Pat.

Chapter 35

The dust raised by a multitude of feet milling homeward after work, and the gasoline fumes from thousands of vehicles in downtown Tehran had mingled into a thick smog which was gradually coming down on the city in an eerie cloak of semi-darkness as Khaled carefully shut the door to his apartment and left the building. He carried nothing on him except a purposeful gleam in his eyes, and the cat-that-got-the-cream smile on his thin lips. As he walked down the street, an orange-crush, one of the local taxis slowed down. A middle-aged woman and a teenaged girl sat in the back seat. A young man occupied the passenger seat in front. Khaled looked at the driver and said, "Shayyad."

The driver tilted his face upward in the traditional way of saying no, and the taxi sped on.

Several other taxis slowed down and Khaled gave and received the same response, until one finally pulled up, and the driver opened the front door saying, "Befarmoidh." Two young women sat at the back, and even if the driver had not pointedly opened the front door, Khaled, unlike other Iranian men of his age would have done, did not attempt to sit with the women. The women usually avoided having to sit beside an unknown man, not only due to a sense of decorum, but to avoid having men rub up against them or even pinch their bottoms if they had the chance.

About two hundred yards before the taxi reached the impressive Shayyad monument, built by Reza Shah to commemorate 2500 years of Persian monarchy, Khaled signaled the driver to stop. He walked away from the monument until the taxi had passed out of sight. Then he turned on his heels and walked to the monument, where he knew his accomplices were waiting.

Nisreen was a dumb broad whom he could manipulate as he wished was Khaled's hope and plan, although she did not have any inkling of it. He had to get something done and she was going to be just another person he would have to exploit. Compared to what feelings he had had for her in the past, he now had no attachment, commitment or obligation to her any more.

True she had treated him with the utmost insensitivity and lack of feeling, but he had no ill will toward her. His pride had certainly been hurt, and the salad-day-love he had had for her had been replaced by a kind of indifference. In fact he had no time for any woman; nor did he have any inclination for sex. Considering the great task Allah had chosen him to perform, she was but a pawn, granted by Him to use and discard when the occasion arose. Now that the occasion had arisen, he had no compunctions about doing just that. He had the gift of the gab, and had convinced her that his absence from her had only increased his desire for her. When it came to sex, he could pretend that he desired her as she wanted to be desired.

He went through their lovemaking convincingly enough, helped on by her appetite which seemed insatiable. Yet his mind was only full of the great responsibility he had on his thin shoulders. His reward would come-in heaven. His commitment to Jihad was so total that he would do anything to attain his greater aim: hukkumathe Islami- Islamic government- for Iran was his all consuming passion. It wouldn't be long, he thought, before the infidels and their lackeys were destroyed or banished. He also had dark thoughts about the B'ahais of Iran. He. like the other more extreme members of his faith, hated the B'ahais, and wanted to cleanse the land of their presence.

As Khaled walked towards the main entrance to the monument, six shadowy figures joined him one after another. They got in a huddle, like the witches of Macbeth, except there were seven witches here. They plotted and planned. As a radical splinter group, they had their own ideas of religion and politics. It was clear from their discussion that they had a singularity of purpose, and a commitment to match. They would walk into the jaws of death if necessary. They would also, without any compunction or guilt, push anybody who stood in the path of their intentions into the abyss of hell, for that's where they belonged, and the sooner they were dispatched, the better. Astute and cautious in their planning, they committed everything they discussed to memory. They kept no tell-tale notes.

In the dim lighting in the Xanadu, the waiters in their starched cream-colored uniforms walked around efficiently attending to the needs of the clientele. Greek cuisine was the specialty of the restaurant, which was always filled with customers of various nationalities.

Abdul, the Pakistani waiter, who recognized Khaled as soon as he walked in with Nisreen, immediately walked up to him whispering in his ear, "This way, sir," and the couple were ushered into a gloomier than usual corner, where there was an unoccupied table with a "Reserved" sign parked on it. "The manager told me that you were coming," he whispered again, conspiratorially.

When Abdul had left them with their order carefully written down, Khaled began, "You know, Nisreen, I think it is time for the world to know about our relationship. I want everyone to know that you belong to me now."

"Is that right? Are you sure you want to be tied down with me. I was wondering when you would take off again, not to be seen for the next couple of years," she giggled coyly.

"Oh, no! No more wandering for me. Besides, I'm not going to take a chance on you again. I don't want you to be snapped up by the next eligible bachelor you meet," he said with the best straight face he could muster.

"Oh Khaled, I missed you so much. I was miserable thinking that you had left me for good," she lied, trying to make it sound as sincere as she could.

"Well, now that we're back together, I want to have a party for all our friends and relatives, and announce our engagement. I want all of your friends and relatives to be there. What do you say?"

"Oh, Khaled, I don't know what to say except that I'm so happy."

"Can we have it at your place," he asked. "We could use the whole building, and invite some of your foreign friends, too."

Nisreen started at the mention of foreigners. She had had a narrow shave, she thought. If he knew how she had been dumped by Bob, he would not have any respect for her, she thought. Little did she realize that Khaled knew every little detail, and had decided to move in on her when she was most vulnerable-on the rebound-which was very lucky for him, a situation which had great potential for his cause.

Nisreen liked the idea. It was time for a party, she thought. She might be able to meet other Americans, she mused languidly. "Of course, darling," she murmured. "Leave it to me. I will organize it. It will be your entry to Tehran's jet set," she said, and Khaled winced. That was the last thing he wanted. He wanted to remain anonymous, nondescript, for the less known he was the better for what he was planning. Yet, he would have to go along with her grandiose plans, or she would suspect that something was not right. She wasn't the brightest spark in Tehran, but she had the innate shrewdness of the designing woman whose top priority was the satisfaction of her own desires. And she did not like to be crossed in matters which she thought she knew everything about. International parties were her speciality, for there were not many parties to which she was not invited. And if she was not invited she would invite herself. She knew her Tehran parties, Khaled had to admit. "You must invite all of your relatives," insisted Khaled. "My Madar and Pedar, too?" she laughed.

"No, silly, I meant the young relatives. Your brothers and sisters, cousins, nephews and nieces are all welcome," he said generously. "We'll spare no expense. It will be a night to remember," he promised, "Yes, it will," he resolved thinking of his plans.

Chapter 36

The stillness of the morning was shattered by the shrill ringing of the telephone in Jordan's room. Thursday was a day when Jordan usually slept late, but Ahmed had told her that he would be in town early that morning, and would call her as soon as he got in. Jordan was sure that it was Ahmed, and hurried to the living room draping her dressing gown over the flimsy nightgown she had worn to bed.

"Halath Khube, Khanum,?" Ahmed asked, using the endearing form of address.

"Khubam, Agha," she replied in mock formality. "Hey, where are you? Come on over. There's a desirable young woman in a half naked state languishing here. Why don't you come on over?"

"Why don't you start off with her and get warmed up. I'll be there as soon as I can," he laughed.

When the intercom buzzed about an hour later, Jordan had showered and changed into jeans and a T-shirt. The coffee was going, and some croissants Jordan had bought at the French Corner Bakery down the street were warming up in the oven.

Jordan trembled in anticipation of seeing Ahmed again as she pressed the release for the street door.

Ahmed surged into the room with a big smile on his face, and took Jordan in his arms tenderly. "I missed you so much sweetheart," he whispered into her hair which was still damp from the shower-she hated hair driers, "Mmm, you smell so nice." He murmured as she led him to the sofa. "Kheili Mothshekkaram," she replied, her love and joy at being near him again adding a trill to her voice.

"Hey, your Farsi is so good. You speak like an Iranian."

"Not anywhere near as good as your English. It's certainly better than the English spoken by some of the natives I know," she joked.

"You mean like the cockneys? That's not much of a compliment," he complained in jest.

Anyway, I've had a longer time to learn the language. And some Americans struggle to understand what I'm saying."

"That's because some of them haven't learned to listen," she pacified him, "There's none so deaf as those who will not listen,"

"There's none so blind as he who will not see."

"You're right," she said, "Ahmad, I'm so impressed with your knowledge of Western literature."

"Well, I don't know about that," he said, his face turning red at the compliment. Poor Ahmad, he's not much used to compliments, Jordan thought and reached out to touch his face. "Would you like some coffee? Have you had breakfast?"

"No, I rushed over as fast as I could before your passion cooled down."

"No fear of that," teased Jordan, "Not with a dashing officer and a gentleman here to fan the ring of fire."

"You have a gentleman in the bedroom, too? I thought it was only a woman."

"Let's go in and see what's in the bedroom," Jordan parried, taking hold of his hand.

And Jordan was surprised at her seeming boldness. It was not like this when I was with Josh she thought. Ahmed made her feel so much at ease. The middle class morality that had had her in thrall in the past was quietly dissipating, and she was beginning to feel comfortable with her body, and their relationship. She had enjoyed sex with Josh, but with Ahmad there seemed to be a new urgency, a new sense of excitement and discovery.

After they had made love, they lay silent in each other's arms, savoring the luxury of ultimate satiation of the body and soul. It was as if neither of them wanted to disturb the magic of the moment of complete fulfillment and the wonder of totally giving and receiving. It was a moment of great power and also of vulnerability which they were unconsciously attempting to understand, until the woman, the hostess, the protective female within Jordan surfaced, "Are you hungry?"

"Always hungry for you," he teased, reaching out for her as she sat up. "Hey, you need energy for what you're doing, and so do I," she said impetuously, and reluctantly disengaging herself from his arms, walked towards the kitchen with Ahmad trailing behind her. The smell of the croissants wafted into their nostrils, and as if on cue, Ahmad said, "You know what? We have an invitation to a party."

"When? Where?" asked Jordan

"Nisreen's having a big bash. She's hooked up again with an old flame after Bob disappeared."

"That's a fast recovery. But hey, that's good for her I guess. I didn't much care for the mood she was in after Bob left her. I'm really happy for her. She is a nice sort, although she sometimes loses perspective, especially in matters of the heart."

"You're too generous. She loses perspective in most matters, but you're right, especially of the heart," Ahmad added. "Anyway, she has invited all of you at the university, too. She wants everybody to be there. Probably wants to show everyone that the loss of Bob doesn't bother her."

"Are we going?" Jordan asked diffidently.

"It's up to you, honey. If you don't want to go, we can make up some excuse."

"No, she's bound to think that I'm trying to drive a wedge between you and her. And especially since she's a close member of your family, we shouldn't…

"Hey, is that an implied proposal?" Ahmad laughed, "I thought I had to do that. I was waiting for the right moment…. …

"Oh, Ahmad," she pounded his chest with her fists laughing.

"OK. Then that's settled. We are going. Will you tell your friends at the university or ….

"Of course I will. Actually some of us haven't been to a party in weeks, and it's time we did. Pat…

"Who's Pat?"

"You know Pat. You met her at our first party, remember. She was with the dark Columbian guy, Jose."

"Oh yes. The bronco-busting, bull-riding gal from Wyoming. Yeah, I remember her."

"You sound as if you don't approve of her."

"Sure, I like her, but you know, we like our females a little mellower."

"Ahmad, how could you? You sound like Nisreen. Not that Nisreen's very mellow."

"I was only joking my dear…" he broke into the Rod Stewart song.

"OK! Anyway, she and her Columbian boyfriend were talking about parties just last week. They were sad that the Friday parties are gone, at least until things settle down…"

"Oh I'm sure they will honey. You can tell them that. The Shah is planning a trip to the USA soon, and he has something up his sleeve. He's not going to run away in fear like he did in the fifties. You know, he's quite mature now, and he will do his best to win back the love of his people, and the glory of the Pahlavi throne. The problem is that he loves his people, and he does not want to hurt them. He has settled down quite a bit over the years."

"How's that a problem?"

"Well, many of the hardliners in his cabinet are asking for a quick and efficient strike at the enemy. It would, of course mean a huge bloodbath. They believe that is the only way out. Reza, on the other hand is trying to placate the enemy with several concessions including a certain amount of power in government for the moderate mullahs."

"Will it work?"

"I hope it will. We all hope it will work and that his trip to the US, whatever he expects from it will probably be the deciding factor. If the moderate clergy can bring the hardliners to heel, and the Khomeini factor is somehow dealt with, it will be party time again in Tehran." he smiled, "and it will be time to bring out the emerald ring my grandmother gave me after she saw you, and get down on my knees for some unfinished business."

"You're making me cry, now," Jordan whispered, averting her tear filled eyes from Ahmad's gaze.

"The thought of marrying me makes you cry?" Ahmad joked. And Jordan thought how wonderful it would be to be married to this crazy, funny guy, who could joke around when everything around them seemed to be crumbling. And something inside her seemed to tell her that it was too good to be true, that something would come between them. The situation in the country had everything to do with it, she consoled herself. Reza Shah would come through just like Ahmad expected, she told herself, and then everything would be all right for them.

Sitting in an Iranian restaurant that was not very fancy, but reputed for its succulent kebab and rice dishes, Ahmad, studying the wine list, quoted Khayyam:

"A loaf of bread, a cup of wine and thou."

As if on cue, Jordan, recalling her favorite poet, Keats, pleaded, trying to get the attention of one of the many waiters flitting around the crowded restaurant,

"O for a draught of vintage that hath been
Cool'd a long age in the deep delved earth,
Tasting of Flora and the country green.

"I'm sure Keats had read Khayyam before he wrote those lines," observed Ahmad.

"That's funny. I was thinking the same thing," opined Jordan.

They ordered Chelo Kebab-flaky, buttery soft aromatic Bhasmati rice with lamb kebabs so masterfully cooked, they melted in the mouth. A huge bowl of fresh salad-crispy green lettuce, vine-ripened tomatoes and other local vegetables added zest to the meal. The ice-cold shiraz wine made it a fine dining experience in a rustic setting making them forget the blazing heat outside, and their concerns about the future.

Back in their apartment, they spent the whole day and night and the next day and the next night in each others arms, getting out of bed only for absolute necessities. It was the most erotic, the most sublime sex, and yet it was so much more than the satiation of physical longing. It was a release of their spirits, their souls that soared beyond gravity, into higher planes where it made them more hungry the more they were satisfied.

Saturday dawn turned the snow-capped Alborz mountains whiter than white, and the stillness of the streets below was rudely shattered by the persistent honking of car horns as each driver fought for an elusive supremacy on the road. Each driver was determined to get ahead of the other, even if it was just for a moment, and just as quickly lost to the next driver who had the same intention to be the king of the road. It made driving a manic activity, and every rule was broken. In the taxis, the patrons sat silently, patiently. The drivers themselves cursed each other and it would seem that they made many mortal enemies before they reached their destination.

Ahmad had woken early, showered and dressed, taking care not to wake Jordan, who still slept the sleep of peace and joyous fulfillment. When he was ready, he sat on the bed and whispered into her ear, "Sleep on sweet maid. Your time is yet to come." And Jordan was wide wake. "Must you leave so soon," she asked plaintively.

"Sadly yes, Sweetheart! I have a meeting at the security division at 6:30.

It's only 5:45, so you can sleep a little longer. You probably need it, too." He smiled, bent down and kissed her.

"I'll call you after the meeting."

"Mmmm…" and Ahmad was gone.

Chapter 37

As Ahmad left Jordan's apartment building, he did not see the dirty looking teenage boy who had been standing inconspicuously in an alcove across the road. Dressed in bedraggled clothes, and scuffed shoes, he looked as if he had spent the whole night drinking in one of the beer parlors downtown, and did not warrant a second glance from the early morning passers-by going about their business. A closer look, however, would have confirmed that he was Mohammad, one of the well-dressed young men who had met Khaled at the Shayyad Monument a few days before. Following Ahmad until he got into a taxi, Mohammad hailed an 'orange crush' himself.

A few blocks down the road the young man got off, and entered Khaled's apartment. The door was unlocked immediately by Khaled himself, who was expecting young Mohammad.

"Salam Aleyikum, Mohammad. How did the vigil go?"

"Well, he left the American woman's house early this morning. He took a taxi downtown, but I didn't want to follow him."

"Yes, that's good. I don't want him to get suspicious in any way. I know he's scheduled for a meeting with Ansari and the others today. All I wanted to know was whether he met the American woman. I'm sure he told her about the party."

"That's probably not all he said or did; he was there two whole nights," started Mohammad, a note of envy affecting his voice.

"OK, that's enough. Concentrate on what you have to do, and don't go about thinking of those American bitches. Your virgins are waiting for you in heaven," admonished Khaled and Mohammad looked away sheepishly. "And don't forget, we are in the holy month of Ramadan," he warned. Then sudedenly he remembered, with a sense of guilt, the sex he had been having with Nizreen the last few days. "But that's all in a good cause," he muttered under his breath.

"What's that," asked Mohammed.

"Never mind," grumbled Khalid.

Chapter 38

The Wednesday evening meeting of the English Unit began as scheduled. The twelve members of the teaching staff made up of nine Americans, a Briton, an Indian and a Sri Lankan sat in their customary three group formation of personal inclination. Jordan, Pat, Ron, Bernard, and Muzaffer, liberals in most matters sat in one corner; their proclivity for getting the job at hand done on time, leaving the rest to the powers that be, drew them close in a bond which extended beyond the office. After work, they usually ended up in some place like the Irish pub or an American bar where they would have a good time observing the foibles of Tehran's expatriate community that haunted those places.

The second group consisted of Ed, Leon and Doug. Conservative to the core, they thought they were the powers that be even though it was just Ed who had some semblance of authority in the department, which was jealously though discreetly held tight by the Iranian boss.

The third group should have been made up of Bob, the quintessential cynic except for the fact that he seemed to have suddenly vanished; the never-satisfied grumbler, he had wittingly or unwittingly admitted that one of his superior officers in Vietnam had dubbed him 'malingerer.' He fitted into neither the liberal nor the conservative group, because 'he is as oily as the slipperiest eel' as observed by Pat, who enjoyed her alliterative jibes at Bob whom she hated with a passion, and the conservative group whom she could never find reason to trust, for they were always critical of everything and everyone Iranian, which prompted her to ask Ed one day, "If you dislike them so much, why don't you leave?" and Bob, who had overheard the remark, answered for him, "It's the money, sweetheart. Who else would pay Ed five thousand dollars a month?" And Ed had grudgingly concurred by his silence.

When Dr. Firooznia walked in, all eyes went to the chair left vacant by Bob.

"So Bob's gone," he said without preamble, and Jordan wondered whether it was only annoyance in his tone, or if it was tinged with a kind of relief, for Firooznia knew that Bob was, in fact a malingerer. He obviously knew that the university was wasting money on Bob although he had never hinted at it; a kind of Eastern graciousness seemed to prevent him from doing so.

Ed was the first to react. "Did you know that he was leaving, and more importantly, has he actually left the country?" he asked, knowing that Bob had at least once gone AWOL since he 'shacked up' with Nisreen.

"The answer to your first question is no! Did any of you?"

The collective shaking of eleven heads answered his question.

"As for your second question, Ed, his friend, Nisreen, called me," Firooznia continued, "She hadn't seen him in a couple of days, and when she went to his room, she found that all his belongings, except for some paperback novels and playboy magazines, were gone. Yesterday I called a friend of mine in Immigration. He confirmed that Bob had boarded a plane to London on Sunday evening."

Jordan's group exchanged knowing glances, for Jordan had told the others about Nisreen's visit to her house. However, Jordan had cautioned them that this information could be misconstrued by some, so they all kept silent.

"Which brings us back to the question about the others," continued Firooznia, "I can assure you that there is nothing for any of you to fear. Iran has had many upheavals in the past, and problems have been quietly resolved. Of course, no one is certain about what will happen eventually. But right now, I want you to know that you are safe, and I want you to feel comfortable here. If you have any problems you would like to discuss with me, you know I'm always here for you. And please continue with the wonderful work you're doing for our students."

"Do you think Khomeini will eventually defeat the Shah?" ventured Leon.

"I wish I could answer that Leon, and I hope it never happens." And everyone in the room knew where Firooznia's feelings lay-something that had never come up before. "But Iran is and always has been a volatile place. Many people and institutions have exploited Iran at various times. One can only hope that the peace and stability of our country will not be disturbed again, for it will take us back to the era of the donkey and the camel once more. We in the field of education, at least, know that peace and stability are the first essentials to progress. But like I said, 'Quien sabe?' as the Spanish say, 'Que sera, sera.' But whatever happens, we will know well in advance, so if there is any danger to any of you, we will do what needs to be done and get you to safety. We will never let any harm come to any one of you."

"Well, Bob's out of it all. Remember how he used to brag about his feats in Vietnam? He's just a yellow bastard after all." Spat out Pat, furious at Bob's intransigence, and a trifle concerned about their situation as well.

"Well, he must have his reasons," condoned Firooznia.

"When he had left the meeting, all tongues came loose, and everyone broke out in a swearing competition-angry with Bob for what he was, and the fact that nothing could touch him now, whereas they were sitting in a situation of uncertainty.

"Well," intoned Ed, "as Dr. Firooznia said, he must have his reasons."

"He must have knocked up his girl friend," mocked Pat.

"If he did, that won't be the last he's heard of her. She will follow him to the bowels of hell. Woman scorned and all that; I wouldn't want to be in his shoes. She even hates Jordan because she thinks Jordan was after Bob," laughed Doug.

"Is that right Jordan," asked Ed facetiously. The fury in Jordan's eyes was only slightly mitigated when Pat placed her arm consolingly on Jordan's shoulder. "Take it easy, girl."

"Fuck him," said Bernard, "We have work to do."

Chapter 39

Id el-Fitr is one of the joyful celebrations in Shia Islam. It is a day of feasting following a whole month of fasting from early dawn to dusk. As much as the turkey's day of doom approaches with the onset of Christmas and Thanksgiving in the Christian world, goats, sheep and cows become the unfortunates on this day, for it is the dream of every family to sacrifice an animal to Allah. The Head of the family slits the throat of the animal and watches it bleed to death. The carcass is cut up into portions, and distributed among friends and family as a gesture of friendship and goodwill. The poor in the community are not forgotten, for they get their share, too.

Feasting on the meat and other delectable goodies, and going to the mosque to give thanks to Allah are the significant acts of merit on this happy day.

After the feasting, the demonstrations resumed, and some of the demonstrators drifted onto the streets once again. Once again, the demonstrators began to voice their hatred for the Shah. "Marg Ba Shah," they thundered, and screamed abuse at the police who were protecting him. The police, however, displayed a great deal of self-discipline and decorum, apparently influenced by the festive spirit; they let the protesters march on without incident.

"Whew, I'm glad that's over," sighed Pat watching from her rooftop balcony a group of protesters marching down the street, "things do seem to be getting peaceful."

Jose, standing beside her, replied, "I hope so, too, Pat. But I wouldn't put any money on it.

Anything can happen. Have you noticed that things happen so suddenly here?"

"You should know," laughed Pat. "Just like home, huh?'

"Yeah, but back home the drug barons are more subtle. When they do not see eye to eye with a politician, they give him a vacation, and he is never seen or heard of again!"

"Yeah, I've heard," giggled Pat.

Chapter 40

The English Faculty of the university was certainly looking forward to the party. Ahmad was, too. The cataclysmic events of the past months were taking a heavy toll on everyone. Sitting in Jordan's living room, Ahmad suddenly announced, "You know what? I'm going to forget about the Shah and Khomeni and everything else. We're going to have a great time at the party tomorrow, right Jordan?"

"Good for you, darling. You deserve it, too." And she went to the kitchen to refill their glasses. As she walked back towards, him, two glasses of Shiraz in her hands, Ahmad broke into Byron's famous lines:

"She walks in beauty, like the night
Of cloudless climes and starry skies"

"Oh Ahmad, it's wonderful to see you so happy again. I wish Iran will have cloudless climes and starry skies again soon."

"I hope so, too, Babe," and Jordan couldn't help but notice the somber tone that his voice had taken on again. It seemed that after a brief moment of escape, his thoughts had reverted to the grim reality they were in fact facing.

Chapter 41

Bernard, Pat and Jose were the first to arrive at house number 66. They did not have to check the house number to know that they had arrived. "Dancing Queen," the ABBA favorite in Tehran was booming out of the doors and windows of the building. As they were getting out of the taxi with the basket of liquor they were taking to the party, the jolly taxi- driver quipped in Farsi, "Don't drink all of it. Save some for me when I take you back." Muzafffer, who spoke Farsi fluently said, "Hey, I'm a good Muslim, and I don't drink."

The taxi-driver shot back, "OK, I'm a good Muslim, too. But this is Tehran, Agha! We will see how you are when I pick you up," and drove away into the night, guffawing generously.

Muzaffer carried the drinks to the enormous pantry, crowded with guests making their own drinks from the endless array of alcohol and mixes arranged on the tables, and spilling over into little baskets on the floor, and on the shelves. A colossal arrangement of Iranian dishes-roasted and fried chicken, lamb kebabs, sabzi polow, Meigo Polow, Shirin Polow and other delectable rice dishes, an assortment of sweets-it was a feast from the

Arabian Nights, but nobody would describe it as such, for the Iranians resented being coupled in any way with the Arabs. The Arabs were Bedouins or camels to most Iranians and the worst insult to an Iranian was to be called an Arab. The Arab invasions had made sure of that. The only thing that they could possibly be grateful to the Arabs for was bringing Islam to their country. Even that was a forgotten thought, for Islam was such a pervasive factor in their lives that they had ceased to think of it as having originated outside their own country. They took it for granted as their religion-the Shia-Islam of Iran- not the Sunni Islam of the Arabs.

Khaled, the host, with Nisreen, coyly hanging on his arm, saw them at a distance and came over to talk to them. "Welcome gentlemen," he gushed, "I'm so happy you're here. How are things at the university?"

Ed answered for them all, "Thank you for inviting us, Khaled-it's Khaled, right? It's great to be here."

"Befarmoidh. Come, eat and drink. Have fun. The dancing will soon begin, and I want to see all of you on the dance floor."

"Oh sure, you will," said Bernard. "Muzaffer can't wait. He's already found a partner," and nodded towards Muzaffer, who was chatting up Farzana, an instructor in the math department. Ahmad, and Jordan arrived a few minutes later.

When the dancing did start, the floor was filled with men and women at different levels of intoxication.

"Befarmoidh, Agha," and the glasses were filled as they became empty. The cacophony from the dance floor – loud rock music, laughter and the speech of men and women enjoying each others' company, their spirits lubricated by the unending stock of liquor which was being imbibed with gay abandon, as if there would be no tomorrow.

Jordan had been dancing with Ahmad for a while, and she was overwhelmed by the noise, the smell of alcohol and pot around her, and the unfriendly glances she was getting from Nisreen, nestling in the arms of her renewed love. She seemed determined to show Jordan that she hated her. "Your cousin really hates me," she whispered, and Ahmad held her closer, protectively, trying to coax Jordan into enjoying the moment.

"Don't worry, Babe. You have nothing to worry about from her. She knows that I've made my choice, and that there's nothing she can do about it. In fact, she had told my sister that she sort of approves of you."

"Wow, that's comforting to hear," laughed Jordan, and as she looked past Ahmad, she caught Nisreen's gaze on her again. Is it hatred for me, or is it just that Nisreen can't bear to see anybody happy, she wondered.

"Let's get a drink and go up on the roof," suggested Ahmad.

"That's a wonderful idea," piped Jordan, "but I need to go to the restroom, first. You go on. I'll join you in a few minutes."

Ahmad picked up their glasses, and went into the pantry. The array of bottles had not diminished. Khaled is really making sure his guests get enough to drink tonight, he thought. He really must be happy to have hitched up with Nisreen again. In shah allah she is very happy, too. That will solve a lot of problems for a lot of people, he reflected amusedly. Spying a bottle of his favorite Shiraz, he picked it up, looking around for a corkscrew, when one of the helpers walked towards him, "Can I get you something, Sir?"

"Well, yes, agha, can you find me a corkscrew?"

"Of course," and he opened a drawer form which he took out several, handing one to Ahmad, a huge grin on his face, "Can I get you a chair?"

"No," answered Ahmad, "I'm going up on the roof. I want to look at the stars."

"That's a great idea. It's a wonderful night to do that," the man agreed, "Here, let me open that for you."

Ahmad gratefully accepted the offer. Opening bottles was not his favorite pastime, especially holding on to two glasses in one hand.

"Kheili mamnoon, Agha," and he gratefully accepted the open bottle.

"Enjoy the stars!"

"Thank you," responded Ahmad, and began to walk up the stairs to get to the rooftop, a flat open balcony which was a common feature of most buildings. The balcony had many uses. Laundry was hung out to dry on lines drawn across them. In the evenings, when the weather was pleasant, families would come up on the balcony to sit and chat, while little children counted the stars, and sang songs to the moon. Men would sometimes come up to enjoy a drink away from their wives and children. It was a place for peace and relaxation, where young lovers could escape the prying eyes of their older relatives and family members. On their way to the party, Jordan said, "It's a lovely night, isn't it? There are billions of stars in the sky. Khaled certainly chose his night well." And Ahmad remembered Jordan's words, as he lightly tripped up the steps, with thoughts of unconditional love in his heart.

Ahmad had hardly left the room when the man who had helped Ahmad turned on his heel and hurriedly left the room. His face had taken on an air of great excitement and a sinister anticipation. He rushed towards the alley on the right side of the house. Three men broke out of the shadows and accosted him, "What's up? What's going on?" they whispered urgently.

"The target's on the roof. In sha allah, this is the opportunity we have been waiting for.

Let's go!"

"Where's the woman?" asked one of them.

"She's gone to pee. Let's hurry."

The four men quietly entered the house. Two of them went straight into one of the bedrooms; one picked up an enormous blanket, rolled it up and stuck it under his arm. The other picked up a baseball bat from a large wooden box containing an assortment of weapons-a long scimitar, a stiletto knife and a two-foot length of bicycle chain. The man with the bat said tonelessly, "We will use the bat, but no sharp objects. We don't want blood everywhere."

"Yes, it must look like an accident." Moving soundlessly, they walked up the stairs, seeking their quarry. The plan had been to isolate Ahmad somehow, knock him unconscious with the baseball bat, carry him upstairs and drop him off the rooftop. Ahmad going up to the rooftop had been a stroke of luck for them. "Hurry," whispered Khaled, "the woman will come back any minute."

The rooftop was almost deserted except for two couples, bodies entwined passionately in two dark corners. Ahmad looked for a secluded spot, and placed the glasses and the bottle on a tiny stool he had brought up for the purpose. I'd better stand in the light or Jordan will disturb those two couples, he thought, as he moved towards the stairway. A gentle evening breeze, still warm from the heat of the afternoon ruffled the leaves on the trees lining the jubes on the street below. Ahmad's keen ears, which were well attuned to the sounds of Tehran at night noticed that the sluices up in the north had not been opened yet. If they had been opened, the sound of water flowing down the jubes would have carried up to him. Tonight the trees will get their water a little late, he thought. That was not unusual. Some days they would open them soon after sunset, while on others, it would open them late, after ten O'clock. Maybe the guy who opened them is late tonight, he thought. That too was not unusual in Tehran.

A night bird screeched in the distance, and its mate answered. Ahmad's thoughts began to wander, from the Shah and his responsibilities, to Jordan and his responsibilities. The present situation in the country was getting more and more complicated day by day. He had to take a decision soon, he thought, whether to see it to the end, or to leave the ship-sinking or not. Right now his responsibility lay squarely with Jordan. He had to get her to the safety of the home she loved. He had to talk to Jordan and make definite plans. I must do it tonight, he said to himself.

Chapter 42

When the blanket descended on his face, he was taken totally unawares. He was a little groggy from the wine he had drunk, but his instinct for survival and the training he had undergone in Sandhurst took over as he swung outward with both arms hitting two of the shapes that surrounded him, but the blanket hindered his movements. The two men whom he had managed to hit grunted in pain, but did not let go of the blanket. Behind him, the one with the baseball bat closed in and aimed blows at his head. He heard the whistling sound of the bat, but there was nothing he could do to avoid the blows. He couldn't see where they were coming from. It did not occur to him to shout for help; it was not in his instinctive nature to do so. With the blows raining down on him, he sank into unconsciousness.

The four men worked silently and efficiently. Each of them held one of his limbs as they carried his lifeless body to the edge of the roof. They heaved in unison and flung it over. A soft thud was heard as the body hit the concrete pavement four floors below. "Khoda Hafiz," they muttered under their breaths, picked up the blanket and baseball bat, and hurried downstairs.

Jordan's step was light as she reached the rooftop. I am on cloud nine, she mused joyfully as she peered into the darkness. She heard romantic giggles from the two corners where the other two couples were standing, and walked in the opposite direction. The glasses and the bottle of wine crashed to the floor as she walked into the stool in the darkness, and she had the chilling thought that something was terribly wrong. "Ahmad," she whispered, "where are you?" Only an eerie silence greeted her. She suddenly felt a chill of fear and screamed, "Ahmad?" and the two couples on the roof, unnerved by the scream ran in her direction. One of them reached the light switch, and the rooftop was bathed in light. One of the men asked Jordan, "What's the problem?" And for a moment, Jordan was tongue-tied. "Ahmad? Where's Ahmad?" and they looked all around them. Ahmad was nowhere on the rooftop. Then there was a cry from one of the men, who was leaning on the short wall on the rooftop, "There's someone fallen down there." And they all rushed to the edge. Jordan didn't have to look twice to realize that it was Ahmad down on the sidewalk. With another anguished scream, she rushed down the stairs.

Ahmad's body lay in a broken heap, blood pouring out of his head, which seemed to have been crushed by a sledge hammer. His arms and legs were at awkward angles. His face, gray brown in the pale light of the street lamps, looked perplexed in death. Jordan flung herself on the lifeless body of the man she loved, and her own body began to shake violently as the gruesome truth hit her that Ahmad was dead. His body was warm, and she felt a strange sensation of loneliness and despair as she broke into uncontrollable sobs. "Someone call an ambulance," she wailed although she had no doubt in her mind that her precious soul-mate was beyond help. She continued to hold him in her arms silently as tears burned rivulets down her cheeks.

A crowd had gathered around her and the still figure of Ahmad, his face beginning to take on the gray pallor of death. The light from inside the building played cruel tricks on his face, which was now lit up and now dark.

The entire crowd from the party had now gathered around them; they all spoke in hushed tones of shock and disbelief. Jordan heard them all whispering, but nothing registered in her mind. She was in complete oblivion, paralyzed both physically and mentally. Suddenly, the shrill voice of Nisreen broke the hush. She rasped in Jordan's face, "You killed him. You pushed him off the roof. You beetch!!! And she broke into a string of expletives in Farsi.

Jordan could say nothing but stare into Nizreen's eyes, which blazed with a fury that Jordan thought even Nizreen was not capable of. When Pat and the others reached the scene, Jordan had collapsed in a heap on the ground. Like in a terrible nightmare, Jordan heard Nizreen's voice viciously screaming at someone to call the police.

When the police arrived about thirty minute later, Jordan was conscious, but all she could say in answer to their relentless questions was, "I don't know what happened."

The four men, the blanket and the baseball bat had disappeared.

Pat and the others helped Jordan up when the police arrived, and started questioning everyone present. Nisreen was screaming accusations at Jordan, and one of the officers was listening to her in rapt attention. They questioned Jordan, who had nothing to tell them. Soon an ambulance arrived, and as Jordan watched in perplexity, they lifted his limp body onto a gurney and placed it in the ambulance. Jordan remembered what Ahmed had said.

They had been discussing Shakesperean drama, and ahmad had said, "You know Jordan, my favorite Shakesperean character is Hamlet. I think I'm a lot like him in some ways"

And now Jordan thought, "Oh Ahmad, if only you had decided to leave it all and go away." Yet, even as she said it she realized the futility of her thought, now, especially, with his vibrant, lovable person transformed into a mass of matter, vulnerable and helpless, which entered her being as if they had been symbiotically joined these past months. She was overwhelmed by the irrevocability of the situation, but could not help murmuring once again, "if only you had," for the might have been was a drug that would numb her raw senses. As the ambulance doors shut with a hiss of cruel finality, she whispered,

"Good night, sweet prince,

And bands of angels sing thee to thy rest"

Chapter 43

Jordan was arrested on the charge murdering Ahmad, an officer of the Imperial Guard, by pushing him off the rooftop. Her repeated plea that she loved Ahmad, and that they were going to be married fell on deaf ears, especially in the light of Nizreen's 'sworn' evidence that Ahmed, her cousin, was, in fact in the process of breaking up with the American woman. He was looking to marry an Iranian girl with money and good looks, which he would not have any difficulty in doing, she added. He was one of the most eligible bachelors in Iran, after all. "He was only having fun with the American woman. He told me last week to look out for a good Iranian girl," she said, and that she had a couple of beautiful Iranian girls lined up. She was lying through her teeth but the cop who was writing down Nisreen's statement did not know that. In fact, he was lapping it up with animated interest, and writing feverishly. The venomous looks that Nisreen kept casting in Jordan's direction sent a cold shiver down her spine and seemed to say, I gotcha, American beech. It was a moment of infinite triumph for Nisreen, which she seemed to savor so much that the tragedy of Ahmad's death did not seem to matter to her at all.

Jordan had not the strength to counter Nisreen's words, for suddenly, her beautiful world of love and her dreams of a joyous future with her beloved had crashed around her as cruelly as the loss of Ahmad's life as his body hit the hard concrete of the sidewalk. She could sense that Nisreen was gloating at her own triumph over an American, and a woman, and was not concerned at all about Ahmad's death.

In the current situation social and political upheaval, the police obviously had bigger fish to fry than Jordan. They were constantly called to look into ongoing events in the country. They did not see Ahmad's death as something even remotely connected with the revolution. It was just another crime they had to investigate as best they could. What gave it special signficance, however, was that an officer of the Imperial Guard was dead, and someone had to take the rap, or some higher up in the government would be asking for explanations. So they arrested Jordan, flimsy as the evidence was for the charge that Jordan had pushed Ahmad to his death. Jordan was taken to the police station for the night.

The next day, she was transferred to the Jamshidabad prison, to be kept there until she could be produced before a magistrate.

The Jamshidabad prison was an enormous structure built in the time of Reza Shah the Great to house members of the Tudeh party and other political groups who did not see eye to eye with the new dynasty. It was a two-storied building with heavily fortified, three-foot thick reinforced concrete walls. Eight feet above ground level was a row of window like apertures covered with glass blocks to let in the light, but not for ventilation. The apertures were glossed over with one inch thick iron grates that had just enough space for a pigeon to perch on, and thousands of pigeons had made the window ledges their home. Pigeon droppings over the years had accumulated on the floor creating a surrealistic white wall along the side of the building.

Inside the building, too, the windows had a similar grate, making escape through the windows impossibile. Along three sides of the hallway were ten by six foot cubicles, each of which provided housing for two inmates. Two concrete beds with a foam rubber mattress, a sturdy pillow, and a rough blanket made up the sleeping facilities. A heavy Persian-styled kettle filled with water and two tin cups sat on a little hole-in-the-wall-ledge. Beside it was a faucet draining into a rough concrete basin. In the corner was a four by five foot bathroom with a shower and a squatting toilet. A narrow gap, facing away from the beds acted as the doorway into the cell. Two concrete hooks on one of the walls made up the closet space. That made up all of the creature comforts.

The door into each room was made of heavy iron bars with a bolt that could be engaged only from the outside. A little aperture at the bottom of the door, similar to a pet-door, allowed the passing in and out of food.

A strict time schedule was always in effect. Powerful amplifiers at each end of the hallways brought in the only sound of habitation outside the prison: the raucous voice of a mullah of a nearby mosque calling the faithful to prayer five times a day.

Chapter 44

It was nearly two weeks before Jordan was presented before a magistrate. Both at the police station and the magistrate's chambers she had been offered tea, fruit juices and Danish pastries. Jordan ate nothing, but gratefully accepted a glass of orange juice.

The magistrate, a stodgy, avuncular man, probably in his early sixties, had a soft voice and kindly eyes. He spoke gently to her, and asked her what had happened. She told him everything as she remembered of the events of the previous evening. She told him that she and Ahmad were in love and had been planning to get married soon. The magistrate looked at her benignly and kept on smiling, and Jordan wondered if what she was telling him was registering in his mind.

The prosecutor, a stern man in his fifties, had a sardonic smile which never left his face. He watched Jordan like a vulture waiting for the onset of death as she spoke. It was obvious that he did not believe a word of what she was saying. Jordan had the distinct feeling that he had already made up his mind that she was more than guilty of pushing Ahmad off the rooftop. His contention was that Ahmad's ardor towards Jordan had been cooling off, and he had asked her to go back home. "His relatives tell me that that he was planning to marry an Iranian woman worthy of his status. I can prove that this murder was the act of a woman scorned," he said, a note of triumph in his voice, and then Jordan knew that Nisreen had done her job well.

At this moment, Jordan couldn't think of what was going to happen to her. All she could think of was the man she loved so much, who was now dead. The wonderful, fun-loving man, whom she loved so deeply, by some strange quirk of fate, had had his life snuffed out like a candle, so suddenly and so unexpectedly, and all she could think of was the injustice and the sadness of it. She wasn't thinking of her own predicament except that she would never be able to be with him again. Why? Why? She kept muttering to herself, scarcely listening to the questions first the police, and now this magistrate kept asking her. She wanted to scream out at them, "Why is Ahmad dead?" She didn't even bother to reply when the magistrate asked her very gently, "Did you push him off the roof?" All she could do was look askance at the magistrate, as if she did not understand his question. The magistrate's eyes were still sympathetic as he said, "I'm sorry, but we will have to detain you until a proper enquiry has been held. You will be kept at the Jamshidabad garrison prison while your case is heard in court."

At that moment the grim reality of the situation dawned on Jordan, and the fear that she might have to spend a long time in an Iranian jail dawned on her.

When the black police truck carrying Jordan veered off the road and entered the prison compound, Jordan who was dozing on the rough metal seat was rudely awakened by the screech of brakes as the vehicle came to a violent stop. A loud bang on the door was followed by the sound of the door being opened, and the first thing she saw was a young male prison officer, and a gigantic woman dressed in the same uniform. "Bia, Khanum," and the woman signaled to her to get off. The handcuffs restraining her were removed by the police officer who had been sitting in the front seat of the truck; he also pulled out of his pocket a little ledger, which the woman prison officer signed. Jordan was led into the prison with the woman holding her arm in a strong but gentle grip.

The officer took him to the women's wing of the prison, and as she passed other cells, she saw Iranian women of all ages and sizes staring at her. Everybody's eyes were focused on her blond hair, but nobody spoke or commented.

Two buxom female guards were in charge of the cell block she was assigned to. At first sight they looked daunting, but Jordan noticed that they kept stealing sympathetic glances at her. "Befarmoidh khanum," one of them invited her in a cultured voice, pointing to her cell door, which was being held open by a slightly built Iranian woman in her early twenties. She was dressed in an orange sweater and blue jeans, not in prison uniform, and it was only after she followed Jordan into the cell and one of the guards had locked the door after them that she realized that the woman was her cell-mate.

"Shoma Amrikai" it was a statement, not a question, and Jordan answered, "Bale, I'm a teacher, an English teacher."

"Khob, good. You good, you Amaerikai. You go home soon, insha allah," she said, as if she was making a wish.

"I'm Jordan," she said, and held out her hand, and the woman held it in both of hers, "I am Fatameh," she said haltingly. And Jordan instantly took a liking to this innocent looking girl- woman, and wondered what she had done to be in prison. As if in answer to her thoughts, the woman said, "I no good. I kill husband, Rameez. I love him, but he drink too much, beat me everyday." And tears streamed down her cheeks.

Their cell was a twenty by twenty foot low-ceilinged room with no windows. Jordan held fatameh by the hand and they sat on one of the beds in the room, for there were no chairs. "You good, Khanume Jordan. You go home soon," she repeated, and Jordan knew that Fatameh already knew who Jordan was and why she was there. The prison grapevine had been busy, she guessed.

The prison guards were surprisingly very friendly and kind to the prisoners. They brought in all the news of what was going on outside the prison, and took great pride in their role of reporters. They obviously were on the Shah's side, and often spoke of Farah and the Shah's children, whom they adored, in the fondest terms.

They were very confident that the Shah would weather the many storms assailing him, and come into his own again before long. Believing that Jordan had killed Ahmad, who was after all a trusted soldier of the Shah, they treated her with a certain coolness, but they also empathized with her as a woman, for they surmised that he had treated her badly-or else why would a woman kill a man?

Fatameh, whom they admired very much for bumping off her bully of a husband, was their favorite in the block, and she was the first to get the choicest bits of news from the outside. In her halting English, Fatameh would tell Jordan everything she heard from her friends. Depending on the news from the outside, some days there would be great rejoicing in the block, while on others there would be a solemn silence. Three weeks had passed since her arrest, and Jordan had seen many of her colleagues. She knew she had the right to ask to speak to someone from the US embassy, but she was filled with a kind of ennui that kept her from making the request. Her gaolers were in no hurry, it seemed, to inform the embassy, but one day, one of the bosomy twins came up to her, and gently said, "Khanume Jordan, telephone."

With great trepidation, Jordan held the receiver to her ear. It was Firooznia, chairman of the English department. "Salaam Aleyikum Jordan…" he began, and Jordan broke into a fit of uncontrollable sobbing. One of the guards put her arm around her consolingly, and the other shouted out to Jordan's cell-mate, "Fatameh, bia bala."(Come here) And Fatameh was soon at her side holding her steady and comforting her.

Firooznia told Jordan that an embassy official would soon be coming to see her, and that her friends at the university were all looking out for her. "Chin up, girl," he said consolingly, "Things will work out. Don't worry. We are doing everything we can to get you out as soon as we can. We will start visiting you as soon as we get the green light from the courts. Is there anything we can bring you?"

Yes, bring Ahmad back to life, Jordan thought ruefully, but said, "Thank you sir. I'm fine. I have some friends here who look out for my needs."

Pat, Bernard and Leon also spoke to her and tried to comfort her.

"Don't fret, Jordan. Johnson, will be coming to see you tomorrow. He has spoken to a good lawyer, who will represent you in court. Their case is built purely on circumstantial evidence. Nobody saw you push Ahmad off the balcony, so it's not going to be in any way possible to prove That you are guilty of a crime. I talked to Ahmad's mother, and she believes that you are innocent. The only problem is that virago, Nisreen. Do you have any idea of how Ahmad fell?"

"I really wish I knew, Bernard. When I went up to the roof, Ahmad was nowhere to be seen.

Whoever pushed him –that's the only way he could have fallen- must have come down the stairs before I went up. Have they been able to contact the two couples that were on the roof at the time? They must have seen or heard something"

"No, they cannot be found. Whoever they are, I guess they don't want to get involved. Do you remember whether they were Iranians or expats?"

"It was so traumatic, Bernard, and I don't even remember that."

"Well we'll keep looking. I've told everybody to look out for them. By the way, I have some Iranian friends who sympathize with the revolutionaries. One of them thinks Ahmad was murdered by one of the revolutionary groups who had it in for him- for his close alliance with the Shah.

I wouldn't be surprised if they were the same group that did Donne in."

"I think so, too. In fact, some time ago Ahmad told me that they had tried to bump him off, and failed. He certainly was a prime target. But you know Ahmad. He didn't think they would have the guts to try something until they were sure the Shah was going to lose."

"I guess they planned it well. We will be on the lookout. If I get any news, I will pass it on to your lawyer."

"Thank you Bernard," replied Jordan, and Bernard was saddened by the unhappiness in her voice. He knew that under the circumstances, Jordan was in a tight corner.

Chapter 45

Johnson, the man from the embassy came to see her the next morning. A giant of a man, with sparkling blue eyes and a cherubic face, Johnson's pleasant features belied his mood. He was accompanied by a skinny, middle aged Iranian in a well-cut Italian suit and shoes that glinted like his black eyes. He looked like an Italian dago Jordan had seen in old movies.

"We got in touch with your mother yesterday," Johnson drawled with a Texan accent. "She wants to come over, but we advised her against it. The next few weeks are critical, and we are not sure which way the wind is blowing."

"What do you mean," Jordan asked anxiously.

"We are not sure if the Shah can weather the storm. If he does, we can get you out quickly but if his government collapses, we will all have to leave fairly quickly. We are advising all Americans to send their families home," he droned, and seeing the terrified look in Jordan's eyes, corrected himself, "It's only a precautionary measure. Are you being treated well, here? Is there anything I can get you?"

"No, thanks, but I don't need anything. The prison staff is quite friendly, and I have no problems with them. All I want is get out of here and go home," she pleaded, as if he had the power to grant her wish.

"I wish I could help you," he said, "the problem is that everyone is confused, and nobody wants to take a decision that will cause trouble later," and added consolingly, "but don't worry Miss Moore. We will do everything we can. I'm confident that we can convince the judge of your innocence, and you'll soon be on your way home. But now, I need to ask you some questions."

The questions took the better part of the morning. Mosallai, the lawyer, asked the questions, and recorded Jordan's answers on a little recorder he had brought with him. Johnson made his own notes on a little notepad, asking a few questions himself.

As they got up to leave, Mosallai asked, "Is the food OK, Khanume Jordan? If you would like anything in particular to eat, please tell me. It can be arranged."

Food was the last thing on Jordan's mind, but she did not say so. "The food's all right, Mr Mosallai, but thank you very much."

That night Jordan slept better, and dreamed of home and her mother. Her mother was making wedding plans, and was showing her some jewelry she wanted Jordan to wear.

"Will Ahmad like these," she asked, and Jordan snapped awake. Reality engulfed her, and she unwittingly whimpered. Fatameh was quickly at her side, "Khanum, you all right? You crying?" Alarm in her voice.

"I'm OK Fatima, thank you. You'd better go back to sleep," Jordan whispered, consoled by Fatemeh's concern.

The call to prayer at early dawn woke Jordan up. Fatameh was lying by Jordan's side, the entire length of her body touching Jordan's in the narrow bed. Fatameh's right arm was draped round Jordan's shoulders. Jordan was filled with love and empathy for Fatameh. A deep sob of love and gratitude unwittingly escaped from her lips. Jordan held Fatameh close to her, and drifted back into peaceful sleep. When Jordan woke up later in the morning, Fatameh was back in her own bed. Later as they had breakfast, Fatameh looked very sheepish and guilty and when Jordan looked at her, Fatameh, looking down at her plate said, "Please don't angry me Khanumeh Jordan. I'm very sorry about last night. I had bad dream."

"You don't have to apologize, Fatameh. It's all right. Don't worry about it. I understand.

Remember I'm your friend. You can come to me any time."

"Thank you. You very kind to me. I like you very much" she replied gratefully, looking away from Jordan in embarrassment.

From that night on, Fatameh would steal into Jordan's bed every night. She was always careful to see that the guards were fast asleep before she moved out of her own bed. They would hold each other close until they fell asleep. Through the thin sheets that covered them she would feel her tremble against her as muted sobs wracked her body. It was the uncontrollable anguish, the sadness and loneliness of a woman in torment, a woman forlorn and miserable, who had no one to turn to but this strange white woman, sharing similar anguish and pain. Although Jordan did not fully understand the feelings of Fatameh, she felt a kind of intimacy, almost a close kinship towards this helpless, fragile looking woman. She admired her for her courage and her refusal to be defeated in spirit by her vicious husband. She held Fatameh tighter and Fatameh woke up. She turned her face upward to look at Jordan, and Jordan reached down and kissed her on her warm, trembling lips. The salt of Fatameh's tears aroused in Jordan a fierce passion and their kiss became intensely passionate. A moan of gratitude escaped her lips, and their mutual longing for relief pulled them closer into a kind of holy communion.

It was Saturday, September 9. The jolly jailer, as Jordan liked to think of Mariam came in much later than usual.

"Why, Khanume Mariam, has your husband left you for another woman?" asked her colleague, Leila.

"I wish he would," complained Mariam, "he gives me too much trouble at night."

Everyone laughed, and Fatameh translated for Jordan.

Then, Mariam looked up, and continued to talk for a full two minutes in a deeply distressed tone, and all of the others listened in rapt attention. No one interrupted or asked questions.

Fatameh interpreted for Jordan. On Friday, the day of prayer, there had been trouble in Tehran. Tens of thousands of people had come out on the streets to demonstrate against the Shah. The Shah and his advisors had lost their patience, temper or both and ordered the protests broken up by any means possible. The army and police had begun to shoot into the crowd, first with rubber bullets, and then with live ammunition. When that failed to disperse the huge crowds, helicopters and tanks were brought in to control the crowd. Some of the demonstrators now had machine guns and other weapons to shoot back with. The resulting carnage had left a hundred people dead and many badly injured on the streets. Video cameras had been on hand to record the death and destruction in gory detail, and the number of martyrs was upped to thousands for the benefit of the international press, which as is their wont, gave the pictures much publicity without checking the facts first. The result was sensationalism of the highest order, and many a Khomeini supporter chuckled in secret that day and afterwards at the success of their coup. Dubbed "Black Friday", the day turned out to be one of the most shameful days of the Shah's entire reign. The action of the armed forces against people who were struggling for freedom from the Shah's dictatorial regime was effectively manipulated by the revolutionaries to look like the work of a power-maddened despot; it seemed that the whole world was in agreement that the Shah was the cruelest dictator in the world, and even the United States, his closest ally was ready to drop him like a hot potato.

It was also rumored that prison riots were imminent, especially in those housing large numbers of political prisoners. And their prison was one of them. Poor Fatameh and the other female prisoners were highly disturbed by the news, and were constantly talking about what they should do if they were caught in the crossfire of the revolutionaries and the armed forces. Although nobody would target them, they would be in the way of stray bullets and wayward shrapnel. Prisoners and jailers, women and vulnerable huddled together and talked late into the night. They made careful plans for putting as much distance as they could between themselves and the fighting if and when the need arose. All they wanted was to get away from it all, to peace and safety. Yet they knew in their hearts that their lives were in an extremely whimsical balance.

For about two weeks after that fateful Friday, life in prison, for Jordan, became a little more tolerable than it had been. Almost everyday, someone from the university would come round to see her, bringing her stories about the world outside.

Chapter 46

The Khomeini campaign appeared to be progressing apace. The Tudeh party, the only possible contender to power was going along with Khomeini; the Communists felt that their first priority was to defeat the Shah. The guerilla militia- the Marxist Fedayeen- as well as the leftist Mujaheddin were forces to reckon with, but none of them could stand alone. They were all biding their time, waiting for a complete collapse of the Shah's power and authority. Until then, it was the story of politics making strange bedfellows, for each of them had their own agendas, but had to coexist with each other for long as it was necessary. When the opportunity presented itself, they would each come out in their true colors. Pondering on this, Jordan recalled what an ancient Chinese General had said, "All wars are based on deception." Khomeini's supporters were numerically greater than the other three factions combined, but they lacked the firepower and fighting skills if it came to a direct confrontation with the Shah's army. So they all treaded softly, avoiding each other's corns.

One day Pat brought Jordan the news that Bigmouth Bob had settled in Texas, where he had found work in an oil company. "The oily sonofabitch," she exclaimed, "I also heard that he has shacked up with a Vietnamese immigrant. Poor woman! But you know what? He's not teaching anymore, and the teaching profession will be all the better for it."

Firooznia, the charming 'professore daneshga' (university professor) often came to visit with Jordan. "I'm very hopeful that you will soon be released,' he said, "in the meantime, are these ladies treating you all right?" he asked, flashing his cutest smile at Leila and Mariam. He then told them that Jordan was innocent of any wrongdoing, and would soon be free to go back to Amrika. He earnestly requested them to make her as comfortable as they could. His charm worked like magic. They vowed in the name of Allah that they would.

And they did. Jordan made two or three telephone calls each week to her mother, and the guards neither listened in to her conversations, nor limited the time of her calls as prison law required them to do.

Fatameh obviously did not need Firooznia's exhortations. She knew Khanume Jordan was innocent the moment she saw her, she had told him.

When Firooznia told Jordan what Fatameh had said, Jordan felt a great love for Fatameh. She draped her arm over her shoulder and hugged her saying, "You're the greatest friend I've ever had," and Fatameh was constantly beside Jordan, talking to her as best she could, trying to make her forget the situation she was in.

The political buzz kept coming in, too. One day it seemed that the Shah was rallying his forces and getting back the advantage he had lost, and the next day it was Khomeini's star on the ascendant.

One day, it was Leila who came in with a cloud on her face. Fatameh, as usual, was the first to notice, and enquired why. She told them that the Rastakizh party had been disbanded. Jordan did not know what this meant, and asked Bernard when he came in the next day. "It was the Shah's own creation. He formed a party to include all those who would support him in bringing the diverse ethno-cultural groups and tribes in different parts of the country together so they could all live in harmony as Iranians."

"So what's the problem?" asked Jordan and Bernard replied, "What really happened is that the party membership was made up of sycophants and diehard supporters of the Shah. All of them were in it just for the patronage. Actually it caused more rifts than unity." And Jordan thought, this Shah was a fraud. Poor Ahmad and others like him had staked their lives for him, while he was only thinking of himself. Bernard, who had his ear to the ground in political matters, added, "It is the poor Ba'hais who will now have problems."

A few days later, Leila came in with the good news that Khomeini had been asked to leave Iraq. Saddam Hussein, fearing the wrath of the US and Iran, had told Khomeini that he would have to leave Iraq unless he was willing to alter his uncompromising stance against the Shah.

Khomeini left Iraq and sought refuge in Kuwait, but here too, he was turned down, whereupon he flew to Paris. Shah supporters in Iran, including Leila and Mariam, thought his star was on a downturn. "Now he is too far away to bother the Shah," Mariam said gleefully.

But in fact, what the two Arab leaders in Iraq and Kuwait had done was give Khomeini a kick up the stairs. France immediately opened her doors to the Ayatollah in welcome. The French, in their infinite wisdom, probably wanted to steal a March over everyone else in making friends with the man of the hour, with their eyes firmly fixated on Iran's oil reserves. Saner individuals in Iran and elsewhere could not see the rationale. The French they felt were fishing in troubled waters. The Great Revolutionaries of Europe had outdone themselves as events would soon prove.

The Khomeini forces probably could not believe their good fortune for Khomeini was immediately thrust into the international limelight, gaining the publicity he could not have dreamed of even if he had all of the Shah's oil wealth-and here he was getting it at no cost at all.

Iranian émigrés in France quickly rallied round Khomeini, and rented for him a very comfortable place to reside in-Neauphle-le-Chateau, just outside the city of Paris. The international press, more interested in the sensationalism of the moment than the possible consequences of his coming into the limelight, rushed to his aid as it were, giving him the most favored spotlight, where Khomeini basked like the proverbial cat that had got the cream. He probably invoked the blessings of Allah on the President of France, Saddam and the Emir of Kuwait, for the way things had turned out for him. He was now ready to launch his god-given task and save Iran from the evils of the West and their lackey, the Shah.

And while the world press converged on Khomeini, the press in Iran decided to abandon the Shah to his fate; a lightning strike launched by newspaper and other media became a spark for all other institutions to implode upon themselves. Schools and universities, banks, bazaars, post offices, railway stations, government ministries and all other institutions essential for the peaceful and orderly progress of human activity came to a dead stop in the entire nation. It was a situation pregnant with the prospects of anarchy, but it was an anarchy that would not come for the Ayatollah was watching very carefully.

The people withdrew into their homes, venturing out only for bare essentials such as food and heating oil.

At Tehran University, the foreign staff and a few Iranians had turned up at the department the next morning. Dr. Firooznia had not let up on his charming smile as he addressed them. "We are officially on strike ladies and gentlemen. The Iranian staff may go home if they wish to. The foreign teachers may come to the office or stay at home, but if you do come to the office, you should do no work."

"What should we do then?" ventured Doug.

"We can party," said Leon, bringing a sardonic grin to Firooznia's face.

"Yes, I guess so," he agreed weakly.

"But remember, no booze," warned Brad, "let's not press our luck." Brad was counting his blessings for being paid for doing nothing.

In her cell, Jordan was getting more and more anxious. The worst part is not knowing what's going to happen, she thought. She was glad for the company of Fatameh, Leila and Mariam. To Jordan, they were not Iranians any more. They were friends-even partners in the quirky game of life. She was not much into praying, but at that moment she said a silent prayer for her beautiful friends.

A few days later, the Iranian oil industry workers joined the rest of the striking workers.

Long lines began to form at gas stations as cars and other vehicles formed queues to fill up. Men women and children stood in lines in the wintry cold to buy kerosene, the household fuel that would keep the stove in the kitchen and the bokari, the traditional space heater running.

The month of November dragged on. More riots, albeit sporadic, and not as extensive as they used to be, and demonstrations continued. In some instances the police opened fire and in others they showed restraint. Buildings were badly damaged and shops were looted. The prime minister, Sharif Emami, appointed by the Shah as a symbol of conciliation with the demonstrators, suddenly resigned, embarrassing the Shah further.

Chapter 47

Reports came down the grapevine of the assassination of people in high places still loyal to the Shah. Officers of the police and army, navy and air-force were suddenly being dispatched by unknown assassins. Still others were quietly leaving the country to safer places-in Europe and other western countries. It seemed the Shah was running out of options and getting war weary, too, for he appeared on TV to make a rare broadcast to the nation. The prison wing was suddenly provided with a large black and white TV, and Jordan was also able to see it, but she had to have everything he said translated to her by Fatameh.

Jordan did notice that the Shah's tone was humble and conciliatory. "I have made many mistakes in the past, and I apologize to you all," he said humbly, "and I promise not to repeat those mistakes. I will be guided by you, the people." He made confessions and promises. He acknowledged the revolution both as king and citizen.

Many people listening to him that day looked upon him as one who wished to make amends for his sins, and even sympathized with him. Leila's body shook with sobs as she listened, and then she smiled and looked at them all with the look of a priest who had heard a sinner's confession. The Shah had done his penance. He was absolved. "Poor man," she sighed, "He is wonderful. He loves us all. Drudh ba Shah." (Long live the Shah!) she exclaimed smiling at everyone present.

Jordan was skeptical, but she held her peace.

In his palace, surrounded by his closest advisers, the Shah smiled an enigmatic smile. One of his closest advisers spoke, "Your Majesty, it is well and good to make promises and ask for forgiveness, but we need to find some way to control the people. If not, it will soon be unmanageable."

It was a bold reminder, the kind which most of his advisers feared to give in normal circumstances, preferring to keep their opinions to themselves and agree with the Shah in all matters. But these were not normal circumstances, and the Shah was aware of that. "Don't worry. Tomorrow is another day," he said cryptically.

Iranian national TV boldly announced what the Shah had meant the previous day. He appointed General Gholam Azari, Prime Minister. Azari belonged to the group of people who believed that the revolution needed to be crushed. The Shah knew that Azari would do whatever it took to bring the country under control. He probably didn't realize that the scales had tipped too far, and tough action on his part would only drive the wedge between him and the people deeper, and that even those who were his allies would be hard put to defend him, for he had reneged on his promises, and withdrawn his confessions and concessions. As soon as the new Prime Minister assumed office, he declared martial law throughout the country. In his broadcast to the nation, the General declared that he would tolerate no lawlessness from anyone, and advised the revolutionaries to lay down their arms and stay indoors. He promised the people that all of their grievances would be addressed by the new government.

The next day, it seemed to everyone that the Shah was losing control of his mental faculties; acting on suspicion that some of his own supporters were working against him, he had thirteen of the hitherto most trusted and well-known members of his power structure arrested and imprisoned. His loyalists were in a quandary, and more importantly, his position was becoming more and more precarious. More of his loyalists were either running away or secretly making pacts with the revolutionaries. It was turning into 'the best of times and the worst of times' if rumor was to be trusted. One day it was the Shah's star that was on the ascendant, and the next day, Khomeini's.

On one day particularly favorable to the Ayatollah, Iranians throughout the country went into an uncharacteristic frenzy of mass hypnosis through suggestion, which was the only possible explanation for what happened. At a given time in the evening, when the sun, going down in the western horizon cast long and strange shadows and gave way to tricks of the mind, many a faithful Khomeini supporter swore that he or she had seen the face of Khomeini in the sky as had been predicted by some tactical genius. Thousands of people were apoplectic in their exhibition of joy, jumping up and down, giving thanks to God for affording them this rare apparition portending the success of "the revered one" in his unrelenting campaign to topple the Shah from power. Ironically, the Tudeh membership, consisting of many non-believers joined in the chorus, not because they loved Khomeini more, but because they loved the Shah less. When he first heard of the impending event, the Tudeh leader remarked, "Here's an opportunity for us to get in with the masses. Let's pretend that we see the man in the sky, and we'll have them all eating out of our hands."

November turned into December, and everybody waited; an eerie calm seemed to pervade the nation, and nobody, it seemed, dared to breathe.

Jordan's hopes of going home were one day very high, the next day lower than ever. Yet, she had within her the will to say 'hold on.'

December is the cruelest month, not April Jordan said to herself recalling Eliot's poem, 'The Wasteland.' She felt she was in a 'wasteland' that even Eliot could not have imagined, for it was purgatory recreated to torment and frustrate, with neither hell nor heaven specified or promised.

The tenth day of the Islamic month of Moharram, Ashura, is the saddest day for Shia Muslims. It commemorates the martyrdom of Imam Hussein, whose death at the hands of his more powerful rivals signifies the struggle between the just and the righteous against the cruel and unjust. On this day, thousands of devotees march the streets bemoaning their loss and flagellating themselves with sticks and chains in atonement for their loss. This year, the Ashura had even greater significance in Iran, for it had come to symbolize the struggle between Khomeini, the just, and the Shah, the unjust. Hundreds of thousands were planning to take part in the processions around the city. Mosques were stocked with enormous supplies of food and water for the devotees, along with medical supplies to attend to the self-inflicted injuries of the more devout mourners. Everything was in readiness, and notwithstanding the solemnity of the occasion, there was a sense of exhilaration as people anticipated it, animated by the thought that liberation day was slowly but surely drawing closer, and that this event would be portentous of victory over the dictator. Events, however, took a totally unexpected turn.

General Azhari, justifiably or otherwise, saw the traditional processions as a potentially explosive event that could lead to violence and bloodshed on the streets. Having consulted with the Shah and the Security Council, he issued a proclamation banning Ashura Processions throughout the country. "This is a necessary step for the protection of the people," he declared.

The Shah endorsed his decision.

Khomeini supporters were incensed. Khomeini immediately recorded a message from his chateau in Paris: "Let rivers of blood flow on the streets. Do not fear Reza or his army. March with courage and devotion for your country and your religion. Follow the example of the greatest of our martyrs, Imam Ali and Imam Hussein. Your blood will help wash away the sins of the tyrant and cleanse you and the country once more. Do not give up your struggle until the tyrant is banished. For those of you who will be martyred, remember your reward will be in heaven."

That evening, the message was relayed through the 'rooftop serenade' as the expatriates came to call Khomeini's messages. The people's animosity for the Shah was fanned into a raging inferno by Khomeini's words. "Allahu Akbar! Drudh ba Khomeini!" reverberated in the streets and in the homes, particularly in the crowded areas of downtown Tehran and other cities.

The world outside got a look into Khomeini's soul when those words were reported in the international media. They realized that the man was as fanatical as he was unrelenting; he was willing to sacrifice thousands of lives for his cause, and more importantly, thousands of people were ready and willing to make the supreme sacrifice.

Oh my God, thought Jordan, what madness is this? What will happen to this country if he comes into power. She recalled what Ahmad had said: "I'd rather not think what the fate of Iran would be if Khomeini came into power."

"I don't want to be around if Khomeini succeeds," she whispered to Fatameh.

And Fatameh agreed.

Khomeini's words had a volatile effect on the people. His words spread like a wildfire, from one end of the country to the other. Children had been made to memorize the incendiary words and repeated them as they played on the streets in downtown Tehran. They seemed to be mesmerized by adult politics.

Chapter 48

Violent protests became the order of the day not just in the big cities, but in the little towns and villages as well. Men left their homes with bands of white cloth tied round their heads as a symbol that they were ready to give up their lives for the cause, and many were shot dead. The women carried red roses and placed them at the feet of the Shah's soldiers even as they were attacked by them; they begged them not to murder their own brothers in Islam.

Pat, Leon and Bernard came to see Jordan in prison. "The news is pretty bad," said Pat, "Many Americans are sending their families home, and everybody's waiting for an official statement from the Foreign Ministry." She knew that this would frighten Jordan very much, but Pat believed that she owed her friend the truth. And it was not as if Jordan did not know what was going on. The prison grapevine kept her privy to the latest developments.

"What about you guys," asked Jordan.

"It all depends on the Foreign Ministry," she repeated, "They have to issue a communique before any organization will take a decision about their foreign staff. Firooznia says that we need not worry until that is issued, so we will wait and see."

Jordan was sitting on her bed when Fatameh came and sat beside her. "Don't worry, Khanum. You be OK." And in her heart, Jordan blessed this wonderful human being, and said to herself that if she got out of her predicament, she would do everything she could to take Fatameh with her to the United States.

As expected, the people defied the ban on processions. If anything, the ban had only made them more resolute for they came out on the streets in the millions not just on Ashura, but Tasu'a, the day before Ashura, as well. To their immense credit, they were extremely disciplined as they marched; the singularity of purpose, namely that of toppling the Shah from power seemed to have replaced their usual boisterousness and taunting words with a kind of chilling calmness.

Very few flagellated themselves as they usually did during the processions. They were all under strict orders from their leaders not to get violent, and no one did. The hapless police and the army looked on from a distance as they had been instructed by the General. They seemed more helpless and lost dealing with the peaceful demonstrators than with the loud and violent ones they had encountered before.

It was the first time in the recent history of the country that Ashura had taken on so much political significance as opposed to the traditionally religious association it had enjoyed before.

The event obviously had a telling effect on the Shah's morale. He summoned his inner circle to discuss the situation. Some suggested that he take a hard line, come what may. He, on the other hand was morally defeated.

The sheer number of people in the demonstrations overwhelmed him, unnerved him. He had been in touch with his American friends, and it seemed to him that their ardor had cooled significantly. The American government was weighing its choices, he thought, and it seemed he was gradually losing favor with them, too. This was not a little uprising which could be quelled by the army and the police. This was a clear and serious statement by the majority of the people. After much deliberation and soul-searching he realized that he had just one option: to leave the country, for the moment at least. Sadly and very reluctantly, he took the decision to leave. The people would accept nothing less.

When the Shah summoned Shapour Bakhtiar to Niavaran Palace, Bakhtiar was more than a little confused. Bakhtiyar had been a strong opponent of the Shah in previous years, although later he had got into the inner circle for political expediency. He now wondered at the reason for the summons.

"Agha," he began, "you and I have had several disagreements in the past, but I have had the greatest respect for you. The time has come when you can actually do something very important for your nation and her people."

Bakhtiar's confusion was increasing, but he thought it better not to interrupt.

"As you know, things have taken a very bad turn in the last weeks, and it is incumbent that I leave the country for a while-my health has suffered what with the strain of events of the recent past- and I need to take my mind off matters of state for a while, so I have decided to leave the country temporarily. The country needs someone who is prudent and strong, able and just to be at the helm, and I can think of no one else who fits the bill as well as you."

Bakhtiar's jaw dropped in surprise, but he knew that the Shah had really run out of options. He was not quite sure whether the Shah was doing him a favor, or placing him under the sword of Damocles, putting him in an impossible situation. To say that Iran was a nation in turmoil was an understatement. It would need a superhuman effort by a real superman to sort things out. Yet he was flattered beyond belief. It was an opportunity he had never dreamed of. Maybe this would be his opportunity to bring honor to himself, his family and the Bakhtiar tribe, and help the nation that he loved regain some composure.

"I shall be greatly honored to accept, Your Majesty. Needless to say, I will employ my every sinew to serve you, the country and our people to the best of my ability in this hour of need. I hope and pray for your speedy recovery, and safe return to the nation."

National Iranian Radio and Television had, by this time, resumed broadcasting news flashes and weather reports. Gone were the foreign programs Jordan had been used to watching. The news itself was very terse and to the point. Hardly any mention was made of the Shah or what he was doing. On the twelfth of January, Khomeini, it was reported, announced a revolutionary council as a shadow government to take over power when the Shah left the country.

Chapter 49

On the sixteenth of January, a somber voice on radio and TV announced that the Shah had left the country. "Shah raft,"(The Shah has left) whispered Mariam as she quietly collapsed to the floor. An eerie silence took over the cell block, only to be shattered seconds later by the booming sounds of fire-crackers exploding on the streets. It was the call to break the fast, repeated many times over. The announcer's words that the Shah was leaving the country only because he respected the wishes of the people, and that he was concerned about their welfare was lost in the noise of the fire-crackers.

Jordan had known right along that it was inevitable that the Shah would leave, and the news did not concern her too much. She called her mother and told her that she would soon be home. "Don't worry Mom. I'm fine. I have some great friends here," and she talked about Fatameh, Leila and Mariam and Bernard and Muzaffer. "They are all looking out for me."

"But what will happen now?" asked Fatameh, terror in her voice.

"I don't know. Khomeini will return soon is what the revolutionaries are saying. I never expected it would come to this."

"Do you think that Shapour Bakthiar will be able to handle the situation in the absence of the Shah?"

"He doesn't have any experience or ability. May Allah protect our country," she whispered, somberly.

Two days later, Jordan and Fatameh were sitting in their cell when Nizreen breezed in like a tornado. She didn't try to hide the pure jealousy and hatred she had for Jordan. "Khanume Jordan," she began, "the friend of you Americans, the Shahanshahi is gone. Soon there be an Islamic government this country. The penalty for murder death, and for your case, it probably will be death by stoning," she continued, watching Jordan like a hungry animal stalking its defenseless prey. Jordan felt weak, and completely intimidated, and reached for the wall to steady herself, but instead of the cold surface of the stone wall, she felt the hands of Fatameh steadying her.

"Khanume Jordan is not guilty of any crime," she said boldly, as she stared at Nisreen, her eyes flashing in utter disgust and rage at Jordan's accuser.

Nisreen laughed as she mockingly glanced at Fatameh, "Oh, I see. The American woman has found a Persian slave. You will both die of stoning unless you do as I say," she continued, "tomorrow I will come with a court clerk who will take down your confession of the crime of killing Ahmad. If you do that, the court will show you leniency. Since you're an American, it will let you go. All you will have to do is to pay compensation to Ahmad's family."

Jordan felt nauseated by the accusation coming from one who definitely should know it was not true. Sadness and anger flashed in her eyes. "But I did not kill Ahmad. How can I confess to a crime I haven't committed?"

And Fatameh stood between Nisreen and Jordan as if to shield her from Nisreen's vitriol.

Nisreen towered over the slightly built Fatameh, who dared her to come forward.

"Is that your final answer," Nisreen screamed taking a hesitant step towards Jordan like a cobra ready to strike a hapless victim, but Fatameh stood her ground and shouted back at Nisreen, "Go away witch devil, or I'll scratch your eyes out!"

Nisreen sensed that Fatameh would probably do just that and quietly edged out of the room, watching Fatameh and Jordan with undisguised hatred. "You will both regret this," were her parting words, and Jordan shivered.

Chapter 50

On Friday morning, Bernard, and Muzaffer, all of whom lived in the Jamshidabad area were standing in line with their five-gallon jerry cans, waiting for kerosene.

"I'm glad I sent my family home," said Bernard, "My little daughter hates a cold house."

"I wish I'd done the same," agreed Leon, an African American, who had opted to stay in spite of warnings from the US embassy that all Americans should leave "Anyway, I've booked them on Monday's flight."

"Thank God I'm not married," agreed Muzaffer, facetiously, "I don't have to worry about keeping the house warm."

"Well, you don't know the difference between a cold bed and a warm one anyway," joked Bernard.

"Jokes apart," said Muzaffer, "What's happening to Jordan? Have you guys seen her lately?"

"I saw her yesterday. Actually the police would like to let her go especially since they don't want any trouble with the American authorities. The Chief of Police for the area is himself trying to send his family to the US."

"So what's the problem?"

"It's that aunt of Ahmad's. She's stirring a hornet's nest. It seems her boyfriend, Khaled, has dumped her again, and she seems to be trying to take out her frustration on Jordan."

"That's terrible. I wouldn't want to be in Jordan's shoes."

"Nisreen visits the prison everyday to make sure Jordan is still there. To make matters worse, she is supposed to have some heavy clout with the Chief of Prisons. He will not agree to let Jordan go without judicial authority."

"Things are getting worse by the day, and it seems our days here are numbered, too. Poor Jordan," added Leon.

Chapter 51

And just as Leon had said, things were getting bad, for when they went to the university on Monday, they were all summoned to a meeting with Dr. Firooznia. "Ladies and gentlemen," he gravely began without preamble, "I'm afraid I have bad news. The Ministry of Foreign Affairs has sent us a memo that all expatriate staff-especially US citizens and British subjects-should leave the country as soon as possible, as the government cannot take responsibility for their safety any longer."

A hushed silence followed, until Brad Foreman broke it. "Will the university make our travel arrangements, or should we do that ourselves?"

"No, Brad. The university will look after it. All you need to do is to hand over your passports to the personnel office. They have been instructed to give it top priority. Your salaries and other final entitlements will be paid tomorrow. The bank has been instructed to transfer all funds in your accounts to your home accounts-unless you need any money to carry with you. If that is the case, you can tell Faride and she will attend to it. "The gentlemen from India and Sri Lanka have nothing to worry about," he added, looking pointedly at Bernard and Muzaffer, "The opposition to the Shah does not see you as a possible obstacle to their dreams of an Islamic government."

In the tense excitement of the moment, nobody spoke about Jordan. It seemed that hey had all forgotten her, even Pat, until Bernard ventured, "What's happening about Jordan? Do you know what is going on?"

A look of fatigue and hopelessness came over Dr. Firooznia. "Yes, Bernard. We have been doing everything we can and will continue to do so. However, you must understand that this is a criminal matter, and in such cases, there's a limit to what we can do."

The tension was so tangible you could scoop it up with a shovel. Dr Firooznia continued sadly, "The biggest problem is that relative of the dead officer. She is raising the devil, and whatever we do becomes innocuous in the light of her loss."

"Her loss!" hissed Pat, "It's more like her spite and vengeance."

"Anyway, let's all hope for the best. I will be in touch with Jordan, and do my best to help her. You may rest assured that even after you leave, Jordan will not be alone." Everybody knew these were not empty words. They knew Firooznia was an honorable man. The meeting came to an abrupt end.

Chapter 52

The next few days were a surrealistic nightmare for Jordan. She tried to get a message to her lawyer, but there was no response from him. The American embassy staff were also unusually silent. Bernard from the university came to see Jordan the next morning.

"The university has advised all expatriate staff to leave the country because they are unable to guarantee their safety. Prof. Firooznia has asked the staff, particularly the Americans and the Brits, to leave as quickly as they can."

"What about you?" asked Jordan.

"Being a Sri Lankan, I will have no problem, which is what Firooznia thinks. Neither will the Indians and Pakistanis on the staff. So we have decided to stay on, and see how things gell," he said. "I will keep you informed of what is happening, Jordan. I'm going to the US embassy today. I hope I will have some news for you tomorrow."

"Oh, thank you Bernard. I could kiss you."

"Promises, promises," said Bernard grinning, "but seriously, I know you'd have done the same for me Jordan. That's what friends are for." The catch in his was unmistakable, and Jordan put out her hand and touched Bernard's face. "I'll see you soon," he said gruffly, and left.

Chapter 53

The news from the US Embassy was not good. They had approached the police, and tried to secure Jordan's release, but everything was chaotic. Jordan's case was particularly difficult as it had already gone to court, and there was no one who could provide legal authorization for her release. No one was prepared to take a chance in a matter such as this. The bureaucracy, which at the best of times was slow and inefficient, was completely stalled by uncertainty and anxiety. No one was ready to stick his neck out taking a decision that could blow in one's face later.

"To make matters worse, Nisreen keeps stirring up the already thick witches' cauldron," reported Bernard on his next visit to Jordan but his sanguine and pragmatic belief in the Newtonian law, that every action has an equal and opposite reaction, helped him to convince her that since she had committed no crime, she would not be touched by any evil repercussions. That's Bernard's Buddhist philosophy, thought Jordan, but how many times had the innocent paid dearly for no fault of theirs. She felt a kind of affinity with Tom Robinson in 'To Kill a Mockingbird,' a book she had enjoyed teaching in her English Literature class back home.

At night, Fatameh would lie by her side and keep telling her "Don't fear, Khanum. You have done no wrong. You are going to be all right."

Jordan found great strength and courage in the ways of this dimunitive, yet courageous woman, who was herself facing great danger. Her empathy for her friend made her involunatarily say, "I will help you get out, too, for you have done no wrong either. Your evil husband deserved to die," trying to console Fatameh, but she wondered deep inside her if any of it would actually come to pass. Jordan actually longed for night time, when she could lie beside Fatameh and forget about the awful predicament they were both in. She recalled a Buddhist image that Bernard had told her about in happier times of the hunter, who was suspended in space hanging from the branch of a tree feeding on the honey from a beehive. Above the hunter's head was an enormous snake poised to strike him, and below him a giant bear, attracted by the honey, now waiting for the man to fall into his grasp. Yet, the hunter was enjoying the moment, and Jordan thanked her fate or destiny that had presented the sweet and kind Fatameh-for without her, she would have given in to total despair.

Everyday snatches of news reached Jordan and the other inmates through their jailers. The jailers were not in the strict sense jailers any more, for they all seemed to be tied up by the common strand of fear and confusion that gripped the great kingdom of Persia, the land of Cyrus, Xerxes and Darius, and more recently of the Shahanshahi, the king of kings. "As flies to wanton boys are we to the gods," mused Jordan, recalling Shakespeare, "they kill us for their sport." How happy and carefree she had been as she first set foot in the land of the Peacock Throne. Look at me now, she said to herself.

Chapter 54

On February 1st, Khomeini flew in to Tehran. As the drone of the jet plane carrying him reached ground level, between three and three and a half million Iranians packing the streets and every little space around Mehrabad airport looked up and chanted in a deafening rumble "Drudh ba Khomeini. Hukkumateh Eslami ba Iran" (Long live Khomeini. Islamic government for Iran.) Their deliverer had arrived.

Shapour Bakhtiar, the PM in whose charge the Shah had left the country, immediately started off on the wrong foot. As Khomeini's plane was circling to land, he issued an order to the controlling tower at Mehrabad to refuse permission for the plane to land. After the plane had been circling the airport for over two hours, he changed his mind and allowed the plane to land. Many of the people who stood rejoicing that day were there not because they loved Khomeini but because they hated the Shah for his mistakes. Many of them did not realize the full implications of what they had wished for; all they wanted was to see the Shah out of their ken. None of them thought of what they were in for with clerical government in command. A few hoped that some compromise would be reached between the royalists and the Islamists, and things would soon be all right for everybody concerned, for Iran had gone through turmoil of all shapes and sizes, but the nation had prevailed. With its two and a half thousand years of nationhood dominating their thinking, nobody saw what was coming.

Shapour Bhaktiyar had put himself in a near impossible situation by accepting the position of Prime Minister. First he lacked the strength of character and the qualities of statesmanship required for the job. Second, conditions in the country had deteriorated so much that there didn't seem to be any room for compromise or negotiation between the government and the opposition to the Shah's regime.

Widespread strikes paralyzed the business sector and brought all economic activity to a near halt. The few workers who did not wish to join the strikes were often intimidated by the sheer force of numbers of those who did. The oil supply had fallen to a trickle; long lines of vehicles waiting for gas had forced distributors to ration the amount sold to each customer. Kerosene, the main fuel used in heating houses, too, was in short supply. People stood in queues to get a few gallons to keep the bokharas going. It was January, and the cold was overwhelming to a people who had gotten used to having plentiful supplies to keep their houses as hot as it was in the heat of the summer months.

Chapter 55

Bernard woke up early with the sun streaming through the huge glass windows of his apartment on Fars Street. It was hardly 5:30 am, but the temperature was nearly eighty degrees. The landlord had told him that the coolers in the apartment could not be turned on because of the kerosene shortage. Through the window he could see the top of Mount Damavand, snow-capped, glistening raucously in thenear-hot rays of the morning sun. Nothing disturbed the peace and majesty of the scene. Sam, his recently moved in roommate seemed to be stirring, so Bernard walked into the kitchen to put the water on. He needed his enormous mug morning tea like an addict craved his fix.

Soon he heard the kettle whistling, and he made a large pot of tea. Sam would soon join him and they would sit in the little balcony and enjoy their tea.

It was 6:30. They had their tea, munching on cream crackers and goat cheese. Sam put away their breakfast utensils in the dishwasher. "Hey, Bernard, I need to get some cigarettes. Do you need anything from the corner store?"

"No, thanks. We can go later and check if they have any fresh lamb. They usually bring it in around eight. I'm in the mood for some kebab, today."

"Great idea. Maybe we can try the recipe I got from Mrs. Kourosh."

Sam had reached the top of the stairs leading down from their apartment, and was about to take the first step down when all hell broke loose. A number of machine guns suddenly opened fire from the left side of the apartment building. It sunded like a dozen pile drivers had started simultaneously under the building. The noise was near-deafening. Whoever was firing seemed to be targeting the Jamshidabad prison complex. Sam bolted back into the apartment and closed the door. "What the hell's going on?" he asked, terror written all over his face. Before Bernard could open his mouth to reply, a bullet crashed in through the glass window, and lodged in the wall about two feet above their heads. Sam and Bernard dove for the floor, and remained prone on the ground. "What the fuck, I thought we had nothing to worry about. Why are they shooting at us?" complained Sam.

"I don't think they're shooting at us. I think we're caught in the cross-fire. I heard they were planning to attack the garrisons to get their friends out and to get hold of the arms," said Bernard.

"Now you tell me. What shall we do? We'll get killed."

Always the practical man who refused to panic, Bernard was in complete control. He was also well enough informed to know that nobody would target them for any reason. "Relax Sam. I'm sure they're not after our blood. There's nothing we can do but just ride it out. It's the occasional stray bullet that will come our way, and as long as we stay out of the way, we'll be all right." And as if in reply, a spray of machine gun fire hit their downstairs door that opened to the road. "The assholes can't shoot straight," screamed Sam, "I'm getting out of here." Sam was obviously losing it, thought Bernard, and spoke to him softly, "Listen Sam, if we try to go out of here, we really will be in the crossfire, and there's no telling what will happen. Let's just lie low and wait a while. It's going to be OK."

The gunfire and the sound of mortars and grenades exploding outside was deafening, but like Bernard had surmised, nobody was intentionally shooting into the apartment. They lay motionless on the floor, their bodies pressed to the ground.

The shooting and the explosions continued for over two hours. Suddenly Sam said, "I've got to pee."

"Crawl to the bathroom. Don't raise your head," warned Bernard.

And then, as suddenly as it had started, the shooting stopped. A deafening roar of human voices rent the air, and then the sound of people running, shouting and laughing. "Allahu Akbar. Drud Ba Khomeini. Allahu Akbar," the people screamed.

Sam and Bernard cautiously stood up, and venturing towards the window, peered out. Men, women and children were milling about in the distance. Laughter and shouting had taken over the sound of gunfire and explosions. "Let's go out and see what's going on," suggested Sam.

"Turn on the TV, Sam. I'm sure there will be some news. Something big has happened!"

Sure enough, the English anchor on NIRT was beaming as he announced that the Imperial forces had surrendered to the people. All garrisons and command posts were declared open to the public. All political prisoners were free to go home to their families.

Bernard's thoughts immediately went to Jordan. I hope she gets out, too, he thought silently. He believed that benevolent thoughts and good wishes could have a beneficial effect on those on behalf of whom they were made. "I need to go out to check on a friend," he said to Sam.

"We'd better wait until things calm down a bit," suggested Sam, and Bernard agreed. His heart told him he should check up on Jordan and see if he could help her in any way, but his head told him that they needed to be careful. It's true the Iranians had no grouse with them, but there didn't seem to be any kind of order in the streets below. It had great potential for anarchy. Still his conscience tugged at him. "Let's just go to the prison and see what's going on."

Sam agreed, so together they got to the road and hailed a taxi. They had hardly gone a mile from their house, when their taxi stopped on the middle of the road with a jolt. The driver, a ball of fat with a huge mustache, got out of the taxi and began rolling away as fast as he could. Sam and Bernard were nonplussed. Then they heard shots being fired from the left. A moment later, an answering barrage of shots was heard from the right. They were in a cross-fire again. "We're sitting ducks inside this taxi," yelled Bernard, "Let's get out and move towards the jube. Get on all fours. We'll have some cover once we get in the jube."

Sam nodded in agreement. They crept out of the taxi and started crawling towards the jube on their right. Shots were still being fired, but it did not look as if they were coming in their direction. They made it to the shallow drain and remained prostrate in the sandy floor. "Thank goodness it's dry," said Sam.

Suddenly three uniformed men on their right came out on the road with their weapons held above their heads. A shot rang out from the left, and the uniformed men screamed. "Nah, Agha." It was a scream of fear and surrender. Six young revolutionaries emerged from the left, relaxed, smiling, rifles and machine guns held above their heads. The leader of the group, a few grenades hanging from his belt, laughingly told the three soldiers, pointing to a youth who looked hardly a day older than twelve, "Sorry, sirs. Osman here is wet behind the ears. He pulled the trigger in the excitement of seeing you guys surrender. He meant no harm," and they all laughed, the three soldiers a trifle nervously. Soon they were all chatting and laughing as they walked down the road, arms draped over each other's shoulders as though nothing had happened.

Bernard and Sam decided to make a hasty retreat to their apartment. The Iranians may have no bone to pick with them, but there was no telling how many armed and nervous twelve year-old Osmans were prowling the streets.

And there were many.

Chapter 56

That whole day, Iranian TV was full of the story of the revolution. All of the terrible deeds of the Shah and his infamous SAVAK were broadcast over and over again. Khomeini's life story, from his early days of standing up to the Shah, up to his triumphant return to Iran was shown with commentary in tones of great reverence. The hopes and the expectations of the Iranian people, and the struggles they had had to go through these last years were explained in great deal.

Words of great admiration were spoken of the many who had died in the cause of the struggle. They would have their place in heaven, declared the speakers. Some of the parents and family members of those who had been taken by SAVAK were spoken of with admiration, tempered with sympathy. Their reward, too, would be in heaven.

Niavaran Palace, the Shah's official residence in Tehran, was thrown open to the public view. The camera panned the special attractions of the palace, lingering in the toilets, where the seats were made of 18 carat gold.

The dungeons, where SAVAK had made merry with hapless anti-Shah suspects received a great deal of attention of the TV crew and commentators. A variety of equipment used by SAVAK interrogators to torture their victims were displayed and described in all of its gory detail.

And suddenly the scene shifted to an undisclosed destination. The Revolutionary Council had decided to mete out swift justice to 'the Shah loyalists who had committed crimes against humanity.' The camera panned a group of about fifteen middle-aged and old Iranian men. They were all bearded, and were garbed in traditional Iranian dress. They looked very somber, very serious. One of them, the leader of the group, stood up and began to speak.

The camera then focused on the audience. On one side was the general public, made up of an enormous number of people, here to watch the proceedings. There were the young and the old, men and women, little children and teenagers, apparently invited by announcements broadcast on the rooftop radio network, as well as the national Iranian TV and Radio. Bernard and Sam had heard the call to the proceedings made as regularly as the call to prayer. Once they had watched it on TV. The announcer had solemnly declared: The Revolutionary Council has appointed a Judicial Council to hear cases against the Shah's officers who were responsible for the persecution of the Iranian people. Many young and old martyrs will be watching from heaven as their persecutors receive their punishment here on earth. The cases against these murderers will be heard at the main soccer stadium in Tehran, starting this evening at six o'clock in the evening, and continue until all of the perpetrators are brought to justice. Those found guilty of crimes against humanity will be summarily punished. The public is invited to watch the proceedings.

The public was present in large numbers. The look of gleeful anticipation in their faces was grotesque. Some of them looked very somber, while others looked puzzled. There were also some who looked amused, as if they were just waiting for the show to begin. They might have been waiting for a movie to start.

The camera panned another group of individuals, mostly middle –aged men and women, standing in a special enclosure. They all looked sad and drawn, and lost. The chief Justice stood up and addressed them: "Today you will see what you have been waiting to see for many years. You will see the terrible people who took away your sons and daughters over the last twenty years. Some of you have been waiting a long time for this day. I can promise you that today you will see justice served. You will see the execution of those who were responsible for the sad end of your children's innocent lives. Be proud and happy that the day has come for the celebration of your children's martyrdom."

When he sat down, the clerk for the court walked into the glare of light with a ledger. He called out a name. Two guards, fully armed, walked in holding a man on either side. The man was dressed in a white prison uniform. The clerk began to read what apparently were the charges against him. He called out two names. A man and a woman in the parents' enclosure stood up. The clerk asked them about the circumstances of the death of their son. They answered, the father, trying hard to hold back his emotions, and the mother sobbing, that their son had been taken away one day, and that they had never seen him again. "Do you see the man who took away your son here?" asked the clerk, and the parents pointed to the man standing between the guards. "Where is their son?" the clerk asked the prisoner. "I don't know," he replied. Two other witnesses were called, and they confirmed that the prisoner had tortured and killed the young man. The Chief Judge asked the accused if he had anything to say before sentence was passed. The man said nothing. He had a bitter, almost mocking smile on his face as he looked around at all of the judges. The Chief then asked the other judges if they had any objections to the sentence of death being passed on the prisoner. Nobody spoke or raised their hands. The chief Justice tapped the table with his gavel. The man was blindfolded and taken to a wooden post in the center of the field to which he was bound.

Six men in uniform took aim with their machine guns. At a signal from the commanding officer, they opened fire. The man slumped forward, still held to the post by the rope round his chest. Two others appeared from the dark background, cut the rope, and carried the dead man into the darkness. The total proceedings had not taken more than ten minutes.

Then they brought in another man, and the process was repeated. And then another. And another.

The first ten men who were executed were not known to Sam or Bernard. "It looks like they've got only the foot soldiers. Maybe the big fish managed to get away."

And as if in answer to their thoughts, the person to be brought in was Nematollah Nasiri, "the Butcher of Tehran." Both Sam and Bernard had heard a great many stories about the atrocities committed by Nasiri.

His name used to be a conversation stopper; people were frightened at the mere mention of his name. And here he was. Sam and Bernard watched mesmerized, as Nasiri was literally dragged in by four heavily built men. The man was babbling and shaking in terror, screaming for mercy, begging for forgiveness. The scene was surreal-nightmarish in its intensity. It seemed that even the judges were affected by the incredible change that seemed to have come over this man, who had mercilessly decided on the destinies of so many people who had come within his grasp. Here he was, crying like a little child.

The procession continued. Officers of the Army and the Air Force, the Police and the Imperial Guard, Former Ministers, Prime Ministers, they all met their nemesis before this hastily drawn up tribunal, whose only objective was to punish all those who had supported the Shah during his reign. "Khomeini seems to have learned a lot of important lessons in France," quipped Bernard.

"How so?"

"Have you forgotten your high school European history lessons, man? Remember Madame Guillotine and the French Revolution? I wonder if he saw some old French movies, courtesy of the French government archives," laughed Bernard.

"Oh yeah, these guys are not wasting any time. They are certainly taking a page out of the French Revolution. Luckily the Shah and his family flew away in their big blue bird, or they'd have suffered the same fate as Louis XVI and Marie A. These guys will soon have the land wiped clean of the Shah remnants," prophesied Sam, in a deep sepulchral tone.

Chapter 57

There was sudden pandemonium inside Jordan's cell block. Two bearded young men, teenagers, thought Jordan, in fatigues, barged in screaming, "Allahu Akbar. Drudh Ba Khomeini!" They carried machine guns, and had grenades hanging from belts round their waists. The excitement of victory and the cock-a-hoop vanity of newly acquired power seemed to radiate out of their eyes. They held their guns and other weapons almost arrogantly, looking for respect in the eyes of the inmates, thought Jordan. Jordan wondered if they knew what all those weapons could do. It seemed to her that they didn't. They hurriedly conferred with the security guard at the entrance to the block, obviously giving him some kind of instructions. They looked cheerful enough, but Jordan couldn't help a feeling of terror creeping up her spine as if a sharp cold steel point was moving up her back. Then as suddenly as they had come, they turned on their heels, and with a loud "Allahu Akbar," marched out of the block.

Jordan and the other prisoners stood with bated breath, not even daring to whisper, as the guard passed on the instructions to the female jailers. Mariam let out a whoop of sheer delight and came rolling down the corridor like a train out of control. "You're free," she shouted, tears of joy streaming down her face, "Fatameh, Jordaan, you're free. You can go home." And Fatameh interpreting for Jordan, held her in a tight embrace. "Khanume Jordan, you go America. No more Iran." And Jordan stood petrified, unable to digest Fatameh's words. In that minute, her world of fear and tension had turned on itself. She was free-to go back home, to her Mom, and the home she could understand and appreciate and wonder at compared to the hard and cold cell that she had known these past weeks. Her new-found freedom was euphoric, and she wanted to just sit down and let the feeling take complete hold of herself. She was drifting into a state of inertia and the events of the last few weeks seemed to have the soporific effect similar to a good drag of marijuana. "I want to sit down for a while," was all she could say to Fatameh.

Fatameh sprang into action. "No!" she cried, fear and urgency in her voice. Fatameh had heard the proclamation on TV that morning. It had clearly said that only political prisoners would be free to go home. The young commandos that had brought the order to the prison that morning had either forgotten, or not understood the difference between political prisoners and others held for criminal offences. That had to be why they had ordered the release of all the prisoners. Whatever the reason, there was no time to be lost. She and Jordan had to grab the opportunity while they could. She had also heardthat the pri son records were being destroyed even as they spoke, so there would be no record of the prisoners that were housed here. All they had to do was get out of the prison and they would be home-free. And then, another fear crossed her mind; a high voltage electric current seemed to pass through her as she remembered Nizreen. She might already be on her way to confront Jordan and taunt her with her evil. "No, we must go now. Nizreen will come." And Jordan was jolted into action, wide-awake to the sheer terror of the situation. "Yes, yes, let's get out of here," she replied, gripping Fatameh's arm.

Chapter 58

Prisoners streaming out of the prison gates, people looking for friends or relatives and onlookers thronged the streets. The uproar was deafening-"allahu akbar, Drud ba khomeini," "bismil il lahi" and other phrases in praise of Khomeini and god seemed to be jostling for dominance. A sudden scream of recognition as prisoners found their loved ones, greetings, laughter and weeping all mingled to create the cacophony. It was a time for jubilation, gratitude, and congratulation, kissing and hugging. For Jordan, it was a time of great confusion as she tried to get her bearings. She was thankful that Fatameh was right behind her; they had agreed that once outside the prison walls, they would not talk to each other or even walk side by side. If Nizreen was looking for her, as they were sure she would be, the two of them together would be a dead give away. Jordan was draped from head to toe in the heavy black chador Fatameh had given her. She was glad that she was not very tall compared to some American women, and could pass off as an average, middle-aged Iranian woman in the heavy chador that Fatameh had chosen for her for that very reason. They all knew that Nizreen would be watching somewhere, waiting to pounce on them.

They had planned exactly what they were going to do. Jordan would go directly to the US embassy. "Get to the embassy as fast as you can," Fatameh had said, "I will be right behind you to deal with Nizreen if it becomes necessary."

Goodbyes had been said before they left the cell. "Come with me Fatameh. I will talk to the embassy officials, and you can go with me to New York and start a new life there."

"No Khanume Jordan," she had replied sadly, but resolutely. I must sell my house and get the money. My father gave me that house when we got married. I will join you after that."

And Jordan knew she was a woman with a cause. She had suffered enough at the hands of her husband, and she would claim what was her birthright. She had a right to it. She deserved it. So Jordan didn't argue. "I hope everything works out for you, Fatameh, and I hope to see you in the US. I will make everything ready for you. You will always have a special place in my heart."

Fatameh had made Jordan practise holding on to the chador so as to cover her blonde hair completely, for that would be a dead giveaway in the sea of black haired women. "Hold tight. Pull down. Use left hand. Keep right hand free."

Jordan hugged Fatameh and held her close for a long time. From the day they met, they were fused in an unspeakable bond-a palpable fusion of two helpless women who had gone together through the corridors of hell as countless women had done before, and countless others would do again. They had nourished each other with the strength and comfort that only a woman could give another, without expectation of reward, all benign, generous and unsolicited, from the very depths of the feminine. And now they had to part, but with some hope of liberation, which they could not yet exult in, for there was still a long way to go. Standing together, they gave each other strength, courage and infinite benison. "Must go, Jordan." It was the first time Fatameh had addressed her without the respectful title "Khanum."

And ever so gently she disengaged herself from Jordan's embrace. It was a moment when they felt as equals, equals in suffering, hope and love.

They left as unobtrusively as they could, Fatameh a few yards behind Jordan, both trying to analyze the multitude in front of them, like prey keeping watch for the predator, the hunted for the hunter. Bodies jostling in the milieu, distracted by voices of emotion communicating with God and friends, Jordan and Fatameh were slowly but surely getting close to their goal-Shemiran street, where Jordan could get a taxi to Takt-e-Jamshid where the US embassy was located.

Chapter 59

Nizreen had woken up early as was her custom. She had dressed up, eaten breakfast, and was spraying herself from head to toe with the Arabian perfume that Khaled had bought her at the bazaar. She was humming a Lebanese song and smiling as she thought of Khaled. There second fling had been good, much better than the first. The sex had been great, and Khaled had been so very attentive to her every need and fancy. He had spared no expense in buying her jewelry and perfumes, shoes, clothes and all kinds of fashion accessories. He must love me terribly, she thought. She, too, had gone the extra inch to please him she thought, thinking dirty as was her custom when a man was not around. He had left so suddenly saying that he was urgently needed in Qum. He'll be back as soon as he has attended to whatever he has to, she said to herself. It never occurred to her to pry. It was his male prerogative to do what he considered important without being questioned by her-even if she was his soul mate. It was the Iranian way.

In the meantime, she had invited another one of her Iranian admirers to share her charms. After a long night of passionate sex, Karim was still asleep in her bed.

The sudden interruption to the regular program on TV brought her to attention. The news came across that the security forces had capitulated. The garrison's were open to the public. And the next bit of news grabbed her undivided attention. "All political prisoners are being set free today. They can go home and join their families with the blessings of Allah, and the gratitude of the supreme ruler of Iran, Imam Khomeini." What if Jordan also got out by chance? And her husband murdering Iranian bitch, she thought venom spewing out of every pore. I must check, she said to herself.

She grabbed the telephone, and feverishly dialed the prison telephone number. The deep hum of the engaged tone grated on her ears. She cut the line and tried again. Again the dial tone droned unconcerned, disinterested in her urgency. Again, and again she tried. She had to get through to her friend, the Chief Jailer, and ask him to make sure that Jordan and Fatameh were not released, for they were not political prisoners but criminals. But the telephone would not oblige.

Nisreen ran into her room and shook Karim awake, and feverishly explained the situation to him.

"Get dressed. We must leave now." And Karim put on his pants and his T-shirt, and laced up his sneakers. There was no time to wash.

Trembling in Frustration and rage she locked her door and stepped out onto the street, Karim trailing behind her. She hailed the first taxi and barked in the driver's face as he slowed down, "Jamshidabad." The driver was unimpressed, for he had a fare that was not going anywhere near Jamshdabad. He turned up his nose by way of denial.

Nisreen jumped right in the path of the next taxi, gesticulating wildly. The taxi was empty, which meant she could ask the driver to take her where she wanted to go. "Jamshidabad," she screamed in joy and anticipation. "Please hurry," she implored in her best cultivated tone of appeal. They both got in.

Chapter 60

Jordan and Fatameh were just about a hundred yards from Shemiran Avenue, their point of liberation. Once they got there, Jordan could slip into a taxi, and merge into the traffic moving south towards Tkht-e-Jamshid Street and the U.S. Embassy.

Suddenly Jordan felt a slight tug at her elbow. "Nisreen," whispered Fatameh "In front, daste chaap" (On your left) Peering cautiously to the left, Jordan saw Nizreen, and a young Iranian man, both scouting the faces of the people passing them by.

Jordan felt rather than saw Fatameh quickly move in front of Jordan. She began walking at a brisk pace toward Nizreen's companion. The man was on her left. Fatameh turned her face to the right as if she were looking for someone herself. She turned her head away and walked right into Nizreen's friend, holding her chador firmly under her chin so it would not slip off her head and reveal her face. The man was taken completely by surprise, and bumped into Fatameh losing his balance in the process. Fatameh collapsed in front of the man, who fell right on top of her in a heap. "Bebakshid agha," she said supplicatingly, playing the role of the docile Iranian village woman; Nizreen, annoyance written all over her face, pulled Karim to his feet, cursing him. "Why don't you look where you're going?" she screamed at Karim. Then she bent towards Fatameh, distractedly apologizing, trying to help Fatameh get on her feet again. "Bad neest, Kheili mamnoon."(No problem. Thank you very much.) murmured Fatameh, standing up on her own, making sure her chador was in place, and turned in the opposite direction, walking away from Nisreen.

The few seconds of confusion were all that Jordan needed to slip past her hunters. She could almost hear the pounding of her heartbeat. Sweat dripped off her face into her hand holding the chador in place. She dare not run for fear of attracting attention. She was hardly fifty yards away from the intersection. Jordan took a deep breath. Not much of a prayer person, she didn't know how to ask god for help! She thought of her Mom, imagining she was there behind her. She almost tripped on the chador. Take it easy, girl, she heard her Mom whispering to her. She so wanted to look behind her, to see where Nizreen was. She might be right behind her ready to pounce on her. Her legs suddenly felt cold, and she thought she would collapse. Again she seemed to hear her Mom say, just a few more yards, darling, and before she knew it she was on the sidewalk of Shemiran Street. Now she risked a look behind her. Nizreen and her companion were nowhere to be seen. Jordan felt a new strength, a new courage, pick her up. She was free of her pursuers.

The first person she thought of was Fatameh. Thank you dear Fatameh, she said to herself as she eased herself into the back seat of the 'orange crush' that stopped beside her; "Takht-e-Jamshid" she said as demurely as she could in order to hide her American accent. The taxi sped away, the driver chanting "Allahu akbar," waving to the crowds of people on the sidewalk.

"Daste chap or daste rasht,?" –to the left or right, and Jordan signaled to the driver that she wished to get off. She didn't wish to leave a trail by asking to be dropped off at the embassy gates. She'd rather trek the distance. Paying the taxi driver with the money Fatameh had given her-she thinks of everything thought Jordan gratefully- Jordan started walking westward. To the west was the University of Tehran, where she had taxied to every morning. She glanced around furtively- it's funny, she thought, I feel like a criminal even though I've committed no crime. Dostoevsky's classic guilt figure, Raskolinikov came to her consciousness. She had nothing to be guilty about-maybe guilt by association, she thought.

Chapter 61

And then, at this moment of relief, and release, a great sadness came upon her as her mind went back to Ahmad. He had driven her to work a few times, down this very street. How happy they had been, often after a night of good food and wine, satiated with lovemaking, they had been in transports of joy as Ahmad drove through the ever present snarl of morning traffic, laughing and making Jordan laugh with his limitless joy and enthusiasm for life, and now here she was creeping furtively away from it all as if it had never existed. A cry of frustration, and defeat escaped her lips.

She passed the International Bank of Iran and Japan, and the headquarters of NIOC, the National Iranian Oil Company. And the very modern looking glass-walled Iranians' bank, black and tall, like a sentinel announcing the approach to her haven, the U.S. embassy.

"On Takt-e- Jamshid, you can buy the most fascinating variety of items ranging from diamonds and emeralds to carpenters' tools," she recalled Ahmad's words. They had come down there one day and Ahmad had bought her a little diamond and emerald bracelet to celebrate their visit to the basement of Bank Markazi, the Central Bank, where the Iranian crown jewels were displayed. Ahmad had told her, "You must see the crown jewels."

Jordan had felt like a poor little girl in an enormous toyshop, where the toys were placed way out of her reach.

Displayed elegantly in 37 beautiful cases were jewels and jewelry of the most unimaginable beauty, variety and opulence, designed and preserved over a period of five centuries, by some of the best jewelers in the world. She had read with fascination from the little brochure Ahmad had bought for her:

Case No. 34

The jeweled Pahlavi Crown was made in 1925 from specially selected gems of the treasury. The number of precious stones set in the crown and their weights are as follows:

3380 diamonds weighing 1144 carats, 5 emeralds weighing 199 carats, 2sapphires weighing 19 carats, and 368 pearls. It was designed by the famed Serajjedin for the coronation of the founder of thePahlavi dynasty, Reza Shah the Great. H. I. M. Mohammed Reza Shah Pahlavi Aryamehr wore this crown for his coronation on 26th October, 1967.

1. The famous Darya-i-Nur or sea of light diamond is the world's largest pink diamond, and takes first place among Iran's crown jewels. Its name is associated with another famous diamond, the Koohi-I-noor or mountain of light. They are said to have been in the possession of the first Mogul Emperor of India from whom they passed on to Mohammed Shah who was defeated by Nadir Shah

in the 18th century. On Nadir Shah's death, the kooh-I-noor was taken to Afghanistan, and found its way into the possession of the East India Company which presented it to Queen Victoria. The Kooh-I-Noor was recut and set in the crown which was designed for the coronation of Queen Elizabeth, the Queen Mother in 1937. The Darya-I-Noor, however, remained in Iran, and after Nadir Shah's demise, it passed down the line, until it came to the hands of Khan Qajar, the founder of the Qajar dynasty, and rested in the treasury of the Qajar's until the beginning of the Pahlavi dynasty, when it became part of the Iranian Crown jewels.

It is a table diamond, pale pink in color, an inch and a half long, one inch wide, and three eighths of an inch thick and weighs 182 carats. It has a frame surrounded by the lion and the sun set with 457 small diamonds and four rubies.

The Darya-i-Nur is the major portion of the "Great Table" diamond seen by Tavernier in 1642. The other portion is a 60 carat oval brilliant set in the middle of the diamond diadem reserved for the use of Empress Farah.

Case No. 26

Jewels assigned for the use of the royal family This case contained an enormous variety of jewels set aside for the use of HIH Empress Farah, the Queen Mother, Princess Shahnaz, Princess Shams, Princess Ahraff and Princess Fatameh. The enormous emeralds and diamonds, exquisite pearls and spinels took Jordan's breath away. The ones that impressed her most were Empress Farah's crown and one of her many tiaras. The crown, made in

1967 by Van Cleef et Arpels was set with 36 emeralds, 34 rubies, 2 spinels, 105 pearls and 1469 diamonds. The total weight of the crown was 1408.9 grammes-about 3 and a half pounds, mused Jordan. "She must have strong neck muscles," she said to herself.

The tiara, which Jordan thought was really exquisite, was set with 7 emeralds as big as giant marbles, and 264 diamonds was made in 1958, also by Van Cleef.

"Can you get that one for me?" Jordan joked, and Ahmad had grinned ruefully.

A week after their trip to see the crown jewels, Ahmad had called her one after noon. "Hey, let's go for a drive," he had said. Jordan was thrilled, as always, to go for a drive. They had often driven to the foot of Damavand Mountain, tall and majestic, topped with winter ice. It was their own special spot of solace and tranquility. They would sit on a thick carpet which Ahmad always brought and spread on a patch of grass by a little stream of water that trickled from the melting ice of the mountain. Birdsong and a gentle, cool breeze suggested a little corner of heaven. A bottle of the best champagne nestling in an ice-bucket took them to the age of Khayyam. 'A loaf of bread, a flask of wine and thou' Ahmad had quoted once.

As they drove, Jordan suddenly realized they had turned right, going downtown. "Where are we going," asked Jordan, already thinking of their little spot near the mountain.

"It's a surprise," he had said, smiling like the sphinx.

They parked by a lrage jewelry store, and Ahmad ran round the car to open the door for Jordan. "Befarmoidh,

Princess," he invited Jordan, beckoning her to the enormous ornate jewelry store doors.

The Manager of the store was obviously awaiting their arrival, as he came out of his little office and walked towards them. "Welcome, Aghaye Ahmad. Welcome Khanum," he invited them, as he escorted them to his office.

They were soon sitting down, and sipping fruit juice served by a pretty Iranian sales associate.

They made small talk for a few minutes, and then Ahmad asked the Manager, "Is it ready?"

"Yes, Agha. It's all ready," he beamed. And Jordan looked and felt a little nonplussed, and looking at Ahmad she saw the look of pleased anticipation in his eyes, as he waited for whatever was ready to be revealed. A moment later, a middle-aged Iranian with a thick mustache wearing the thickest bifocals Jordan had seen, walked in through a little door holding a jewelry box in his hands. He bowed to everybody in the room, and handed the box to the Manager, who opened it, examined it for a moment, and nodding approval, gave it to Ahmad. Ahmad immediately shut the case, without looking at it, and somewhat ceremoniously, presented it to Jordan. "It's a little surprise for you darling," he said almost shyly. "I hope you like it. But if you don't like it, Agha Shiraz will design it the way you like." And the man who had carried in the box, looking embarrassedly at Jordan, mumbled, "Yes, Madam. Just tell us if you want it changed, and we'll do it for you."

And Jordan, pretty embarrassed herself, opened the box. "Oh, Ahmad," was all she could say as she gazed at the magnificent creation lying in the box.

The most gorgeous bracelet Jordan had ever seen lay on the blue velvet lining of the jewelry box. Seven exquisitely faceted emeralds, each the size of a lima bean, were embedded in little rustic looking silver nuggets, hinged together in the most ingeniously inconspicuous manner to make an enormous working piece of jewelry. The nuggets were so designed that that the mint green light of the emeralds bounced off the silver and the strategically placed diamonds surrounding the emeralds. The entire ensemble reminded Jordan of the green waves of the Caspian Sea bouncing off the rocks in a spectacular area of the beach Jordan and Ahmad had visited in the summer. When Ahmad lifted it out of the box and placed it against Jordan's wrist, she could almost smell the sea and feel the warm breeze on her cheek. "It's so beautiful, Ahmad," she whispered as if saying it aloud would break the spell of this fairy tale moment. "I'm so glad you like it, darling," said Ahmad, and turning to the designer, said, "Shiraz is one of the best jewelry designers in Iran today. He is an old friend of my father's, and has designed most of the jewelry my father gave my mother. Since I couldn't give you Farah's tiara, I thought the next best thing would be to have this designed by Shiraz."

"Thank you so much, darling for being so thoughtful," she had said, and so generous, she now thought, for the bracelet would have cost at least twenty five thousand dollars.

Ahmad turned to Shiraz, standing shyly away from them, "Congratulations, Shiraz on a superlative creation. And thank you for making my future wife so happy."

Jordan swallowed the lump in her throat, and dabbed at her eyes, the memory overwhelming her.

And Jordan's reverie was broken for she had arrived at the gates of the United States Embassy.

Chapter 62

The African-American commando, all spit and polish and neat uniform standing quietly a few yards away from the gate looked incongruous against the motley crowd walking about on the street, chanting and screaming, and Jordan felt she had reached the pearly gates themselves. Jordan released her chador a crack to let him see her blonde hair, and he hurried to the gate and let her in. The moment she entered, she tripped on her chador which she had almost let fall around her feet, and the commando, hastening to support her asked, "Are you all right, Ma'am?"

And Jordan replied with all the bravado she could muster, "Never felt better," as she swooned to the ground.

Chapter 63

After a preliminary meeting with the front desk staff, Jordan and two others who had been unable to leave before revolution day walked around the embassy grounds. Another commando, assigned for the purpose, accompanied them and explained the layout. "The brick building over here is the chancery. The grey building on the right is the Ambassador's residence, while the one slightly behind it is the residence of the deputy chief of mission," he explained.

"What are those smaller buildings all in a bunch?" asked Jordan.

"Well, they are little bungalows for what we call transients and official visitors. You guys will be staying in one of them."

"The swimming pools look great; it's a pity we will not be able to swim in this cold weather."

"No, but you can enjoy a game of tennis if you like," suggested the commando.

Tennis and swimming were the last things on Jordan's mind. All she wanted was to get on a plane and get back home, but she said nothing. She hadn't disclosed the nature of her ordeal to anyone. Only Johnson knew the circumstances of her presence, and he had advised her not to talk about it. Jordan was certainly not going to do so.

Around six o'clock they walked into the restaurant which was adjacent to the enormous commissary. The wholesome goodness of American food was overwhelming after many months of Iranian prison food. She tried not to look too greedy as she wolfed down the meal with gusto.

Lying in a comfortable chair, she fell asleep almost immediately, but the most eerie of nightmares assailed her, and she awoke in a sweat. Nizreen and two burly Iranian men were pursuing her with a thick rope while Fatameh was behind her, screaming encouragement. "Run, Jordan, run faster!" but Jordan was unable to move. She awoke in a sweaty panic, and then realization dawned on her. She was safe. Thank you, dear Fatameh for your courage and support. Remembrance of her dear devoted friend gave her the strength and comfort to get back to sleep. "God bless you, Fatameh," she whispered into her pillow, "be safe, dear friend."

The next morning, Jordan called her Mom from the embassy. "I'll be home within a week," she announced, and after she had told her mother as many of the details she could think of, she felt she was back in her mother's living room.

All of the 'residue' at the embassy, the term a staff member coined in levity for all those who had not been able to get away on time were assembled in the chancery, and one of the senior staff members addressed them. "No one should leave the embassy grounds under any circumstances. If there is anything you need, please give me a list, and one of our Iranian staff will get them for you."

Jordan told him in private about all her personal effects which were still in her apartment.

Jordan had instructed her landlady, who had visited her a couple of times in prison, about all that she wanted to take back with her if and when she got out. The landlady had promised to pack them in suitcases and put them away in a safe place. Jordan called Bernard, who with Muzaffer, had gone to the apartment and met the landlady. True to her word, the landlady had packed everything in two large suitcases, which she had handed over to Bernard. There was also a little leather briefcase. "This contains her jewelry and important documents that I found in her desk drawer-passport, work permit and some photographs and check book," she explained, conspiratorially. "I talked to Dr. Firooznia, and he paid me the rent out of her salary. He told me that all of her dues have already been transferred to her account in the US."

Chapter 64

When Bernard and Muzaffer went to see Jordan at the embassy, they could hardly recognize her. The time she had spent in prison had exacted a heavy toll on her, but one day of freedom and the feeling of liberation had done wonders. She looked exuberant, and sounded very cheerful.

"You're looking great," said Bernard, and Muzaffer agreed. "Thank you guys; and thank you so much for being there for me, Bernard. You've both been such good friends, and I will never forget you."

"Won't you come back when things get better," asked Muzaffer.

"You think things will get better? I don't really think so. Too much has happened, and it's not easy to forget so much sadness."

"Is Fatameh going with you," asked Bernard, who knew of Jordan's plans to get her to the US.

"No, but I've already started working on it. I talked to the Deputy Head of Mission, and he said there is a good chance of getting her there. In fact he promised to do everything he could when I told him about her situation."

"That would be great, She's a very nice person, and this is no place for her, especially now with the Islamic government that everybody's talking about."

"Do you think it will come to pass?"

"That's certain. These guys are crazy. They don't know what they are wishing for. The Shah and his father took the country forward by a hundred years even though they made some foolish mistakes. Hukkumat-e-Islami will take it back a thousand," said Muzaffer, himself a devout Moslem. "I've seen it in many countries in the Middle East. In Saudi Arabia, the kings keep the people under absolute servitude. They are absolute dictators who cannot survive without Islamic government."

"Poor Faride and others were so hopeful of the Shah continuing in power. I wonder what will happen to them."

"Oh they will eventually get out of Iran. Everyone who has some means will leave the country."

"What I can't understand is why some women were against the laws passed by the Shah which were actually favorable to women. The 1967 Family Protection Bill allowed women, under certain circumstances, to sue for divorce or refuse her husband a second wife. It banned the traditional practice of temporary marriage, and upped the legal age for marriage for girls.'

"Yes, but all this was twisted by his enemies to look anything but favorable to women. It was made to appear as if it was the Shah's proclivity to ape the west. Moreover, women, who were for the most part denied education, believed that the old laws were actually meant to protect them from injustice. They didn't realize that the laws were made by men, for men, in a completely male-dominant society.

After they had left, Jordan went back to her apartment and went through the contents of her briefcase. The emerald necklace which Ahmad had given her was in the jewel case, and the green gems looked for a moment like Nizreen's wicked, envious eyes. Jordan shuddered as she slid the bracelet into the case and shut the briefcase.

The American Embassy was a hive of activity. None of the staff could be contacted and Jordan and her new friends had to be content with the tidbits that fell from the mouths of the commandos and lesser mortals in the embassies hierarchy. They did meet one of the attaches who assured them that they would be able to fly home as soon as things were arranged without ruffling anyone's feathers. There was a revolutionary government in place, after all. And the US embassy had to tread softly.

Chapter 65

Three days had passed since Jordan entered the safe haven of the US embassy, three days that had given her the opportunity to reflect on the events of the last year. The more she thought about them, the more she realized the futility of even trying to comprehend them. Meeting Ahmad had been the most wonderful thing that ever happened to her, and she looked at the days she had spent with him as the happiest in her life. The two of them had come from two completely different and seemingly incompatible worlds and yet their relationship had seemed such a natural-almost symbiotic-relationship. Their lives had collided in a glorious cascade of light and warmth, and they had shared the same magnificent orbit for the briefest possible time, but other forces and gravitational pulls had worked against the path they were seeking and drawn them irrevocably apart. She did not want to dwell in the past, to lament her situation or even the death of Ahmad. He had died doing what he wanted to do even though he was confused at times whether he had made the right choice. But having chosen a path, he had never veered away from it, and his death was the supreme sacrifice. His infinite loyalty wouldn't have wanted it any different, she thought.

Her thoughts came back to herself-where did she stand now? What should she do? Of course, she would return home to the safety and protection of things, people and places she knew and understood better, but part of her would remain in Tehran, with the beauty and the grandeur she had first flown into. At the time she had been unaware of everything that lay beneath, all of the terrible things that had taken place-the clash of wills and destinies of men and ideologies, and the awful consequences that inevitably followed. What she had experienced would always be with her and would always color the way she lived, thought and did things in the future, yet she was determined to choose the positive and bury the dark and the unpleasant. If there was one thing she had learned from Ahmad, it was that life should be lived to the fullest, in the moment, without regret for the past or doubt about the future. The joy of having known him would give her the strength and fortitude to carry on.

Ahmad's mother and siblings were planning to settle in the USA, and once she went back she would resume contacts with them. Unlike Nizreen, they believed in her innocence, and for Ahmad's sake she would do everything she could to assist them in every way she could. And Fatameh. She had already spoken to one of the undersecretaries, who had assured her that Fatameh would have no problems getting a refugee visa to get to the US.

Jordan called Fatameh at her home and gave her the good news.

"I am with my parents now. I told them that I want to go to the US, and they are happy. I am going to sell my house soon," she reported elatedly.

In the heat of the phenomenal events that had taken place in the country, nobody cared to ask about her husband. Everybody was rejoicing in their liberation, Fatameh told Jordan. "I will come to the embassy as soon as I can to start working on my visa," she promised.

"I will not be here when you come because the embassy is trying to send us back as soon as they can make travel arrangements for us. When you come to the embassy, please ask for Mr. Johnson. He will help you." Jordan promised.

Traveling out of the country was taking more time than Jordan, or the embassy thought. Mehrabad airport had shut down, apparently on the orders of the Revolutionary Council which was concerned that foreign elements, led by the US, would attempt an invasion to topple Khomeini, who had hardly had the time to acclimatize himself to his newly acquired power. Many in Iran expected him to withdraw to his enclave in Qom, and leave the politics to those who knew something about it. But not so Khomeini. He was setting himself up as the supreme ruler of the country. He would have it no other way.

Chapter 66

The Mujaheddin and the Fedayeen, both leftist elements, and Tudeh, the most leftist of all were hoping for a piece of the pie, but Khomeini had no intention of sharing anything. When Shapour Bakhtiar had attempted to start a dialog, Khomeini curtly replied, "First resign. Then we will talk."

Fortunately for the prime minister, he knew when to accept the inevitable; he knew that his very life now hung in the balance, so he secretly left the country and sought refuge in France.

In the meantime, both the Mujaheddin and Fedayeen were doing their best to rub western noses in the ground. The British embassy had been attacked and set on fire. Some kind of punitive action against the Americans, whom they saw as the root of all their problems was imminent. The French, who had given refuge to Khomeini was the favored western power, and the Revolutionary Council was negotiating with them on how to restore nomalcy in relations between Iran and the west. Neither Khomeini, nor the Revolutionary Council, which had suddenly and unexpectedly been thrust into greatness had the diplomatic finesse to carry on any meaningful discussion.

Khomeini's Revolutionary Council was attending to what they considered their first, most important duty. Just like the leaders of the French revolution had engineered the methodical slaughter of all those they thought were 'enemies of the revolution,' so, too the Revolutionary Council, in their infinite wisdom, decided to summarily deal with their enemies. Kangaroo courts were immediately set up, and hundreds of the Shah loyalists who had not been able, or did not choose to leave the country were rounded up. Former Prime Minister, Hoveyda, during whose stewardship the army had opened fire on a group of protesters, was among the first to be hauled before the Islamic court. The trial lasted not more than thirty minutes, and he was found guilty of crimes against humanity, the penalty for which was execution by firing squad. Revolutionary guards with their faces covered, marched him to a marked spot against a blank wall, and shot him. The portly, French educated hexagenarian took it very calmly, a thin smile on his face as he stood up to his executioners.

"I thought he had left the country," said an embassy employee who, with Jordan and a few others of the 'residue' had been watching the macabre proceedings, broadcast live on National Iranian Television. Before the broadcast began, the anchor had apologized to the nation: "We are unable to bring you this program in color since we are having some technical difficulties." And Jordan thought Nizreen would certainly miss the gory details in living color.

As the high-ranking officers of the army, the police, former ministers, prime ministers, all walked the terrible walk of death, Jordan, who had declined to watch after she had seen the first execution could not help wondering if Ahmad, too, would have suffered the same fate if he had survived. The thought made her tremble.

The executions continued for over a week; the gruesome tally was close to a thousand.

On the day of the revolution, the armories throughout the country had been opened up, and the people walked in and picked up whatever weapon took their fancy. Boys as young as twelve were touting pistols and rifles. The Fedayeen and the Mojaheddin were armed to their teeth and strutted around like ponies at a horse show. Stories abounded of people shooting others by accident. In one case, a teenager had pointed a gun at a group of his friends and ordered them to put their hands up. When the friends refused to obey, he had laughingly pulled the trigger, and the burst of fire from the machine gun mowed down the friends and some others standing by. "I guess they all died laughing," commented Muzzafer wrily, when he heard the story, which was not by any means an isolated incident. "The monkeys are playing with the razor," observed Bernard, remembering a folk tale from Sri Lanka.

Bernard and Muzaffer were walking down Jamshidabad avenue, when a peculiar odor assailed them. It didn't take long for Bernard to identify the aroma. "I smell whiskey," he said, confusion written all over his face. It was the smell of liquor, for when they reached Hotel Intercontinental, they beheld a most uncommon sight: a row of men and boys were carrying cases of liquor from the hotel's cellar and smashing them against the rocks and stones in the drains. The wine, the whiskey and brandy flowed down the wadis making the air heavy with the strong fumes of the alcohol. Two young Phillipino housemaids were standing by, eyeing the bottles that had escaped the demolition squad. Seeing the women's interest in the bottles, one of the men asked,

"You want?" and the women stepped forward smiling, and picked up a few bottles and wrapped them in a shawl they carried.

"Give telephone number, I bring you more." He offered with a sly wink, and the women complied, laughing coquettishly. Romance was in the air!

"What a waste," cried Bernard, and the young man heard him. "You want?"

"No, no Agha," cried Muzaffer, horrified.

"Speak for yourself," said Bernard, walking towards the young man, who gave him two bottles of Hennessey brandy. "Give me telephone number. I bring more," he said under his breath, and Bernard hastily scrawled his phone number on a scrap of paper, which he gave the young man.

"I come tonight. Give money," he said.

Around ten that night, Bernard answered the phone and gave the address of his house to the man, who arrived an hour later with a case of Chivas Regal Scotch. "How much?" asked Bernard.

"How much you give?"

Bernard pressed two thousand rials, the equivalent of thirty dollars into the amateur liquor vendor's hand, and the man smiled in satisfaction. "My name Vahid. Call me if need more."

Thank goodness for private enterprise, thought Bernard, who knew it would be impossible to get a drink anywhere else in town after that day's happenings.

Chapter 67

Back at the US embassy, rumor was rife among the civilian 'residue' housed there. They could get nothing official about American plans for the immediate future except a promise that they would soon be sent home. Jordan, more than any other, felt the urgency to be on her way, for she knew that anything could happen. Ahmad's mother had been to see her in prison, and assured Jordan that she was convinced of Jordan's innocence.

"After Ahmad's death, it is very difficult for me to continue to live here. I am afraid for myself and my other children. I want to go to the US, or any other place far away from here."

Jordan took the old lady's hands in hers, and tried to comfort her. "I know how you feel, and I think that's the best thing to do. I will do everything I can to help you when you get there."

"I have already handed in our passports to the embassy, and am sure it will work out soon. We will meet in New York, Jordan."

"Of course, we will. We will visit the Empire State building together," she said to Ahmad's kid sister, tussling her hair."

"I'm so glad you got away. My sister, Nisreen is crazy. She has now officially joined the Ayatollah's party." And Jordan shivered, for she had seen Nizreen's determination to make Jordan suffer for something she knew Jordan hadn't done. She had also seen on TV what the Ayatollah's party had done to the Shah loyalists. Jordan shivered and the apprehension showed on her face; and this time it was Mrs Khosravi's turn to comfort Jordan. "You're safe now. She can't do anything to you." And Jordan tried to find comfort in her words, but she felt a cold sweat of terror all over her body.

During the past months of crisis, the US had not intervened on behalf of the Shah. Most loyalists felt that the US had very badly let down her friend and ally, and could not fathom the reason behind US thinking. Maybe the US thought that the defeat of the Shah was inevitable, and non-intervention would guarantee her some opportunities for dialog with the new government.

Khomeini, in the meantime, was trying to bring a semblance of order to the country. Confusion reigned everywhere. There were still little pockets of resistance from unyielding Shah loyalists, mainly the rank and file. Sporadic gunfights on the streets had been reported in downtown Tehran. The Fedayeen and the Mojaheddin had carved up Tehran between themselves, and were patrolling the streets, now almost completely deserted, except for the food shoppers, and those looking to buy kerosene for their homes.

And then Khomeini spoke to the nation. He congratulated the people on their victory against cruelty, injustice and oppression. "God has helped you get rid of a despot who sought the destruction of your culture and your religion. He has liberated you from Reza, the puppet and lackey of the west. You can now live in peace, and most importantly in the Islamic way, under Shariar law." And the firecrackers went off again, forcing the few stray dogs on the streets to look for cover.

He then called upon the people to join him in putting the country back on track. "We have to start working hard to make the Islamic Republic of Iran economically strong. We will weed out the saboteurs and the lackeys of the west. You must all work hard for the progress of your country."

Some people who listened wondered how much progress would be forthcoming. Would it be from the frying pan into the fire?

As events showed, the 'weeding out' part continued unabated. Men were arrested by squads of masked Fedayeen, and summarily shot. The revenge and the bloodletting had just started. Khomeini's call "to make the streets red with blood" had only just begun.

Then, in the morning of February 14th, Khomeini announced that the firearms in the hands of the population should be immediately returned to the closest mosque, for he realized that the Fedayeen and the Mojaheddin would soon be a thorn in his side. "All weapons should be returned immediately. Your new government will employ soldiers of the Islamic Republic, and only they will bear arms."

"The Mojaheddin, the Fedayeen and even certain belligerent members of Tudeh pooh poohed Khomeini's words and concealed their weapons from the Revolutionary Guards, who suddenly raided the houses and meeting places of those they suspected of belonging to those organizations, and the criminal elements downtown. But an enormous portion of the Shah's armory was unaccounted for, yet no one would tell, for each group had its own ways of ensuring the loyalty and silence of its membership.

The Fedayeen, at this time, was seeking ways of showing the west, especially the US, what was what. A majority of its membership consisted of college students who had been sufficiently indoctrinated into believing that until the US stopped interfering in Iran's affairs, no progress was possible. "They must be taught a lesson they will not forget," one of its vociferous leaders was exhorting a group of about two hundred students, who were all ears to the speaker. Fired with the enthusiasm of their new found power and emboldened by the kalishnikovs and the grenades they carried, they decided to storm the US embassy and take the entire staff hostage until they could get a 'Hands off Iran' assurance from the US Congress.

Chapter 68

Jordan and her friends were by the tennis courts, having an impromptu get together with some members of the embassy staff. Some of them were playing a game of tennis, if you could call it that for it was clear that they had never played the game before. "Here's a Jimmy Connors serve," said a man and hit the ball clear over the trees in the vicinity.

Jordan's new acquaintance, Katy, said, "And here's a Chris Evert return," as she tried to hit but completely missed the ball.

Jordan, watching her fellow citizens' histrionics amusedly, suddenly realized that something was wrong. Hearing a sudden commotion at the embassy gates she yelled to the others, "Listen. Something's happening," as loud voices in Farsi and Irano-English came clearly to their ears. The voices were hostile, belligerent, commanding. The tennis players dropped their rackets and their jaws fell open when a commando came rushing from the direction of the main gate shouting, "Get inside. The embassy is under attack."

Jordan and her roommate ran into their apartment and locked themselves in.

About fifty students, most of them in their early twenties had entered the embassy premises, which they had entered through the main gate. They all carried American or Soviet built automatic and semi-automatic weapons, but they were all smiling in the most relaxed and affable manner. The leader, tall and broad shouldered, and blessed with Iranian good looks had, like all the rest in the group, a band of white cloth tied around his head, covering his forehead; an automatic weapon was slung over his right shoulder. Speaking in perfect English, with a flawless American accent, he addressed the commandos and other embassy officials. "Gentlemen, we are here to see the Ambassador. We mean no harm, but we insist on seeing the ambassador immediately."

The assistant secretary for internal security, an enormous man of forty some stepped forward offering his hand, "I am Wilson, Assistant Secretary for internal security. You are Mr..?"

"Ali."

OK, Mr Ali. First, do you have an appointment with the Ambassador?

"No, but we must see him. Like I said before we mean nobody any harm." And Ali's tone certainly seemed to promise a lot of trouble unless they were taken to see the ambassador.

That's when Wilson saw a larger number of similarly dressed young men dropping off the embassy walls, which they apparently had scaled from Takht-e-Jamshid Avenue.

"Let me see if His Excellency is available," he said, picking up the intercom.

Sitting in the main communications room, the Ambassador had already seen and heard what was going on at the gate through the closed circuit TV connecting every part of the embassy grounds, and when he heard Wilson's voice on the intercom, he replied, "Yes, Wilson, you can let three of them come in, but they must leave their weapons outside."

When the massage was relayed to the group, Ali and two others chosen by him put down their weapons and walked into the inner sanctum of the embassy, the Ambassador's office, where the ambassador sat, his fingers beating a steady rhythm on his enormous glass topped desk. "Come in," he invited in his most affable tone and the four men entered.

The Ambassador stood up and began, "Salam…" but Ali cut in almost brusquely.

"Mr. Ambassador," he said, "We, the Student Front of the Islamic Republic of Iran are taking over the United States Embassy with everyone within its premises hostage."

To the credit of the Ambassador, the announcement brought forth no visible reaction from him. "All right, Mr. Ali. Seeing that you have over two hundred fully armed men within the premises, and my first objective being to avoid any unnecessary bloodshed, I do not challenge your declaration. However, on behalf of the President and people of the United States of America, I wish to record my strong and serious objection and condemnation of your action, which is tantamount to waging war on my country, for you have violated international law by hostile trespass on the property of the United States, a friendly country, and posing a threat to her citizens. Now, if you and your friends will sit down, we can talk and see how the issue that has brought us to this unfortunate situation can be resolved, I sincerely hope, peacefully."

"As I told your officials at the gate, we do not mean harm to anybody unless you force our hand. We are here to make a formal request, better still a demand of the government of the United States. I have a document here, the contents of which are to be conveyed to the President of the United States. He must give us an undertaking in writing that the United States will not act in any way that will undermine the interests or the actions of the Islamic Republic of Iran. Until we receive that undertaking, your embassy will remain under siege, and everybody in it will remain hostages."

Ali had just finished his speech, and the Ambassador was about to speak when the telephone in the room began to ring shrilly. Wilson, who answered the phone, listened for a few seconds looked at the Ambassador and said sheepishly, "It's for Mr. Ali, Sir. The Head of the Revolutionary Council wishes to speak with him."

The four occupants of the room fell into an awkward silence as Ali put the phone to his ear. They could not hear what was being said by the Head of the Revolutionary Council, but it was clear that Ali was not happy with what was being said. He began by protesting very strongly, and suddenly cut the line. The telephone rang again, and Ali immediately picked it up as if he had been expecting the call. This time Ali listened carefully. He looked wild and very upset, but he listened. He listened for a full ten minutes, trying at intervals, to interrupt what he was being told, but it was obvious that he was being shouted down. Suddenly his voice became very respectful as he said into the phone, "Bale, Agha."(Yes, Sir.) Ali sounded completely subdued. He abruptly cut the connection and stood holding the receiver in his hand for a full five minutes. He replaced the phone in its cradle, and walked grimly and decisively to the Ambassador. He walked up to the Ambassador, and virtually snatched the document that he had given him earlier. "The Chairman of the Revolutionary Council wants to speak to you," he said through clenched teeth.

Outside the ambassador's office pandemonium reigned. Several gunmen were walking around herding the staff and visitors into various offices, and locking the doors. The American commandos had laid down their weapons on the orders of the Ambassador. Nobody at the embassy was about to give the trigger-happy gunmen an excuse to use their weapons. "Swallow your pride, and remember that your duty is to protect U.S. citizens. Right now, the only way you can do that is by acting with restraint," he had announced on the intercom just as the three 'visitors' were being shown into his office.

Chapter 69

In her room, Jordan and her friend watched through a window as the Fedayeen marched around the embassy grounds. One of them looked familiar, and as Jordan watched him, he suddenly looked through the window and their eyes met. Recognition seemed to light up his face, and Jordan almost lost consciousness of the world around her. Panic took over as she wondered if it was one of Nisreen's friends looking for her. Then she lost sight of him.

A minute later, there was a knock on her door, and before Jordan could tell her friend to ignore it, she opened the door, and Jordan beheld a young man, white headband, semi-automatic weapon and all standing in the doorway. A scream arose in her throat, as the young man addressed her in a pleasant voice, "Khanume Jordan, can you remember me? I am Sa'ad. I was student in your English class at university. Salaam Aleikum, Miss Jordan. It's so nice to see you."

Jordan walked up to the young man with bated breath. "Oh yes, Sa'ad, I do remember you. I'm so glad to see you." I can't actually tell you how much, she thought. "How are you?"

"I'm fine, Miss Jordan. I hope you're all right. Did you have any trouble?" he asked, sincere concern in his voice.

"I'm all right, Sa'ad, thank you," she had to make a great effort to sound all right.

"Are you going home, to the USA?"

"Yes, I'm hoping to leave soon."

"Will you come back? You are a great teacher, Miss Jordan. We all respect you very much, and think people like you can help our people a lot. I hope you will come back. And Miss Jordan, I'm sorry I missed some of your classes. I enjoyed them very much, but I had to join the revolution. You see, my elder sister was attacked by the Shah's goons many years ago; she is crippled and has never left the house since she was hurt. One of my brothers was taken by SAVAK, and we never saw him again. That why I had to join the revolution."

"I'm so sorry to hear that, but why didn't you tell me? I wish I had known."

"It was too dangerous. I had to change my name after my brother was taken away. If SAVAK knew of our connection, my life would have been in danger, too."

"I'm very sorry," Jordan responded.

"Why you not go before?" he asked, and Jordan knew she was treading dangerous ground. She changed the topic, asking him what he would do now. "I don't know. After Iran come back to normal, I go back to school, I hope."

"What's going on, Sa'ad? Why are you guys here?"

"Fedayeen decided to take over embassy, and take everybody hostage. It's as you say a hush-hush operation. Only we know about it. I'm sorry Miss Jordan. You know how are things between Iran and America. But I'm sure you all will be OK. They told us no shooting or violence. Maybe just a week or two. Then everyone free to go."

And Jordan felt as if her dreams were fading away before her. By tomorrow, word would be out that the US Embassy was being held by the Fedayeen. Most importantly, Nisreen would know, and she would do anything to lay hands on Jordan once again.

It was surreal, like the plot of a horror movie. Here she was all agog awaiting her ride back home to safety, and the unthinkable had happened. Destiny seemed to have played a hand, and Jordan was again back in square one. Who could help her now, she wondered.

Sa'ad suddenly came back to the present. "Miss Jordan, I really hope that you will soon be home, insha allah. Good luck. Koda hafiz," and he was gone.

Koda Hafiz-May God go with you-thought Jordan wrily. What could God do now? She was in the hands of Allah!

"Hey, imagine meeting a student in this mess. Was he a good student?" asked Jordan's roommate, but Jordan didn't seem to hear the question. She literally staggered to her bed, and lay down in a heap.

Chapter 70

The ambassador held the receiver to his ear and said, "Hello, this is Robinson speaking."

On the other end of the line, the Chairman of the Revolutionary Council introduced himself to the ambassador. "Your Excellency," he began, "the Revolutionary Council of the Islamic Republic of Iran wishes to apologize to you and the staff of the United States Embassy for the unexpected, and totally uncalled for event that took place today. Neither the Revolutionary Council, nor our Supreme Leader, Ayatollah Ruholla Khomeini was aware of this unwarranted action on the part of the group of people who now occupy your premises. The Supreme Leader, and the Revolutionary Council deeply regret what happened today. The supreme Leader, in fact, just spoke to Mr. Ali, the leader of this foolhardy venture, and we have jointly instructed him to withdraw from the embassy compound forthwith. We have given him two hours time to withdraw with all of his forces. We should be grateful if you detain him in your office for an hour to give his soldiers the impression that you are actually discussing the modalities of what he has already asked you to do."

Rather confused by the request, the ambassador began, "But why, ….?"

Chuckling gravely, the Chairman explained, "It's a cultural thing, Your Excellency. We do not want Mr Ali to lose face before his troops. He has been a very strong supporter of the revolution, you see."

From his own point of view, the ambassador certainly 'did not see' why he should accommodate Mr. Ali in this way, for he had criminally trespassed on his country's domain, but in his role of diplomat, he had to relent, and assured the Chairman that he would accede to his wishes.

Ali and his two aides sat with the ambassador and Wilson for an hour discussing mundane to topics such as the weather and Persian carpet weaving, at the end of which he stood up, stifling a pretended yawn. "It was nice talking to you, Mr Ali. I hope that some day we willhave the opportunity of meeting under happier circumstances."

Chagrined and completely subdued, Ali had lost the cock a hoop appearance he had when he walked into the Ambassador's office a half hour before. His red face was wrinkled like a sheep's stomach hanging in a butcher shop; his mood was no different. His irritation atthe way things had turned out was not helped in any way when the ambassador declined to shake the hand he stuck out as most Iranians did as a matter of course.

Once outside the office, he got into a huddle with his two companions and swore them to secrecy over what had transpired in the ambassador's room. Resuming his swagger, his voice boomed over the megaphone that one of his foot soldiers handed to him, "We have achieved the purpose for which we came here. We are leaving now. Get all the men to fall in by the main gate. Allahu Akbar Drud ba Khomeini!"

And they all trooped out of the embassy.

Chapter 71

Nisreen arrived at the embassy gates just as the troops were marching out. Seeing Ali, obviously the leader of the group, at the head of the march, she sidled up to him and tried to get his attention. She was completely unaware of what had transpired in the embassy compound, and was not prepared for the cool reception she received from Ali. He was not only in a foul and bitter mood, but also had more important things to think about than to listen to this middle-aged woman whom he had never seen before as he led his troops away from the scene of his debacle. He brushed her aside and walked resolutely leading his troops.

Fatameh, on the other hand, had also heard what was going to happen at the embassy that day, and had rushed there to see if she could help Jordan in case things got out of hand. She had a cousin among the group that had scaled the embassy walls, and had sworn to assist Jordan to get away in case Nisreen managed to 'capture' Jordan again. But as things turned out, there was no need for any intervention, and Fatameh's joy knew no bounds as she observed the treatment Nisreen received from Ali; it was the icing on the cake for Fatameh. From a telephone booth round the corner, Fatameh called the embassy and asked to speak to Jordan. When Jordan answered the phone, Fatameh, giggling like a little schoolgirl who had got straight A's at school, said, "Salam Aleiykum Jordan. Are you well?" and Jordan, hearing the voice of her beloved friend broke down in an uncontrollable frenzy of heart rending sobs followed by hysterical laughter.

"Fatameh, is it you? It's so wonderful to hear your voice, dear friend." And Fatameh told her about what had happened right down to the frustrated efforts of Nisreen to cashier the assistance of Ali.

"Is Nisreen still around?" she asked, terrified.

"No, don't worry. She has left. She looked lost and defeated. I don't think she will bother you again."

Jordan came up to the embassy gates and saw Fatameh standing outside, a seemingly frail figure, belying the strength, courage and fortitude Jordan knew lay beneath. They enjoyed each other's company, laughing and chatting, reveling in the magical, freedom they had found at last. The fear and anxiety, the uncertainty of the past months had taken a heavy toll on their bodies, for they looked gaunt and weary, as if they had journeyed through a seemingly unending desert in a state of parched desperation. But they had lived through it all, lending each other the strength of each other's friendship and loyalty, sharing each other's pain. Now they faced a new beginning, a beginning that promised happier and more joyous times, far away from the misery they longed to put behind them.

"When you come to the USA, I will help you enter a college and study for a career," promised Jordan.

"Yes, I am looking forward to that. When I left high school, I wanted to go to college to study business, but my parents didn't like the idea. I was eighteen, and my father thought that I would not be able to find a good husband if I delayed marriage beyond age twenty.

And they arranged my marriage. Maliki was a good husband during the first year of our marriage. Then he started drinking and gambling. Later, he began losing at the casinos and became very irritable. Nothing I did would satisfy him. He would get angry and start beating me." Her red eyes were a lambant pool of bitter tears, which she tried to hold back with little success. Jordan let her cry. Fatameh needed to unburden her soul, she thought. She listened without encouraging or restraining her. It had to come out of Fatameh's own volition; it had to be her own purgation.

"It was my twenty-first birthday. That morning Maliki wished me a happy birthday. He told me, 'We will celebrate tonight.' So I cooked a great dinner-all the things he likes-chelo kebab and fried chicken, a fresh salad. I got his favorite beer, and made bhaglava for dessert. I took out the candelabra we had received as a wedding present. I was so happy, and I waited for him to come home. I waited and waited. The memory was too painful and Fatameh stared out into space, as if hypnotized by the emotions she recalled.

"I fell asleep at the dinner table... He finally came home at two in the morning. He was drunk, and he was angry. "Why are you all dressed up," he mocked, and he began to beat me. His hand got entangled in my hair, and he began to pull at it as if to pull it all off. I was being shaken up like a rag-doll. I lost my footing, and tried to steady myself by grabbing at the table. My right hand came in contact with a heavy object-it was the candlabra. Something snapped inside me and I brought the ornament down on his head. It caught him on the back of his skull with such force that I thought my arm came out of its socket. Maliki hit the dining table and everything went down with a crash. I fell in a heap, my hands reaching out for Maliki, and I lost consciousness.

Hours later I woke up in a police holding cell. The police told me that Maliki was dead. I was charged with his murder."

It was as if a great burden had been taken off Fatameh. "This is the first time I told anyone what happened. At my hearing, I did not say a word. I thought I deserved to die, for after all, I had killed my husband."

"Yes, but it was an accident. Don't you see, Fatameh, you couldn't have willfully killed your husband."

"Yes, Jordan, I thought about it a lot, especially after I met you. The love and friendship you gave me has shown me that there is hope for me whereas before that I just thought of myself as a murderer who deserved to be punished. I have so much to thank you for."

"So what will you do now?"

"I guess I'll find a nice man in America, right? Maybe I'll get married and raise a family."

"It's great to hear you say that, Fatameh. I will introduce you to some nice people when you come to New York."

"I'll look forward to that, Jordan. Thank you very much."

This time they said goodbye with greater hope that they would meet again, and pick up the threads of their lives which had come very close to being irrevocably cut off.

Chapter 72

It took a week for the embassy to get all the paper work done for the transit crowd housed at the embassy. Two embassy vehicles drove them to the airport, and took them through customs and immigration as embassy employees. The officials manning the posts were all newly appointed after the revolutionary government had come into power. Wet behind the ears in immigration and customs procedure, all they did was to appear brusque and business like. It occurred to no one to check the circumstances under which Jordan, a college teacher at the hotshot University of Tehran was leaving now, when all of its foreign staff from the west had left weeks before. Had they checked, they would have found that she was wanted by the police for the murder of an Iranian officer of the Imperial Guard. That was what police records would say. Jordan, on the other hand, would carry the sadness of what had really happened that grim and fateful night, when the man she so deeply loved had been cruelly murdered.

Epilogue Part A

It was a beautiful Indian Summer day in New York. Jordan was anxiously scanning the faces of the arrivals at the JFK airport terminal; about a half an hour before, she had heard the announcement on the PA system that the Air France flight from Tehran had landed.

Jordan and Fatameh saw each other at the same time. They ran towards each other with whoops of delight, and held each other in a tight embrace. "Welcome to New York, Fatameh. I'm so glad you're here."

"I'm so glad to be here, Jordan." And they both dabbed their eyes. "OK, let's not waste time. Let's not keep that guy I promised you waiting."

They both burst out laughing.

Epilogue Part B

It was November 1979. Fatameh was attending ESL classes at the Adult Learning Center in downtown Albany, waiting to join the State University in the spring of 1981. She was holding down a job at the Museum on Washington Avenue.

Jordan had given up teaching and started a career in business. She was working at the State Capitol where Josh had been working before she left for Iran. She had never seen him, although she sometimes wondered where he was and whether he had found the stability he had been craving for. But she was constantly reminded of Ahmad, for his family had also settled in LA where they had many relatives and friends. Ahmad's kid sister called her at least once a week, and they talked about Ahmad, as well as Tehran then and now. Sheherazad, Ahmad's sister would tell her about school, and about the American boys in her class, some of whom she thought were very cute, 'as cute as some of the Iranian boys I knew back home' she said. And Jordan's mind reached nostalgically back to the cutest of them all.

"So Jordan, do you have a boyfriend?" Sheherazad asked precociously.

"Well, yes, I have many boyfriends now," she replied, thinking of the casual dates she was having-nothing to write home about, she thought, and added, "Nobody steady yet."

It was, in fact, too early to think of any one who could fill the void left behind by Ahmd's passing. It would take quite a while, she said to herself. "But you must find someone, soon, Jordan. It is good for you. You must forget the sadness of the past," said Sheherezad Jordan was overwhelmed by Sheherazad's maturity, and concern. "I will, dear, I will." She promised, smiling into the phone.

Jordan and Fatameh would meet occasionally in downtown Tehran for lunch, and talk about their memories, and dreams for the future. Fatameh was in fact seeing a cute Argentinian from her ESL class. He was hoping to be a doctor some day, and Fatameh was dead set on a career in business, as she had told Jordan when they were in Tehran.

One day, as they were having lunch, there was a news flash on TV about Tehran. The US Embassy had been taken over by Iranian militants, and they were holding everybody at the embassy hostage. The announcer was reading a list of demands the militants were making for the release of the hostages. "Those guys are crazy," declared Fatameh angrily, "I knew those revolutionaries didn't know what they were doing, the idiots."

"I don't know about that," said Jordan, "but I'm sure glad I'm not there any more."

Jordan and Fatameh looked at each other as if a great weight had been lifted off their souls.

Printed in the United States
By Bookmasters